MONIA MAZIGH

Farida

a novel

translated by
Phyllis Aronoff & Howard Scott

MAWENZI
HOUSE

We acknowledge the support of the Canada Council for the Arts for our publishing
program. We also acknowledge support from the Government of Ontario through
the Ontario Arts Council.

We acknowledge the financial support of the Government of Canada.

Cover design by Sabrina Pignataro
Cover photo: gianliguori / Aerial view of Tunis, Tunisia stock photo / iStock

Library and Archives Canada Cataloguing in Publication

Title: Farida : a novel / Monia Mazigh ; translated by Phyllis Aronoff & Howard Scott.
Other titles: Farida. English
Names: Mazigh, Monia, author | Aronoff, Phyllis, 1945- translator | Scott, Howard,
1952- translator
Description: Translation of: Farida. | In English, translated from the French.
Identifiers: Canadiana (print) 20240469852 | Canadiana (ebook) 20240469925 | ISBN
9781774151747 (softcover) | ISBN 9781774151754 (EPUB) | ISBN 9781774151761 (PDF)
Subjects: LCGFT: Novels.
Classification: LCC PS8626.A955 F3713 2024 | DDC C843/.6—dc23

Printed and bound in Canada by Coach House Printing

Mawenzi House Publishers Ltd.
39 Woburn Avenue (B)
Toronto, Ontario M5M 1K5
Canada

www.mawenzihouse.com

CONTENTS

Author's Note

This novel is not autobiographical. Farida and the other characters are fictional, the fruit of my imagination, research, and reading. However, I have drawn inspiration from historical facts to try to create characters that are as close as possible to reality.

Part of this book was written in Vancouver during a writing residency in the house of the famous Canadian writer of Japanese origin, Joy Kogawa. I wrote and revised several chapters in the childhood bedroom where Joy Kogawa often looked out the window at a tree in the neighbour's backyard. That bedroom became the office where I spent hours looking out the same window and writing.

The old house came close to being torn down in 2006, but thanks to the efforts of a number of citizens, politicians, and members of the local community it was saved. So I was able to write while watching people walking by in the little back alley where that tree still stands, a cherry tree, weakened and old, but still alive. It's a miraculous tree. During the Second World War, when Joy Kogawa, still a child, was forced to leave her home to go to an internment camp for Japanese Canadians in the little village of Slocan in the Kootenay region, she put her arms around that tree and begged it never to forget her. I looked at that cherry tree every day thinking about that innocent little girl who in her immense sadness made a wish to the tree and to the wind that swayed it. Forever marked by that painful event, Joy Kogawa would see her wish fulfilled years later when, having regained her freedom and won recognition for her literary talent, she came back to revisit the vestiges of her childhood.

Joy Kogawa's story is one of extreme injustice but also, like so many other stories around us, one of perseverance. Perhaps it is enough to look at the trees and smell the flowers and, above all, to remember to make wishes. It was to keep stories like that alive in my memory and in the hearts of readers that I decided to write this novel.

BAB SOUIKA

1941-1964

I feel the blood of youth
Boiling in my heart
New winds are rising in me
I listen to their song
Listen to the growling thunder
The rain that falls and the symphony of the winds.
And when I ask the Earth,
"Mother, do you hate men?"
She answers me, "I bless the ambitious
And those who like to take risks.
I curse those who do not adapt
To the vagaries of time and are content with leading
A dull life, like stones."

ABOUL-QACEM ECHEBBI (1909-1934)

Chapter 1

Farida

I was lying on the bed in the raised alcove. The muslin curtains were draped over the edges of the mattress. I waited patiently in the dark, counting the regular beats of my heart. A muscle in my left thigh suddenly began to twitch. I massaged it gently with my fingertips and the movement stopped as quickly as it had begun.

Aunt Hnani and Aunt Zohra had led me gently into the dark bedroom, holding me by the waist and the arm. There were lighted candles in each corner of the room, their slender flames dancing with the movements of our shadows. A heavy scent of amber rose from the incense burner and filled the air. With great care, my aunts removed the *keswa*, which their friend Khadija, who was blind in one eye, had spent years embroidering. That wedding *keswa*, made up of two pieces that barely met over my belly, weighed heavily on me. Hundreds of silver sequins and embroidered flowers and foliage formed a sparkling pattern on the white silk. The *blouza* squeezed my breasts together and pushed them forward. It closed in the back with little hooks, and when Aunt Hnani finally unfastened it, I almost cried out with relief at being released from its torture. The *sirwal* covered my legs down to the ankles. A long ribbon of fabric held everything firmly in place. I had to walk with my legs apart like a little boy in pain after circumcision, the yards of heavy material restraining my movements.

Once I was freed of these trappings, I felt as light as a sparrow at the beginning of spring. Fortunately it was warm in the room, or I would have been freezing. Wearing only white cotton underpants extending to my knees and a cotton *merioul* covering my bosom, I became aware of my near nakedness in front of the two old women, and I blushed.

Aunt Hnani came over and began to undo my hair, which the *hanana* who had applied my henna had spent hours braiding to make it behave. The jasmine flowers woven into my braids began to tumble to the floor one after the other like hailstones. I could still feel a few flowers tickling my neck. The subtle fragrance of the dried flowers mixed with that of the amber. I suddenly felt like fleeing from that bedroom where my fate would be sealed.

Aunt Zohra, bent double, squinted and grimaced as she rummaged in the small checkered cardboard box that had been shown to me each time my trousseau was mentioned. "Hnani, are you sure you brought the nightgown?" she asked.

"Oh, yes, my dear Zohra! It's at the bottom . . . wrapped in the red scarf. Look again, you'll find it."

The red scarf had belonged to my mother. Remembering my Ommi, I felt a pang. She had gone too soon, taken by pneumonia, which came like the sirocco wind, sweeping away everything in its path.

Aunt Zohra squinted even more, she could hardly see in the increasing darkness of the room. Finally, with a smile on her lips, she came toward us holding the white garment I had tried on at least five times. Its collar was adorned with a *shebka*, the lace made by Aunt Hnani with thread from Scotland. The sheer cotton voile fabric would soon be slipped over my naked body and would keep me company during this fateful night.

I recalled Aunt Hnani sitting on the blue wooden bench by the lemon tree in the inner courtyard of our house every summer, her little pink cushion on her lap, stitching patterns she had learned by heart as a little girl. One bare foot tucked under her thigh, the other one dangling, she would work in silence. I'd watch her out of the corner of my eye while reading an article in *La Dépêche tunisienne*. I found the pages of the newspaper in the kitchen. Aunt Hnani would throw them out with the potato and carrot peelings; when she wasn't looking, I'd hide them in the pocket of my dress. Sometimes the paper smelled of fish. The fishmongers, butchers, and market gardeners used the newspaper to wrap their products for the customers. Every morning the little clerk, Mohamed, delivered a basket filled with soaked chickpeas, a piece of pumpkin, a few potatoes and carrots, a handful of peppers, some nice red tomatoes, and a big green striped watermelon or some oranges from Menzel Bouzelfa. Sometimes he would sometimes leave me a few intact pages of the newspaper that were not stained with mutton grease or reeking of the little red mullets fished off La Goulette. To thank him, I would slip him a piece of *halwa chamia* or a stick of Meunier chocolate my brother Habib had traded me for one of the bananas he was crazy about.

I was happy to be able to read. My brother Habib stayed in his bedroom. He read in Arabic and in French. But I loved French. When he was in a good mood, which occurred from time to time, he would loan me one of his books and I would savour it like an almond *baklawa*.

When my mother, may God bless her soul, was still alive, she turned a blind eye to my love of reading. Deep down, she wanted me to learn to read and write. With Ommi's coaxing, Baba had agreed to send me to the school of the "Francisses," as we called French people, as long as I was accompanied every morning by my brother Habib. That was over now. The person who had protected me from my father's dictates was gone, leaving a gaping wound in my heart that no one could heal. Ommi was no longer there. My aunts came to replace her. They were kind, but they were not like Ommi. They simply wanted me to behave myself and get married. "Girls from good families get married, they have a husband and children, they don't go to school like the *gaouria*."[1] Their answers did not satisfy me, I was left wanting.

"And what about Habib? Why can he go to school and not I?" I would answer, in a manner that bordered on insolence.

"He's a man, he'll have to work one day to support a family, but you're a girl, why would you need to go to school?"

So I kept quiet. The conversation stopped there. We had come to a dead end. I felt as if I were at the bottom of a well, where I could see only my own reflection. If I answered that reading was my life, they wouldn't understand. If I told them that reading was my oxygen, my reason for living, they would burst out laughing and shake their heads in astonishment. So it was better just to keep quiet. Keep quiet and retreat. Or else look up at the sky and watch the clouds go by in silence.

After Ommi was gone, Baba again started to say things like "Girls are

---

1   *Gaouria* or *gaouri,* vernacular words to designate foreigners, usually Europeans.

supposed to stay at home" and "Farida has read enough books . . . it's enough now." He also started talking about marriage. I had just finished my primary school certificate. Only two of us Arab girls had graduated: Wassila Fourati and I. I wanted to go to the *lycée*, I wanted to be a teacher like Thérèse Chemla, our neighbour, who used to come visit us when Ommi was still alive. When I made the mistake of talking to my aunts about my dream, they looked at me with surprise, as if I had uttered a terrible swear word. Aunt Hnani said, "Remember, *ya binti*, Thérèse is Jewish, but you're Muslim. Muslims have their own traditions. You won't ever become a teacher." I so wished Ommi were still alive to whisper words that would let me dream again.

Since then Baba hadn't stopped talking about Kamel and marriage. "Your cousin Kamel has always been interested in you. He takes care of our land. He has money and will make a good husband for you. I'll arrange things for the two of you."

I did not want my cousin Kamel. He was ignorant. He had gone to school for a few years and had been expelled because he could not get beyond fourth grade. As children, we had played together in the big courtyard of our house. The family of my uncle, Sheik Salah, lived upstairs and we lived downstairs. Kamel always wanted to win, and when he lost he would start whining and kicking. I did not like Kamel and I did not want to be his wife.

Aunt Zohra and Aunt Hnani had left. From the little window, I saw their silhouettes gradually disappear into the night. Before leaving, they had put perfume on my body. It was rose perfume, from a blown glass vial that had belonged to Ommi. She had kept it in a special place on her dressing table and used it occasionally when she was invited to a wedding. "Come here and I'll put a little perfume on you, you'll smell nice," she would say to me while sitting at her dressing table applying kohl to her eyes. She would reach for the vial of perfume and I would go to her, almost running, and she would dab my hands with the stopper. I would breathe in the fragrance wafting from my hands. Ommi would smile at seeing me so happy, and I would walk out into the courtyard holding my hands to my nose, afraid that the scent would dissipate too quickly.

But now, lying on the bed, I wanted to be rid of this perfume that enveloped me and made me feel as if a *jinni* had sneaked into my soul. I heard footsteps on the marble tiles of the patio. I stiffened. The door opened with a creak that made my heart beat wildly. The muscle in my right leg started twitching again. I no longer tried to stop it.

"When your husband comes to you, let him do what he wants. You belong to him now. You're his wife," Aunt Zohra had whispered in my ear when she buttoned my nightgown. I had remained silent, my eyes averted, too shy to answer her.

The footsteps came toward me. I heard my name spoken in the dark. The smell of alcohol mixed with the scent of roses on my skin. I felt the *rouzata* I had drunk during the evening rise in my throat, ready to spurt from my mouth.

"Farida, come here, beside me!"

Kamel's arms pulled me toward him. "You belong to him," Aunt Zohra's words kept echoing in my ears.

I didn't belong to anyone. I belonged to life. I belonged to death. I belonged to words and books. But it was too late. Kamel's voice was insistent, like his hands, which were clutching at my body.

"Farida, I can hardly see you, come closer!"

He lay down beside me. He took off his *jebba*. He was naked except for his underpants, which made him look like a kid at the beach. I could see the sparse hair on his chest. I shuddered. I didn't want to become Kamel's wife.

His hands were searching for my mouth. I didn't resist. The rose perfume and the smell of alcohol mingled. My fingers clutched the mattress. Kamel mumbled some incomprehensible words. He rubbed against me. I didn't move. Then suddenly, he got on top of me.

"Take off your nightgown," he ordered. "I'm going to show you that I'm a man."

That was the last thing I wanted see of Kamel.

Chapter 2

Farida

On the seventh day of our wedding celebrations, I was seated in our courtyard on the blue bench, which was adorned with hand-embroidered cushions for the occasion, and all the women were gazing greedily at me. The lemons on the tree nearby had not yet turned golden against the green foliage. Soon their brief lives would end, pressed into lemonade to quench our summer thirst. The band Kamel had hired, which he had praised endlessly to Baba and my aunts, consisted of three men, all hiding their eyes behind big dark glasses. The one in the middle played the *oud* and sang in a melodious voice; the one sitting on his left held a *darbuka* on his thigh, striking it with rhythmic, staccato blows, and the third member was beating the *tar*, a tambourine, whose little jingles danced to the rhythms of the songs.

"Are you sure they're blind?" Aunt Zohra had asked. "Maybe they're pretending in order to get a good look at our guests."

"*Salli Al Nibi, ya Khalti* Zohra!" Kamel reassured her. "I would never allow anything like that. They're Jewish musicians. They're blind, and everybody is talking about them these days. Their songs and their music are remarkable."

Aunt Zohra had murmured a prayer. The expression on her face showed that she was not convinced by Kamel's words. But her mind was already elsewhere. Everything had to be ready for that seventh day. The whole family would be present to share our happiness. Everyone wanted me to be happy. No one wondered if I really was. And yet, anyone who looked could see that the sadness in my eyes was infinite. The sparkle went out of them the day the notary presented me with the marriage contract and asked me, in front of Baba, sitting beside me, and all the women in our sitting room, if I accepted Kamel as my husband.

Kamel was waiting outside with the men. From a distance, I could see him smiling and puffing out his chest like a ram ready to fight. His new shoes, bought at the Italian store Chez Carlo, the most expensive in Tunis, made him look even more arrogant.

I was wearing a light white burnoose whose pointed hood covered my hair. Aunt Hnani had given me a pretty mirror with a silver frame to hold in my hand. "Look at your beautiful face, it will bring you happiness," she had said.

I studied my face and all I saw were my eyes. Dull. Sad. Defeated. Not a trace of happiness. Alone, I was unable to confront my father. Even my brother Habib, who might have been my natural ally, was indifferent to my fate. Only his own life counted for him. His studies and his reading were enough. He had the double advantage of being male and an only son. And I, the daughter, existed only for marriage.

The notary, a man with a gentle, feminine manner, turned to me and said, "Farida, daughter of Si Laroussi Ben Mahmoud, do you accept Kamel, son of Sheik Salah Ben Mahmoud, as your husband according to the law of God and the tradition of his Prophet?"

Girls from good families do not answer when the notary asks them this question, because when you love a man, you are not supposed to say it. It's bad manners. Only girls with loose morals talk about such things. My aunts had taught me that lesson in a subtle way. Just as they themselves had learned it according to our traditions and customs. In fact, I had nothing to say. My battle was already lost. An unequal battle I had no chance of winning.

And why couldn't I be like Cosette, Victor Hugo's heroine, who married Marius, the young man she loved? Why say yes to an ignorant man who would never understand the world in which I immersed myself each time I read a book? A vindictive, arrogant man who loved only himself.

The musicians filled our courtyard with songs that alternated between joy and melancholy. It was as if they had guessed my state of mind. The words consoled me:

layam quif erri'h fil birrima, lili ya lil,
Fil barrima, chargui wa gharbi ma dimash dima . . .

"Life is like a weathervane in the wind . . . the east wind, the west wind, nothing lasts forever . . . "

It was a song by Sheik El Afrit, a Jewish musician from early in the century. My mother would sometimes hum it while she sewed our clothes, moving her feet up and down on the treadle of her Singer sewing machine. For a few minutes, I felt a bit better, carried back to the comforting memories of childhood.

Aunt Hnani came over and, in front of all the women, said, "Stand up, *ya lella* Farida! You will step over the fish to ward off the evil eye from you and your husband."

The ululations of the women were deafening. What I really wanted was for the evil eye, if it actually existed, to catch Kamel and take him far away. Obviously, my prayers were in vain. I stepped hesitantly over the platter of big silver mullets caught in the sea that morning.

"Again, again! You have to step over the fish seven times so that the evil eye goes away and only happiness remains."

Aunt Hnani held me by the arm to help me step over the big platter. I obeyed. I had no choice. Once, twice, three times . . . and finally, one last time to complete the seven steps to happiness. I endured the smothering kindness of my aunts, the orders of my father, the indifference of my brother, and the boorishness of my husband. Soon those fish would be scaled, cleaned and cooked in a couscous that would be served to all our guests.

Two or three women stood up and performed a few tentative dance steps. Plates of little cakes began to circulate, followed by glasses of mint tea. Tongues were loosened. Whispers gave way to bursts of laughter and sly looks became sympathetic. The party was in full swing. For a few moments, I was alone, lost in my thoughts.

It was already a week since I'd married Kamel. A week that felt like an eternity. Every night, it was the same story. Every night, the same ordeal. Kamel would get on top of me and show me he was a man. His breath stank of alcohol. His hands were rough, without love or gentleness. He repelled me. A vulgar man, that was who I had married. Before proving his virility to me, he would go and drink wine at Café La Joie in Bab

Souika, where they sold tea and coffee to poor people in the daytime, and in the evening, behind closed doors, alcoholic drinks to those who were a little richer.

And it mattered little that my uncle, Kamel's father, was a sheik who taught the Quran at the Al-Zaytuna Mosque in the medina of Tunis. In any case, Kamel hid his true colours. But my cousin Fatma, Kamel's sister, had told me before my marriage that her brother drank. She had often seen him come home drunk in the evening. Fatma was my best friend. As little girls, we would conspire to foil Kamel's dirty tricks.

Fatma couldn't read any French, and read only a little Arabic. Her father, my Uncle Salah, didn't allow her to go to school. When we got bored playing with dolls, she would say, "Let's play school." I was always the teacher and she the pupil. I would act very serious and say in French, exactly the way Mme Lacroix, my teacher, did, "Mademoiselle Ben Mahmoud, sit up straight and take out your grammar workbook."

Fatma wouldn't react. I could tell from her look of despair that she hadn't understood a word. She felt a bit humiliated, a bit jealous, but she would soon get over it and say, "You know what, Farida, speak to me in Arabic, I'll understand better."

I would regretfully go along with the compromise and we would continue our game in our mother tongue while still pretending to be the French teacher and the little Arab student.

Chapter 3

Farida

"Farida, Farida, Farida . . ."

I was in the kitchen pretending to peel potatoes. My aunts Hnani and Zohra had hired a *carroussa* and were leaving for Hammam-Lif to spend a few weeks with their cousin Daddou, who was married to one of the bey's ministers. Hammam-Lif, a few kilometres from Tunis, was a little village nestled at the foot of Mount Boukornine. Winter was milder there. Mineral waters flowed from deep within the mountain to fill the public baths with their warmth. They were enjoyed by people from the city who wanted to get away from the humidity of the Tunis winters and the damp in the walls of the Arab houses.

My aunts were going to visit Daddou and listen to the latest gossip about the prominent families of Tunis—marriages, births, divorces, and deaths—and go to the hamman and bathe in those waters, which were said to be a miraculous cure for their chronic rheumatism and persistent pains.

When they left, I found myself alone in the kitchen. How I hated those chores. I had no idea where to start. Cut the meat into pieces, but how large? Big or little? Maybe medium-sized? What spice should I use, dried coriander or powdered cumin? My head was already spinning. Ommi had never made me go into the kitchen. She would let me read peacefully. As a result, I was lost every time I found myself in that room, with the ingredients piled on the counter, the *kanoun* to be lighted, and a meal to be prepared.

"Farida, can't you hear me? I've been calling you for a while."

I was holding the earthenware jar of olive oil, about to pour it on the onions I'd been labouring to dice. Kamel was standing in the doorway.

"Why are you using so much oil? You don't need a ton of it. The jar won't last till the end of the month. At this rate I'll have to buy you a whole tank of oil to keep you going."

"This is exactly the amount needed for a good potato ragout," I answered automatically in my defence, but I knew I was just saying whatever came into my head and I really had no idea how much oil to use to brown the onions, which were now swimming in oil.

Kamel was not pleased. He muttered a curse between his teeth. I heard it. He was calling me a bitch. I pretended I hadn't heard him.

"I'm famished, hurry up, I need to eat." He withdrew to the sitting room.

I wished Fatma were there to help me. She was so at ease in the kitchen. She knew how to combine spices, gut a chicken, scale a fish. In a few hours, the cooking utensils would be put away, the peels thrown in the garbage, the *kanoun* lighted in the courtyard with the food simmering gently on it, and a bucket already filled with water standing beside the mop to scrub the floor. But today she had gone to visit a cousin on her mother's side, which meant a day of hell for me in this dimly lighted room where wreaths of dried red peppers, braids of garlic, and bunches of bay leaves hung on the wall beside little jars of olives.

"You call that a potato ragout?"

Kamel had just awakened from the nap he had taken while I finished preparing the food, and his eyes shone with anger. He had taken off his *jebba* and thrown it on the sofa, and was wearing only an undershirt and underpants that went down to his knees.

I sat down at the *mida*, ready to eat. In the centre was the dish of potatoes and meat swimming in a dubious-looking mixture of oil and water. I said nothing.

"I told you not to put in so much oil."

"It isn't the oil. The *kanoun* takes too long to light, and the potatoes were wormy, they were almost rotten." I was groping for an excuse, but things only got worse.

"Do you think I'm an idiot or what? What does the *kanoun* have to do with it? And why are the potatoes rotten? They were fine when I bought them at the market. You left them in the basket too long, that's why they aren't good. It's the amount of oil, I told you that at the beginning."

"It's not my fault, you always buy food that's half-rotten and you stick your nose into how much oil I use to cook—"

I hadn't finished my sentence before Kemal's hand came down like a knife, missing my face by a hair. The potato ragout was now all over the *mida*. Kamel's sudden movement and my reaction had overturned the dish.

"You ought to keep quiet and learn to cook."

"And you ought to buy good-quality fruit and vegetables and stop spending money on alcohol and shoes."

This time his fist got me in the shoulder and nearly knocked me over backward. He stood up, threw on his *jebba*, and left, saying that this time I'd gotten off easy, but next time I would get a beating.

It was funny. His words hadn't frightened me. But the blow had hurt. I looked at the red mark it had left, and tears welled up in my eyes that I couldn't stop. I would go tell my father about it. I would say his nephew, the husband he had chosen for me, had dared to hit me and that I would not live with a brute. I would say I didn't want to go back to live with Kamel even if he promised never again to raise a hand against me. I was not a peasant woman who would allow herself to be beaten. I was Farida Ben Mahmoud, a *beldia*, a daughter of the bourgeoisie of Tunis, who despite her unhappy lot intended to defend herself and demand respect.

Chapter 4

Farida

My father was sitting across from me. I told him what Kamel had done to me during our argument. As usual, his right eye was wandering, and I couldn't tell whether he was looking at me or at the wall. He seemed to be in a bad mood, and his moustache was quivering. Drops of sweat ran down his temples, although it wasn't hot in the room, which he used as both his office and his bedroom since my mother's death. Before then, it had been a closed room, used to store old things we didn't know what to do with. Now Kamel and I had my parents' bedroom and my father had put his business papers in this room at the eastern corner of the courtyard, where he spent his days, when he wasn't at his office in Bab Souika.

"What do you want me to do for you? You are under another man's responsibility now."

I had half expected this answer, but I had hoped he could still save me from Kamel's clutches. "Baba, may God keep you, Kamel raised his hand against me. He dared to hit me. I don't love him."

My father burst out laughing. A sardonic laugh that hurt my ears and that I wanted to stop immediately. I didn't understand this sudden change in him. What was happening?

"You've read too many French books, Farida. But you're a woman now, not a little girl. A woman who is married to her cousin, Kamel Ben Mahmoud. You saw how much your husband spent on the seventh day of your wedding celebrations. Nobody's ever seen such quantities of fish, couscous, watermelons, and cakes on offer for the guests. People still come to my office and tell me what they've heard in the neighbourhood about the ceremony. I'm still proud. And don't forget the band. We're the second family, after the Ben Ammars, to hire those musicians. What more do you want?"

I had known he would again give me all kinds of stories about money and prestige. But I wouldn't be taken in. I wanted to be rid of Kamel, whatever the cost. "But Baba, he pushed me hard, violently. He left a bruise on my shoulder." And to make the point, I tried to show him the spot where it still hurt.

But my father didn't want to look. One eye was directed toward the wooden bookcase where his books were carefully arranged and the other was gazing off into the distance. "That's nothing. It's just the passion of youth, he'll calm down. You'll see. If you complain every time you have a disagreement with your husband, your family life will be hell. Kamel is a good husband, you need to take the time to get used to him."

"Baba, Kamel isn't good. He drinks. He comes home drunk every night."

He started to laugh again, but stopped short. "A little alcohol doesn't matter. God is merciful and indulgent! But who told you he drinks? Maybe it's sweat you smell. What do you know about alcohol?" His face darkened again and he knitted his brow. Sweat was still running down his temples.

A light breeze came from the half-open door to the courtyard, giving me courage. I didn't mean to tell him that Fatma also knew, but it was too late, her name slipped out. "My cousin Fatma told me, even before the wedding."

I hadn't even finished my sentence when my father exploded like a firecracker on the day of the Eid. "Fatma is a parasite. She's jealous because you're married and she's still looking for a good match. Your brother Habib isn't interested. Maybe she'll be an old maid. That's what she deserves!"

Why such hatred for Fatma? It was as if he were speaking of a stranger, or even an enemy. I wanted to say that Fatma wasn't yet sixteen and it was better that she wait rather than end up with a husband like Kamel. But I didn't dare, I was too scared. "Fatma is my cousin, Baba, I love her, and she doesn't lie. And why would she lie about her own brother?"

"Because she's jealous and she doesn't want you to be happy. Only your father knows what's best for you, and that's being with your cousin Kamel. He's strong, he doesn't waste his money, and he takes care of our land. He thinks of his family." Baba came and put his arm around my shoulder, the one Kamel had hit. I still felt a burning pain in it.

"Farida, my dear daughter, forget what Kamel did. Yes, he acted brutally. But you mustn't let it upset you. Calm down and things will work out. You've only been married a few months. You have to be patient."

I forced myself to smile. To hear my father speak of patience, when he himself wouldn't wait an extra minute for his morning coffee. When he would fly into a rage if he found a speck of dust on his books or on the table in his sitting room. Why should I be the only one who had to be patient? No, I couldn't be patient. I needed a way out, but I couldn't find any.

Chapter 5

Habib

My sister Farida has married that brute Kamel. I've known she was unhappy. I could see it in her eyes, in her manner, in the way she stared at me as if she was asking for help. But I couldn't do anything for her. I couldn't confront my father. It was all his fault. He was the one who wanted that marriage so that his fortune would be preserved and would remain in the family.

Farida was intelligent, too intelligent for Kamel. She's read most of my books. I loaned her quite a few, but I knew that she stole some of them to read in secret and then carefully put them back in place. I pretended I didn't notice, because I didn't want to add any unhappiness to her life. Farida should have gone to secondary school as I did, as the French girls did. She was capable. But now it was too late.

Farida thinks I'm selfish. She never told me so, but I heard her talking about me with Fatma, that *ifrita*, that mischievous girl. They were sitting outside my room. They didn't know my window was open and I could hear them. I was lying on my bed reading Stendhal's *Le Rouge et le Noir*, fascinated by the tragic fate of Julien Sorel, the hero: his passion for his mistress, his ambition to move up the social ladder, torn between the Church and the army, both of which he was drawn to. Unable to choose between my father and my own ideals, I experienced Sorel's conflicted feelings as if they were my own.

Their conversation came to me in snatches through the old shutters, like a distant murmur. I put my book down on the bed and leaned toward the window to listen.

"I don't want to marry Kamel. I just want to continue my studies. But Baba won't listen."

"I don't suppose there's any point asking Habib to help you? The only thing he knows how to do is read. Stories about *gaouri*, maybe love stories, with mistresses and lovers." Fatma burst out laughing.

Farida let out a long sigh. "Frankly, I don't know what Habib thinks. He doesn't talk much. He's the only one I have, now that Ommi is gone, but I have a feeling he thinks only of his future. Soon, he'll get his diploma from Collège Sadiki. What an honour! Oh, if only he'd talk to Baba and convince him to change his mind. I would be grateful to him for the rest of my days."

"He won't do it; he's too afraid. You remember when we used to play hide-and-seek? He was always the one who would come out of the dark little room first, because he was afraid. We would stay there crouched behind the crocks of oil. Kamel could never find us and that made him furious."

My father's footsteps returning to the courtyard cut short Farida and Fatma's conversation. They hurried off to the kitchen.

I picked up my book again, but Stendhal had lost his hold on me. Farida and Fatma's words were buzzing in my ears. Wasn't I my father's only son, the one who should one day take the reins in our family? But Baba was set on that marriage. He trusted Kamel. He saw his nephew as his true successor instead of his own son, who cared only about reading and writing poems. Baba was a tyrant. He didn't listen to anyone, least of all his schoolboy son. He spent his days in his office in Bab Souika, where he received the small shopkeepers and poor people of the neighbourhood who came to borrow money.

"I'll loan you ten thousand francs on condition that you bring me the deed to your house. That's your collateral." How many times have I heard such words when I passed his office on my way to school? I was ashamed of my father's lack of scruples. I couldn't look him in the eye for fear of seeing my own weaknesses. I'd put my head down and continue on my way. From a distance, I would hear the person who had just received the promise of a loan singing his praises.

"May God protect you, Si Laroussi, just give me time to go home and I'll come back with the deed. I'll pay back your money. Don't worry, I will soon receive my share of the inheritance from my mother and your money will be repaid down to the last centime."

I knew that the man's promises were exaggerated, and that, like many before him, he would probably end up losing his house. My father was a moneylender. That was how he made his fortune. People would come the first time to borrow a thousand or ten thousand francs, then another time and still another. Once the total borrowed was close to the value of the house, my father would send the deed to his lawyer friend, Shlomo Fallouss, and together they would initiate legal proceedings to recoup the money by taking ownership of the store or house.

What my father did was base and contemptible, and I looked forward to the day when I would graduate and could get far away from that man who thought only of getting rich at the expense of the poor and unfortunate.

Since the beginning of the war, business in the country had been going downhill. It was worse than the Depression of the 1930s. The fall in the prices of the country's main agricultural products—wheat, barley, olive oil, and wool—was spectacular. Everything was becoming more expensive, and people were becoming poorer, including the family of my Uncle Salah and his son Kamel. Everyone except my father, that is. He was hoping Kamel would perform miracles with the family land. But this time, I'm convinced, he was making a mistake. There are major political and economic upheavals coming and Kamel won't understand anything.

I couldn't help Farida. Fatma tried to blame me, but she was forgetting that it was my father who controlled everything. The only thing I had control over was my reading and my exams. I was determined to succeed in order to be able to go away as soon as possible.

Fatma was too clever. How was she able to guess what kind of books I read? She couldn't even read French. But she was always with older people, her other cousins and her mother. She heard all the gossip and knew all the rumours. Farida was not like that. She was an intellectual, unlike other girls her age.

Chapter 6

Kamel

That scatterbrain Farida went and told her father, my Uncle Laroussi, about our argument. She thought I was scared of him. Not a bit. On the contrary, my uncle is on my side, and he always will be. At least, as long as I make money for the family.

The business is not doing well. The land doesn't bring in the income it did in previous years. Farmers can't sell their wheat at the usual price anymore. Europe is still at war and the merchants at the souk are saying that the Germans will soon be coming here. Just as well, they'll boot out those damn Frenchmen who've been stealing our wealth for years. Every year they tell us the prices of wheat and barley are dropping. They're lying, they're exploiting us. Soon the farmers who lease our land won't be able to pay the rent. I don't know what I'll do.

But also, Romdane, my tenant, is shiftless. He spends his days napping. Instead of working harder and producing more, he hides behind lies to avoid paying his rent. I'm going to have to find someone to replace him. Yesterday at the café, my friend Lamine told me about an Italian family that's looking for a plot of land around Jedeida to raise cows and produce milk and cheese. I'm going to ask Lamine to introduce me to this Italian. I'll have to put Romdane Jlasssi and his children out, or else in a few years they'll take over our land without paying a centime. That *goor*[2] thought he was smart, but he was forgetting that I'm the intelligent one, I, Kamel

---

2 *Goor* or *goora* (feminine), pejorative, used by some city-dwellers to speak of common people or those living in villages.

Ben Mahmoud, who appreciates beautiful women and Italian shoes.

Farida is too skinny for my liking. She's like a wooden board in bed. She doesn't move or say a word. I can't forget Samira, the girl from Rue Zarkoune. Always ready, always passionate. She says nice things to me, things that make me forget life's problems. She adores my shoes, she sometimes polishes them until they're shiny as a silver coin. She sits on my lap, strokes my hair, kisses my neck, massages my feet and my back. After we make love, still naked, her breasts shapely, her legs crossed, she lights a cigarette and, almost laughing, says, "You shouldn't come see me anymore, you're married now and your wife will be jealous."

"My wife can't do anything, not in bed and not in the kitchen. I can't give you up, Samira. You're like a magnet."

She gave her loudest laugh, the laugh I adored, open and vulgar, which made her even more beautiful, showing her white teeth with the gap in front. "*Ya hallouf, ya* Kamel! I adore you, you sly little pig." She threw herself on me. Her lush body excited me. She covered me all over with little kisses, and all I wanted was to make love to her again.

Farida feels I'm stingy. Maybe she thinks I find money in the lanes and souks of the medina. She lives in her *gaouri* books, books about things that aren't from our culture, books that brainwash her. She can't even cook a decent meal. The other day, her potato ragout was a disgusting combination of water, oil, and half-cooked pieces of potato. The meat in it was full of fat that wasn't melted. More fat than meat. It was awful. She blamed me for it. She really doesn't know me. She thinks she's a *beya*. I don't have as much money as my Uncle Laroussi, who extracts money from people like a bloodsucker and accumulates houses and stores. Maybe she's forgotten how her father makes his fortune.

Farida had better shut her mouth and accept her new life or one day I'll give her a beating she won't soon forget. Has she forgotten I'm her husband? Or maybe she thinks I'm like her brother, Habib, that weakling. He too thinks he's a god. Too smart for us. All he needs is to change his name and religion and become a Frenchman. But I know what Habib's problem is. He's a big baby. He's afraid of his own shadow. He'll never be able to go to bed with a woman. The only thing he knows how to do is read books and do his lessons. The other boys in the neighbourhood used to laugh at him. They would grab the *chechia* off his head and toss it from one to another. I can still see him running back and forth trying to get it back while the boys played with it and laughed. Finally, when they'd had enough fun, they would throw it on the ground and Habib would sheepishly pick it up. He would walk away, his satchel under his arm, the *chechia*, a bit crushed, stuck back on his head any old way. From Rue Kaadine, he would hurry toward Rue de Pacha, and then continue along Rue Dar El Jeld, crossing Rue Bab Bnet, to finally arrive at Collège Sadiki, which he's been going on about ever since he was accepted there.

But books and reading don't bring in a centime. I go every week in my *carroussa* to Jedeida and meet with Romdane, his sons, and the workers in the fields. Fall, winter, spring, or summer, in rain, wind, or extreme heat, it doesn't matter, I don't get any respite. I have to go there and inspect the work, or that shiftless Romdane and his sons will lie to me and say the harvest isn't good this year and they can't pay the rent for the land. And of course I deserve a few little pleasures, like a new pair of shoes from Chez Carlo or a few glasses of wine at Café La Joie before spending an evening or two in Samira's arms. I deserve more than that, but one day they'll see how important I am to the whole family, including my uncle, who will kiss my forehead for preserving our land and keeping and increasing the money of the Ben Mahmoud family.

Chapter 7

Farida

Luckily my aunts Zohra and Hnani were back from Hammam-Lif and I didn't have to cook anymore. They quickly took things back into their competent hands. They made a different dish every day, a delicious dish that we would savour, which put an end to Kamel's constant grumbling and complaints. My aunts didn't bother me; they even told me that until I had a child, I would still be considered a new bride and would be spoiled. So I prayed to God day and night that I would not have a child.

Every morning when Kamel went out to the land, I'd go back to bed and catch up on the hours of sleep I'd lost with him. It was always the same scene, him on top of me like a horse in rut, and me silent, waiting in the dim light for him to get it over with. When finally, he threw himself on his back panting with pleasure, I'd roll to the other side of the bed and put my nightgown back on. Kamel would quickly fall asleep, as if he were paralyzed by the love he looked for in me. I would remain awake, thinking of a man who would truly love me, with whom I could spend the evening nibbling salted chickpeas or chestnuts roasted over a low fire in the *kanoun* and discussing the most beautiful passage of a book or reading a poem describing our sadness or our happiness. Unfortunately, Kamel's loud snoring added to my nightly torments, and I had a hard time waking up to make coffee for Baba and serve one to Kamel before he left. But as soon as he closed the door behind him, I'd slip back into my bed, reassured by my aunts' presence, and find the sleep Kamel had taken from me the night before.

Sometimes Fatma would come and wake me up and I would spend the morning with her, happy to be together. One day she came with her hair braided, wearing a pretty dress that went down only to her knees, a dress I didn't recognize. Her pale skin contrasted with her dark eyes and hair. The new dress accentuated her ample bosom. Fatma was beautiful, with no resemblance to her brother Kamel—unfortunately my husband— with his nasty look of a scrounging rat.

I took her hand the way I used to when we were kids, and led her to my little sitting room. Everything was orderly. The big Italian baroque armchair of carved wood that my father had given me, with its wine-red and ochre velvet cushions, and the matching chairs. Their gilded wood made them look even more opulent. In the middle, there was a small white marble table with a solid base the same colour as the wood of the chairs. And against the wall, a bookcase Baba had ordered from the same cabinetmaker, still filled with his books in Arabic.

"Where did you get the new dress?" I asked.

Fatma remained standing. She twirled around twice to show the fullness of the skirt, which fit closely at her tiny waist. Her fast twirls revealed her firm white calves.

"It's so beautiful on you. You're not afraid your father will forbid you to wear a dress like that?"

"Who do you think I'd seduce? Habib doesn't look at anything but his books, and the men in my house are my little brothers. You know I rarely go out." A veil of sadness fell over her face.

"Don't worry, Fatma. You're still young. You're only sixteen. Don't be in too much of a hurry. Eventually you'll find a good match. A man who will love you, that's what counts."

Her cheeks turned red. "And you think such a man exists?"

"Why not? There are plenty of men from good families. You just have to be noticed at a wedding, by the mother or sister of one of them, and you'll see, it will happen."

Her eyes brightened. "As a matter of fact, I wanted to tell you my cousin Rafika is getting married in a week, and you're invited. And I'm planning to wear this dress on one of the evenings."

I knew Rafika. She was Fatma's cousin on her mother's side and some-times came to visit us with her mother and sisters. She lived not far from us, near the great mosque of Al-Zaytuna. Her father had died when she was young, and her mother, Kalthoum, had gotten remarried to Am Chedli, who had a *chechia* shop on Rue de Sidi Ben Arous and was fat and good-natured and praised by everyone. He had raised Rafika as his own daughter.

"But you haven't told me where you got the dress."

Fatma stood up again and turned from side to side to show off her figure. Everything about her was lovely, her full breasts, her plump arms, her bright face, her dark, silky hair. Fatma was a great beauty; all she needed was a husband who would love her. While I, thin and not especially attractive, had been married for several months to a man I did not love.

"I sewed the dress myself. I cut it the way I wanted it. My mother helped a bit with the sewing and fitting, but I did almost all of it myself."

I was astounded. I knew Fatma was good with her hands—cooking, making pastries . . . and now sewing. "But where did you get the pattern? It looks like a dress from France."

She made a face, laughing at my naïveté. "My dear Farida, you live in your books, but I'm practical."

She laughed and held out some crumpled pages from a fashion magazine, *Le Petit Écho de la Mode*. The issue was a few months old. On the cover, it said in big letters that it was published every Wednesday and cost ten cents.

I still didn't understand. "But where did you find this?"

Fatma motioned to me to lower my voice. "I went out alone the other day, not far from our house. I really felt like having some roasted chickpeas and none of my brothers were home. So, without anyone knowing, I put on my *safsari* and went out. I bought the chickpeas, and they were in a cone made of the paper that you're holding. When I saw the dress, I knew I had to copy it. I had to wear a dress like the ones the beautiful French ladies wear. We're beautiful too, aren't we?"

I looked dumbly at the paper in my hand. Four drawings of elegant women. One of their dresses was similar to the one Fatma was wearing. A tight waist and buttons in the front. Short sleeves that barely covered her arms and a skirt that ended at the knee. I was amazed. Here was a girl who didn't know a word of French but who could make a dress for herself based on some images on a crumpled piece of paper. "Fatma, you are amazing. You'll have to make me a dress like yours."

"I'd be glad to make one for you, Farida."

I was so impressed by Fatma's determination that I had forgotten Kamel and my woes.

Chapter 8

Kamel

I had made an appointment with Lamine at the café on Place Halfaouine. I left home early, after a quick cup of coffee Farida had made for her father and me. A disgusting coffee, with no froth, which was not a good sign. She probably made it while she was still asleep and couldn't tell the sugar from the salt. All she likes to do is sleep and read. There's no limit to her laziness. This morning I didn't have time to bawl her out, and also her father was present, but I'll take care of her later. It was nothing like the coffee with sugar from Samira's magic hands. The little brown bubbles on it make me want to take another sip and the drops of geranium flower water Samira adds are almost intoxicating.

But this morning I forgot my sufferings as an unhappy husband and hurried to Place Halfaouine, stopping in front of Lamine's barber shop, where he was sitting waiting for me. There was a yellow canary singing sweetly in a small cage hanging on the wall, and Lamine was whistling to encourage it. When he saw me coming, he took a comb from his back pocket and fixed his hair, gesturing to me to wait.

"*Sbah el Kheir*, Lamine," I greeted him, "Are we going?"

"Yes, just a minute! I want to tell my apprentice to clean the floor and wash the scissors, combs, and blades."

The young apprentice came out of the shop in a grey knee-length smock and a *chechia*, with a broom in his hand. He greeted me with a nod. "Don't worry, *Arfi*," he answered his boss respectfully, "I'll do as you say."

"Very well, and if someone comes for a haircut, offer him a cup of coffee or tea and tell him to wait for me. I'll be back in an hour."

The apprentice nodded. Lamine whistled a last few notes to the canary, and we left to go meet the Italian, Monsieur Giuliano, who was interested in renting our land.

There were shops all along our way. The butcher, Am Salem, was hanging up sheep heads, whose lolling tongues and dripping saliva made them almost look alive. Ox feet that had been singed, scraped, and washed were displayed on the counter to attract customers.

"Good day, Am Salem. The ox feet look fresh, I'll take one or two to make a *hargma*."

"Whenever you want, just tell me, *ya* Si Kamel."

"I'll come back and get one later."

"With pleasure! I'll always have something good for you."

With the back of his hand, he waved away the flies congregating on the fresh meat.

A skinny cat was washing its face in the sunshine in front of the store, waiting patiently for Am Salem to toss it a piece of fat or for a mouse to come out of the grocery store next door.

We were almost at Place Halfaouine. The Saheb Ettabaâ Mosque shone like a jewel in the midst of a sea of poverty. The stores surrounding the ground floor of the mosque were opening their doors. Carts were stopping in front of them and child apprentices were placing merchandise on the cobblestones for older, stronger workers to take inside. Men wearing *jebbas*, with turbans on their heads, were hurrying up the stairs to the mosque, where sheiks were probably teaching the Quran or the *fikh* in *halakat ilm*. A woman in a *safsari*, her face hidden by a *khama*, was walking on the other side of the street, her little boy lagging behind her.

We reached the café on Place Halfaouine, which was shaded by plane trees. The patio of the café was already full of men sitting at the tables talking animatedly. Lamine and I found two chairs and sat down. I took out my watch and checked the time. "What time did the Italian say he'd be here?"

Lamine mopped his forehead with a handkerchief. "He'll be here, he said he was coming early in the morning, he didn't give me an exact time. He'll come. Look, there he is, I see him coming."

A man wearing trousers and a checked jacket and looking a bit lost in the hubbub of the café came toward us. He was almost completely bald, with a few strands of hair carefully combed to the side barely covering his shining skull.

Lamine stood up and motioned to the Italian, calling in a loud voice, "Monsieur Giuliano, Monsieur Giuliano, we're over here,"

The man seemed reassured, and came toward us smiling.

Lamine began to speak. "Monsieur Giuliano, this is my friend Kamel Ben Mahmoud. He is the owner of some nice land on the shores of the Medjerda, in the valley near Jedeida. You can ask him all the questions you want, and I really hope you'll do good business together." He was getting ready to go. "I left the shop with the apprentice. I don't want to miss my regular morning customers."

I held him back with my hand. "Stay for a few more minutes. I'll buy you a coffee. Garçon, two—no, three—coffees!" I turned to Monsieur Giuliano. "A coffee for you, Sir?"

He smiled. "Yes, a coffee, y'achek," he replied politely.

He spoke the Tunis dialect almost perfectly. I was very glad, because I only knew a few words of French and I didn't want to do business in a language that wasn't my own. I had been afraid Monsieur Giuliano would speak to me in French, as some Italians who've lived in Tunisia for a long time do. "So, you're looking for land to raise cows and make cheese?"

Monsieur Giuliano, still smiling, explained that he was from Sicily and had come to live in Tunis with his family when he was five years old. Since then, they had lived in La Goulette, in a two-bedroom apartment in a building his uncle had built. His father and his uncle lived there with their wives and children. He had left school at fourteen and started to work for another Sicilian, who sold cheese and spices in the Marché Central in Tunis. Little by little, he had learned to make Sicilian cheese and ricotta. Now he had some savings and a wife and daughter to help him, and he wanted to buy some cows and rent land to set up a farm to produce milk and make cheese from it.

I listened in silence as Monsieur Giuliano told me his life story, and I imagined the farm he wanted to build on our land and how it would make the land more profitable. I would get rid of Romdane Jlassi, that idler who was always telling lies about the crops, and replace him with this Italian, who seemed honest and ambitious. "There's a small house on our land. You could live in it with your family. You'd only have to pay rent for the land."

"What about water? Is there access to the Medjerda River?"

"We have a well, but the river is close. The only thing we don't have is a stable for the cows."

Monsieur Giuliano did not appear too disappointed. "I can build one. My uncle has promised to help me. I have an idea of how to go about it."

We were practically in agreement on everything. The rent, the date, and even a commission when the business did well. Lamine had drunk his coffee and left in a hurry. I was delighted to have met this Italian. Our land would be in better hands and I would have a regular rent and maybe some profit as well.

"I want to start the work in a month."

"I have to get rid of the current tenant first. After that, we'll sign a contract for several years."

Monsieur Giuliano shook my hand and we agreed to meet again at the same time and place in two weeks.

Before I left the café, the owner, a guy I knew vaguely, announced to the clients that a new *Karakouz* show would begin at onset of Ramadan. That was still a few months away, but I promised myself I'd come see it. I loved the puppets.

Chapter 9

Habib

I was walking to Collège Sadiki, the jewel of Tunisian education. The country's future lawyers, teachers, doctors, and jurists studied there in order to contribute to the advancement of the country and free it from the clutches of French colonialism. No boy from our family had ever gone there. I was the first one. My father's cousin Jalloul Ben Mahmoud had nearly gone there, but tuberculosis took him at a very young age. I got to know *Ammi* Jalloul when he came to live with us in the last days of his life. He was emaciated and weakened by illness, and with each breath he came a little closer to death.

My father visited him only rarely, while my uncle, Sheik Salah, was calculating the share of the inheritance that, according to Islamic law, would come to him after Jalloul's death. Once Jalloul left this lowly world, which according to my Uncle Salah was not worth much, how many hectares would be added to their respective properties, the land that the great patriarch Mahmoud Ben Mahmoud had acquired at the beginning of the century and that had since fed the family—and fuelled their arguments. Jalloul was the only one in the family who was not interested in the land or in the endless quarreling between my father and his brother. He read day and night. Even sickness did not deter him from his quest for knowledge. He was a delicate young man, gentle, with fine features. A sensitive person. A stranger in a family that was divided by money and obsessed with appearances and social status. His father, the elder brother of my father and my uncle, had died young, and Jalloul,

his only offspring, had inherited his father's share, one third of the land
near Jedeida. Young Jalloul had become the object of my father's and my
uncle's greed. Fortunately, his mother was able to protect him from that
hell by giving him a lot of love and a good education. No one understood
Jalloul's immense knowledge, nor his refinement, his boundless compassion. They saw only the land he possessed, and they were waiting for one
thing: for him to die, so they could get their hands on his share of the
inheritance. And Jalloul died in horrible conditions, abandoned by his
cousins, misunderstood by the rest of the family, having lost his father
and then his mother. His life was snuffed out early, like the flame of a
candle blown out by violent winds.

I would sometimes visit Jalloul in his dark room. They had given him
a bed with a straw mattress and a small bedside table. My aunts Hnani
and Zohra, who were also at the mercy of my father and my uncle—and
who, although theoretically entitled to his land, would receive nothing
from their brothers—took care of him as best they could. I would keep
him company and talk to him about my studies. A book in his hands,
he would smile feebly and always ask the same question: "When are
you going to go to Collège Sadiki?" His weak, teary eyes spoke volumes
about his suffering.

"Soon, Ammi Jalloul," I would answer. "Insha'Allah, in a few years."

And as if by a miracle, his eyes would light up, his breathing would
stabilize, and his face would be filled with a smile stolen from death.

"Make sure you don't let yourself get caught up in the family's scheming and endless quarrels. You will lose your soul. Go to college and
become a teacher, earn your living and get away from those monsters."
He stopped short, tired from talking too much, tired from the heavy
words and the painful thoughts. I held his hand and moved closer to kiss
him. To kiss his delicate fingers that didn't know how to hurt, that knew
only how to hold a pen and turn the pages of books.

At the touch of my lips on his fingers, he closed his eyes and stopped
talking. My tears flowed in silence. I wanted that moment to go on forever. I wanted to hold onto that image of two people sitting in a room
where death and speech were waging a ruthless battle that would soon
end with the victory of death.

When Jalloul died, my uncle and my father pretended to grieve, each
in his own way. My father by distributing thirty meals to poor people

living in our lane in the medina, and my uncle by reciting suras from the Quran for three days. Two years after his death, I entered Collège Sadiki, a dream of Jalloul's that had never been realized during his short life, but that I was able to give him as a posthumous gift.

In the distance, I could see the twin domes of the college, like two breasts pointing to the sky, and the minaret, standing tall like a jealous guardian of Islamic traditions. The college represented a kind of uncertain compromise between East and West, between French and Arabic, a union of two worlds that had been watching each other for centuries. My friends were in the large courtyard with its stone pillars with black and white marble arabesques. They were in little groups waiting for the start of classes.

"Did you finish the Arabic essay on *Kalila wa Dimna*?" Hedi Zakour asked quietly.

Hedi was my best friend. We got along famously. His father had a little vegetable shop. His background was humble compared to my family's, but certainly with simpler and more peaceful relationships, for which I envied him at times.

"Yes, I finished it. I'll read it to you during the break."

The bell rang, and we lined up in silence to go to our classroom at the end of the corridor, where the French teacher was waiting for us with his usual serious air and invincible authority.

Chapter 10

Farida

Fatma's cousin Rafika's wedding was simply magnificent. It almost made me forget the unhappiness of my marriage to Kamel. But in the midst of those days of gaiety and celebration, an upsetting event put an abrupt end to my happiness. That event would mark me for life.

The festivities went on for three days. We were almost a delegation: Fatma, my aunts Hnani and Zohra, Fatma's mother, whose sister was none other than the mother of the bride, and I. Of course, there were other women invited, some of whom I knew and others I was seeing for the first time. The house where Rafika lived with her mother, her stepfather, and her half-sisters was in the middle of the medina. A lovely house, with an inner courtyard with ochre and blue tiles on the walls and a marble floor. The wooden doors of the bedrooms contrasted with the whitewashed walls, on which branches of jasmine climbed, whose mauve-tinted white flowers filled the air with their perfume in the evening. The young girls would gather the blossoms and string them together into necklaces to scent their necks and bosoms.

Aunts Hnani and Zohra were spending the days in the kitchen with old acquaintances, preparing dishes to be served to the guests in the evenings. Taking advantage of my sudden freedom, I spent my days with Fatma and the other girls, some of them married and others dreaming of marriage. I stuffed myself with *mloukhia*, lamb stew, and sausages in tomato sauce with capers and preserved lemons. I ate constantly, delighting in these delicious dishes that, sadly, I couldn't make myself.

In the evening, they would sprinkle the marble floor with cold water from the well in the centre of the courtyard. When it was dry, the floor would be covered with kilims, sheepskins, woolen blankets, and cushions. The guests would sit cross-legged on them or lie leaning against the wall, and at night they would sleep there under the stars until morning.

When the evening meal was finished, the bride would sit in the centre, surrounded by her female cousins and other relatives and neighbours, and the *hanana* would decorate her hands with henna paste. "There's no bride without henna. It brings good fortune, and above all, green is the colour of fertility," said the old woman, who would moisten the paste with her saliva until her lips were stained wine-red, and apply it with care to Rafika's plump little fingers. Rafika kept smiling at the guests.

At the *hanana*'s words, Fatma looked into my eyes. I knew what was in her mind. How come I was still not pregnant? Had the henna not brought me good fortune? "Don't you want to put on a little henna?" she teased.

"No, I still have some on my nails from my wedding, it takes a long time to fade away. I'll put some on for your wedding, I promise."

Fatma blushed. She was really beautiful. She had put on the dress she'd made, which accentuated her generous curves. She was radiant under the jealous gaze of the other girls.

When the women began to sing and the girls to dance, Fatma joined in. Each time she twirled, I would see girls whispering behind their hands, their eyebrows raised at her boldness. But Fatma couldn't have cared less. She danced with all the more enthusiasm.

There were no men in the house, only women and children. Rafika's stepfather, Am Chedli, was sleeping at the home of one of the neighbours who had opened their houses for the many guests. We had seen him when we arrived at the house on the first day. He was a fat man with fleshy lips, laughing eyes, and a goatee. Fatma and I, wrapped in our *safsaris*, were getting out of the *carroussa*, with my aunts and Fatma's mother ahead of us. "*Zaritna Al barka, zaritna Al barka!*" he had said in greeting with every step we took through the vestibule to the bench where we could rest. He pretended to avert his eyes, as a mark of respect for the women, but I could easily see that his gaze rested on Fatma. Her face was radiant and he was clearly stirred by her beauty. In the evening, when I shared my observation, Fatma burst out laughing. "But I need someone who isn't married. That one's already taken. And he's my aunt's husband, with a daughter who's almost the same age as I am."

All the men in our family, my father, my brother Habib, and even her own brother Kamel, were wary of Fatma. They found her dangerous, with her lively intelligence, her easy manner with people, and her sometimes brazen behaviour. They seemed to feel threatened by Fatma, but I didn't really understand why.

There was one night left of the wedding. Every evening after the meal, the sweets, the gallons of tea, the singing and dancing, we would lie on the rugs and blankets in the courtyard and try to sleep. The old women were in the large rooms inside the house, but we stayed outside with only the starry sky to watch over us. I always stayed close to Fatma. Our pillows and nightgowns touched each other. Since my recent marriage, I went almost unnoticed in the group of girls. I was no longer a little girl now, but I was not a woman either. I was between two worlds, belonging to neither.

Suppressed laughter, muffled whispers, the refrain of a song hummed endlessly came from every corner of the courtyard, keeping us awake for hours. Every once in a while, one of the older women would burst angrily out of a neighbouring room and order us to keep quiet. Silence would descend for a few moments, and then gradually the sounds of feet, hands, and arms moving under the covers would resume, and this would continue until the first light of dawn.

When I woke up in the morning, Fatma was not beside me. I looked around and all the other girls were still asleep, their hair spread out on the covers, silk shawls covering their bodies, their lips parted. They would soon be awakened by grandmothers, mothers, and aunts, to begin the last preparations for the *tasdira*, the great day when the bride would wear her sequined and embroidered *keswa* and the guests would all come to admire it and wish her good fortune and joy before she went to live with her husband.

Finally, I saw Fatma returning. She was coming from the washroom, walking as if the *kabkabs* on her feet weighed a ton. Her face was white as a sheet. I didn't know what was the matter with her. Maybe she hadn't been able to sleep.

"What's wrong? Are you sick?"

She didn't say a word. There was none of her usual gaiety in her eyes.

"Did the *mloukhia* give you a stomach ache? I'll go make you some mint tea. You'll see, that will make you feel better."

Fatma wouldn't look me in the eye. I didn't recognize the cousin I'd grown up with, who had shared the secrets of the house with me, my childhood friend who would pretend to understand French, who had sewn the beautiful, clinging dress that had shocked the other girls and made them turn green with envy. This was a stranger in front of me. I began to panic. "Fatma, what's the matter? I'm going to call your mother, *Khalti* Kmar, she'll send one of the boys to buy some herbs to boil. You'll see, you'll feel better."

The mention of her mother gave her a start, and she placed her hand over my mouth and motioned to me to stop talking. "No, not my mother! She mustn't find out."

I still didn't understand what had happened to Fatma. What if the stories of *jinn* and sorcery my grandmother, and then my mother, had told so often on winter evenings were true and what if the "other people," as my mother called them, had frightened Fatma when she was in the washroom, and what if her soul had been kidnapped by a *jinni* who refused to return it? If all that was true, what would we do to get the old Fatma back?

Fatma came over to me. She crouched beside me, grimacing as if she had an invisible pain, and brought her mouth close to my ear. Her eyes wide and her mouth sad, she whispered, "I'm a woman like you. Am Chedli has taken everything from me. I no longer have anything to offer."

Chapter 11

Fatma

Farida had fallen asleep. I could hear the faint whispers of the other girls. One was speaking of a ring she had admired on a guest the evening before. She found it beautiful and wanted one just like it. I heard her say that maybe her future husband would give her one that was as lovely and elegant. An emerald set with zircons. Always the same dreams, always the same wishes. I didn't want a ring. I wanted a man who would love me. I needed love and attention, not the vacant gaze of my father, the suspicious gaze of my brother Kamel, or the embarrassed gaze of my cousin Habib. A gaze that would linger on me. That would love me for who I am without any fear.

I was having trouble digesting the *mloukhia*. The women had put too much oil in it. Even the lemon juice I'd squeezed onto the viscous green liquid hadn't dissolved all the oil in my stomach. I couldn't stop burping. I felt like vomiting.

I couldn't sleep and I suddenly needed to go to the toilet. Maybe then I would feel better. Without putting on my *kabkabs*, I set out for the *douiria*, which was between the main bedroom of the house and the kitchen. I knew the way perfectly and I couldn't go wrong in spite of the darkness lighted only by a few rays of moonlight. I groped my way along the walls so as not to trip over anything the girls had left on the ground by.

As I approached the *douiria*, I heard a faint whisper, as if someone was calling my name. I turned around quickly and saw Am Chedli in the dark. I was sure it was him, it couldn't be anyone else. The round face, the stocky body, even in the semidarkness I could recognize his silhouette.

"Fatma, Fatma, come here."

I was afraid. I had never seen him without his *chechia*. A man without a *chechia* was a man with his family, a man at home.

I didn't know what he was doing here in the middle of the night. We were all women and children. The men were sleeping at the neighbours'.

"Come here, Fatma, come; I need you."

I took a step toward him to see what he wanted. He took advantage of my closeness to grab me and pull me toward him with both arms. I wanted to cry out to get free.

"Keep quiet, or everyone will think you came to see me."

I didn't know what he was talking about. Again, I wanted to shout, but he put his mouth against mine and kissed me violently. I shuddered. I didn't want this kind of love. "What are you doing, Am Chedli?"

I tried to get away from him. We were in the vestibule, where a candle was slowly burning down. I recognized the little bench usually reserved for guests. He wedged me against it and began to touch me all over my body, my neck, my arms, my belly, my bottom, and my legs. I didn't know what to do. If I cried out and ran away, I would be shamed in front of all the women in the house. I could already hear them talking about me. "She was asking for it." "Did you see that dress she was wearing?" "*Wallah*, you'd think it was a dress for a *gaouri*." "She shouldn't have provoked the men like that." "After all, a man can't help looking." I would be the shame of the house. I had asked for it, hadn't I, and I'd have to pay the price for my brazen behaviour.

And my cousin Rafika, the bride, and my Aunt Kalthoum, Am Chedli's wife, what would they think? That I had seduced their father and husband? What would happen to my poor Aunt Kalthoum? Would she believe me or her second husband, who had taken her out of poverty and given her a good life with a comfortable house, lovely healthy daughters, and the status of a respectable woman. Thoughts whirled around in my head. Meanwhile, Am Chedli's hands were moving all over me. He was all over me with his kisses, his saliva, his moustache, his goatee. I resisted, I resisted and I pushed him, but I was dealing with a man. No, I was dealing with a rutting animal.

"You're so beautiful, Fatma, your freshness, your body, your eyes, you're driving me crazy, I adore you."

Violence and love. I'd never dreamed of that. How dare he speak like this while he was doing me harm? Am Chedli, the model of respect and gallantry. The new father of my cousin Rafika, who would in a few hours be giving her away in marriage like any good father, was on top of me on a wooden bench soiling me with his hands, crushing my body and tearing my soul into a thousand pieces.

Chapter 12

Monsieur Giuliano

I returned home pleased with my meeting with the Arab. I wasn't ready to believe everything Kamel said, but, still, he seemed somewhat honest. In any case, the land seemed good. I asked my Uncle Paolo, who's lived in Tunis since 1890, for his opinion. He knew these Arabs better than I did, and better than old Fabio: their scheming, their dishonesty, their lies, the way they treat their women and children. He's always warned us not to trust them. We were caught between the French on one side and the Arabs on the other. The French gave us a big "slap" in 1881 when they surprised us by signing the Treaty of Bardo. We'd been present in Tunisia longer than the French. Sicilians and Italians had been established here for centuries, with our fishermen and coral fishers on the coast, our clothing shops, and our businesses in El Grana. All that was us. But the French always acted superior to us, as if they had more right to the country than we did.

By the grace of the Madonna, I'll rent this land and make my cheese and sell it in the Marché Central of Tunis. I'll earn my living like a Frenchman and I'll show old Fabio what I'm capable of. He has always underestimated me and never believed in me. He would tell me, "Go sell *limonata* and *biscotti* to the Arabs in a makeshift stall in front of the Marché Central. You're not good enough for a trade, you're too stupid." I'll show him I can do better than a mere stall in the street. That my daughter Graziella and my wife Lorena can live decently. Maybe we'll even be able to buy a small apartment in the new neighbourhood of

Lafayette in Tunis. I would leave La Goleta in spite of my love for the Saint-Augustin-et-Saint-Fidèle church in La Petite Sicile. I would forget the misfortunes of my childhood. The brawls in the neighbourhood streets. The dirty, barefoot, snot-nosed kids playing with a ball in front of the buildings. I'd forget all of it.

We'd go to mass every Sunday and come back and eat together, with a good wine from Grombalia and some fried freshly caught triglia with tomato sauce and zucchini. We'd work together and I wouldn't have to take orders from old Fabio anymore. My dear Lorena and Graziella would work with me, always faithful, always loving.

I'd do anything to get out of that building in La Petite Sicile. Dark, dirty, crawling with kids, whose mothers shout at them from their kitchen windows all day long. "How did you get so dirty?" And then a slap here and a whack on the bottom there. ""What are you crying for? Come here and I'll give you something to cry about." And the kid would cry harder and the mother would swear on her father's head that she'd tear out his tongue if he didn't stop. And the father would come with his belt and add to the kid's suffering. I saw and heard these scenes all day long. Sometimes I would cover my ears with my hands in a vain effort to block them out. My father did the same as the other fathers in the neighbourhood. And the women, talking from their windows while hanging out the wash, their children's patched pants and their husbands' underwear. "Have you heard? Claudia had an argument with her husband last night. He beat her all night. I heard the blows and the shouts. He's always getting drunk and beating her. He's jealous. He saw her talking to the fishmonger in the market and accused her of being his lover. Poor Claudia. One day she'll be in a coffin and her kids will be orphans, poor *donna*." Rumours, bad news, men brawling after leaving the bistro, women gossiping, children fighting in the street. I didn't want that life anymore.

I'd buy a nice apartment and take Lorena and Graziella away from that nightmare. Everything would be clean, calm, well-maintained. The French and the Jews built nice houses. They sent their children to Lycée Carnot on Rue de Paris. Sunday afternoons, they drove around in their beautiful cars or just went for a walk. I'd like to do that, and erase old Fabio from my memory. Go out on Sunday afternoon arm in arm with Lorena, stroll around, look at the cars, admire the lovely new buildings with their blue shutters and wide balconies, where an old man might be sitting who'd greet us with a nod. I would forget La Goleta, its violence, its cramped quarters, the dark looks of old Fabio and his heartbreaking words day after day. But before that paradise and that new life could become a reality, I would have to rent the land from Ben Mahmoud and start up my cheese business.

The TGM train had stopped at La Goulette. A crowd poured out of it into the little station like a swarm of flies. French civil servants, Italian workmen like those in our building, and a few Arabs—women in *safsaris* carrying baskets, with their children running around, men in *jebbas* shuffling their feet in their *babouches*, and others who looked a bit better off, wearing European dress, their noses in the air.

The autumn sun was beating down, burning my skin. The heat was humid and sticky. I mopped my forehead with my handkerchief. The smell of the soap my lovely Lorena used for the laundry refreshed me for a few moments. I tried to make my way through the people who were all trying to get out the iron gate of the station at the same time. I finally got to my usual route, along Avenue du Cardinal Lavigerie and then Rue Jean Jaurès. I could already see the Church of Saint-Augustin-et-Saint-Fidèle smiling at me, with its tall campanile, its steeples, and its whitewashed walls. Always beautiful and charming, the interior with its wonderful frescoes as well as the exterior. My Uncle Claudio had told me that the frescoes had been painted by the brother of the mafioso Alfonso Capone in penance for the sins of his *famiglia*, but I couldn't believe it. May the Madonna protect us! Images of my little Graziella in her beautiful lace dress at her communion are still etched in my memory. I quickened my pace. I was eager to tell Lorena of my meeting with Kamel Ben Mahmoud.

There was a deathly silence in front of the building. None of the usual racket of children running in and out, racing down the stairs past the adult residents clinging to the wall or the banister to keep from being overturned. The cacophony of women shouting insults and gossip from their balconies was absent. The shutters were closed. What had happened, I wondered, praying to the Madonna that nothing terrible had occurred. I noticed little Alfredo, a neighbour's son, sitting under the fig tree in front of the building, scratching on the ground with a little branch. "Alfredo, what's going on, why isn't there anyone outside?"

He barely looked at me, absorbed in his digging. "It's old Fabio, he fell down off the ladder when he was fixing the roof. He died right away."

I could hardly believe my ears. Fabio, old Fabio, couldn't have died so suddenly. Fabio, who had never had a kind word, a smile, or a gentle touch for me, who had beaten me. Old Fabio was no more. For all his dreams of rising high, he had ended his life at the foot of a ladder. My father was dead. I turned, leaving little Alfredo to his labours, and entered the building to be with my family in this misfortune that had befallen us.

Chapter 13

Farida

I couldn't believe what had happened to my cousin Fatma. I came back from the wedding sad, my heart as heavy as the day my mother died and her body wrapped in a white shroud was carried out on a board on the shoulders of my father, my uncle, and other men of the family. Fatma hadn't said another word after she told me what Am Chedli did to her. We attended the wedding as if it were a funeral. No laughter, no joy, no sparkle in our eyes, not a word. All that was missing was tears. They were kept inside. The women laughed and Fatma's heart was bleeding. The girls danced and Fatma's body was suffering. While the bride was getting ready to spend her wedding night with her husband, her stepfather had destroyed my cousin's body, defiling it with his hands and his breath and imprinting in her memory and her flesh words that would never be uttered.

Rafika's wedding ceremony had been carried out in accordance with tradition. It would be talked about for months and years. For Fatma, Rafika's wedding was a death sentence, the night her fate was sealed. A night she would remember all her life. What would she say when a man came and asked for her hand in marriage? That Am Chedli had been quicker than any other man and had violated her? That Am Chedli, a respected merchant liked by everyone and affectionately called Si Shidula by all the artisans of Rue de Sidi Ben Arous, was in reality a pervert who had raped Fatma, his own daughters' cousin? And if he had done it to Fatma, perhaps he had done it to other young girls. All of them forced into silence. A silence that could turn into a scandal that would blow up and apparently the first that occurred to Kamel.

"You have to go see a midwife. I need to know. That would be the best news of my life."

Until that day, I had never thought I would become pregnant. As if babies came from heaven or as if I believed Kamel's manhood would have no effect on my body.

Chapter 14

Kamel

I slowly disentangled myself from Samira's arms. Her bedroom hadn't changed, the same cathouse clutter that I usually found so stimulating. But not today. The perfume bottles lined up on her dark wood dresser, some full, some half-empty, little gifts from her transient lovers, didn't arouse my desire, and the black hair cascading down her arched back and her provocative poses in front of the mirror didn't make me want to take her and make her mine again and again. Nothing had any effect.

My mind was fixed on one thought: Farida was pregnant. Mongia, the midwife, had given her the news a few days ago. I'd made Farida pregnant. Another life was growing within her. A new life that had come from me and found shelter in her belly. Who would have thought it? My cousin Farida, who did not want to love me, who did not respond to my touch and withdrew as far from me as possible every time I took her, was pregnant. I would soon become a father, Farida would give me that gift. The body of that woman who couldn't love and couldn't cook had been able to conceive a child and she would give it to me. While Samira, whose body, whose breasts and thighs, were made to be desired, to be touched and caressed, gave me nothing. A tree that bore no fruit. A flower with no scent. A plot of land with no water. That's what Samira was. Yet I loved her and could not be without her. But today, things were different. Something had changed.

Samira took me in her honey-coloured arms again and gave me one of her most beautiful smiles. Her left eyelid was twitching. I avoided her gaze.

"What's the matter with you today, aren't you well?" She pouted like a little girl trying to choose between a piece of chocolate and a caramel. "You don't love me anymore, is that it? Or are you thinking about your wife? I know, these respectable women always end up getting the upper hand." The sparkle went out of her eyes. She glanced over at the bottles of perfume as if they reminded her of the succession of men who had passed through this dim room that smelled of tobacco, perfume, and damp.

I didn't answer. I put my pants on again, and my *jebba*, which I'd thrown on the blue velvet chair. "It's not what you think, Samira. Yes, it's my wife. But she's not the one I love. It's the child in her belly. That's who I'm thinking of."

She leaned back on her arms, her head on the big pillow, and hid her breasts under the pink sheets we had rolled around on dozens of times, mad with desire. She picked up a heavy wool blanket that had fallen beside the bed and pulled it up over her naked body. She was trembling slightly and I could see she had goosebumps. I looked away to avoid seeing the tears welling up in her eyes.

A loud burst of laughter filled the room. Samira, always surprising, always unpredictable. Never sad for long. Still covered with the blanket, she reached for a cigarette and picked up the silver-plated lighter I had given her, bought at a high price in the Souk El Birka, the jewellers' market. The flame quivered with her breathing. She inhaled deeply and let out a cloud of white smoke that rose to the ceiling, which was speckled with green spots of mold. "You have to buy me a *mabrouk*. I give you pleasure and it's your wife who gets pregnant."

More demands. But this time I couldn't say no, I would buy her a gift as she asked—a dress, a gold bracelet, or perfume again. "What do you want, my sweet?"

I felt desire return. I approached her. She moved away and went and sat on the blue chair, her bare legs crossed, her upper body still hidden under the blanket.

"I want a house in La Marsa, facing the sea. I want to hear the murmur of the waves in the evening with a glass of mint tea in one hand and a cigarette in the other. It was my childhood dream. Get me out of this dark room, this pigsty of Sidi Abdallah Guech. Your little boy who will soon be born is worth more than that, isn't he, *ya azizi?*"

I was speechless. Samira had made strange demands, but this was one too many. A house in La Marsa was the last thing I'd expected her to ask for. I could never afford such a gift for her. Not even if the business with Monsieur Giuliano went wonderfully well.

She came over to me. The blanket had fallen to the ground, revealing her bare shoulders. She put her cigarette in the pink ashtray decorated with little hearts, which already contained a few butts. "So, what do you think? A little house in my name, where you can come visit me whenever you want, where I'll put my life as a whore behind me and become a respectable woman like your wife. What do you think, *ya azizi*?"

I could never do such a thing. Where would I get the money? My Uncle Laroussi wouldn't allow it. He controls all the money that comes in and goes out. He counts every *sourdi*. No, anything but a house!

"We'll talk about it, Samira. You know, there's a war on, everyone is talking about it. The Germans are going to land here. Business is not as good as you think. You'll have a *mabrouk*, that's for sure. But a house in La Marsa . . . "

"Nothing is impossible. God is great and generous! You'll see. I'm going to pray for you, for your wife, and for the boy who will be born."

I really didn't want to look at her. I was soon going to meet with Monsieur Leduc, the bank manager. I was going to ask him for a loan to build a stable on our land. Business would have to be good, the money would have to flow, and the family would have to get rich, in spite of the French who'd colonized us and the Germans who were at our gates.

Chapter 15

Habib

"The Destour Party is our only hope of freeing the country from the French protectorate, this protectorate that is plunging us deeper and deeper into the Dark Ages. We are suffering doubly from the horrors of war; on the one hand, the continuing French occupation, and on the other hand, the Axis troops that will soon be landing. In addition, the Anglo-American front wants to turn Tunisia into another battlefield. All those forces want a piece of our flesh. Even the Italians want our flesh. Believe it or not, the Italian ambassador has offered Si Moncef Bey the cancellation of the Treaty of Bardo and proposed negotiating a new treaty with Italy! And what about the poor Tunisian people in all that? Worn down by poverty and misery, our youth killed by the French gendarmes. My friends, we have to unite against our enemies. Remember that we have a nationalist bey. However, there are some around him who are not worthy, they only want to look out for their own interests."

There was grumbling throughout the room.

"The cowards! We should kill them all!" my friend Hedi responded impulsively to Bahi Louzir's words.

We were gathered with other young people who supported Destour. Hedi had told me he was going there and that I should join the movement of young nationalists. I really didn't want to. Not that I didn't believe in the demands of the movement, but I did not see myself involved in political action. I'm a lover of Arabic and French literature, a dreamer. I'm a poet, not a nationalist activist. Despite my reservations, I agreed to go with Hedi to the clandestine meeting in the back of the grocery store of Si Ahmed Louzir, the father of Bahi, one of the major organizers of the Destour Party.

Hedi could no longer contain his anger. He held out his open hands in front of him as if to say he was waiting for the French gendarmes to squeeze the triggers of their rifles and kill him. His defiant gesture was met with applause.

Bahi stood up and went over to him to congratulate him for his courage and fearlessness. "If we had more young people like you, dear Hedi, we would not be where we are today."

Indeed, Hedi, with his growing boldness, was becoming the hero of the day. But there appeared to be no place for poets who were writing verses and who did not say much else.

And as if Bahi had read my thoughts, he turned to me. "I'm happy to see you again, *ya* Habib, you should always come to our meetings. Destour needs people like you, sincere patriots."

Bahi was tall and husky. He was wearing a grey coat that was missing a few buttons. His glasses were broken on the left side, a wire holding the two pieces together. He was younger than I, and we knew each other only by name. What we had in common was Collège Sadiki.

"Thank you for your confidence, dear Bahi. As you know, I'll soon finish my secondary studies, and then I plan to get my degree in literature. I don't know if I'll always have time to come to meetings, but I'll do what I can."

"Yes, our nationalist movement needs your words, your keen mind and your great intelligence, *ya* Habib."

I smiled without answering. My life would be elsewhere, far from politics, I was sure of it.

Hedi, his cheeks red, his hair dishevelled, looked like a worker who wanted to repair his machine but whose toolbox was lacking what he needed. His eyes lit up when he saw Bahi talking to me. He came over and joined the conversation, which was becoming strained because of my lack of enthusiasm.

"Si Bahi, as you correctly stated, we have a bey who's a brave nationalist. It is rumoured that he is ready to defy that brute . . . that . . . Resident-General, Esteva. The bey is waiting only for popular support. We have to get out and demonstrate, express our anger and show our people the way. We're no longer afraid of anything."

There was whistling from all directions. Hedi was getting fired up, and his spark was spreading through the whole group.

I quietly made my way to the exit, my schoolbag under my arm. A corridor led out from the back room, with a small lightbulb that barely lighted the narrow space. I waited patiently in the dim light for Hedi to come and join me. All I wanted was to get out of that place and go back to my room and my books.

Chapter 16

Fatma

My cousin Farida was pregnant. I heard her cross the courtyard in her *kabkabs* every morning, rushing to the bathroom to vomit. Poor thing, even her body couldn't tolerate Kamel, it violently rejected him. When the midwife came to examine her, my mother and my aunts Hnani and Zohra were present. My mother asked me to leave the room. "These are matters for women," she said.

I blushed. My mother didn't know what her sister's husband had done to me. But I pretended I didn't understand. I too had become a woman, but with no wedding or ceremony. I became a woman without baklawa or *rouzata*, I became a woman on a wooden bench in candlelight, under the rough, heavy body of Am Chedli. In spite of my pain, I learned to live with that secret, which only Farida knew. Yet I was able to rid myself of the stain that man left on me. I didn't let Am Chedli take all of me. I didn't let that monster mark me forever.

As soon as we got home from that horrible wedding, I decided to go see the *dégasa*.[3] She lived with her son not far from our lane. I had met her once by chance in front of our door when I was leaving to take my little brother to the *kuttab*[4] and she passed by. Her sleeping baby was in a shawl on her back. She had tattoos on her tanned face. She approached and spoke to me, looking into my eyes. The intensity of her gaze was

---

3   A generally pejorative name given to peasant women who came to the city and worked as clairvoyants or fortune tellers.

4   Quranic school where young children go to study with a tutor called a *meddeb*.

deeply disturbing to me. "Would you have something to help me?" she asked in a dialect I could barely understand.

All I had was a few pieces of *makroud*[5] my mother had wrapped up for me to give to my brother's *meddeb*. "I don't have any money, but do you want some *makroud*?" I tried to avoid her piercing eyes, which frightened me a bit.

Without even an answer, she reached out her hand and practically tore the paper the pastries were wrapped in. "May God open his door to you, my daughter, and may God help you as you've helped me."

Her quick reaction took me by surprise and encouraged me to continue the conversation in spite of the inquisitive stare of my brother, who was eager to join his friends at school. I ventured to ask her, "Where do you live?"

She had already opened the little package and bitten into one piece. Her two front teeth protruded slightly, making her look like a field mouse. Her mouth full of semolina, dates, and honey, she gestured to the end of our lane. "I live with my son in the *zaouia*[6] of Sidi Boukari. See the green door at the end of the lane? I'm poor and I'm trying to raise my son. My husband died last year, he was hit by the *tramfaille*."[7] She took another piece of *makroud*, adjusted the shawl holding her baby, and continued speaking as if we were old acquaintances. "I do laundry in people's homes. If you need me, I can always come to you. I don't ask a lot. Just a little food for myself and my son."

My brother wanted to go, he was pulling on my *safsari*, and I was afraid someone from our lane would recognize me and tell my mother about my conversation with this *dégasa*. To tell the truth, I didn't know if she was really a fortune teller. She seemed like one, but she could also have just been a poor woman.

"Come see me if you need help, down there, the green door, near Sidi Boukari." After repeating this several times, she gave me a last cryptic look and then went on her way, her hips swaying, her baby still on her

---

5   Diamond-shaped Tunisian pastry made with semolina containing dates and dipped in honey.
6   Tomb of a saint. Often visited by women to pray for the marriage of young girls or the birth of a child. The site can sometimes become a dwelling for the poor.
7   The term for the tram in Tunis in vernacular Tunisian dialect.

back, and her *melia*[8] trailing on the cobblestones. She was holding the
pieces of *makroud* she hadn't eaten.

I had not forgotten that woman, and it was to her I turned to cleanse
my body of the stain from Am Chedli. I went to see her without saying
anything to anyone, not even Farida. Taking advantage of siesta time,
when everyone was in their room, I put on my *safsari* and left to go find
the woman I now called a *dégasa*. I went in through the green door, which
was ajar. I gave it a gentle push and found myself on a patio with a large
door leading to the tomb of Sidi Boukari. It was said he had been a pious
man who took care of poor people and gave them herbs to cure them
of their illnesses. There were always women visiting the *zaouia*, lighting
candles and reading the Fatiha on the soul of the holy man. The other
rooms of the house were occupied by poor families. In the room where
the tomb was, a woman was lying on a mat on the ground, covered with
her *safsari*. Only her feet were visible, hardened and cracked from walking. It was not the *dégasa*. There was a row of candles in front of the
tomb, some of them partly burned down and others unlit.

I found her in another, smaller room with a tiny window protected by
iron bars. I recognized her immediately. She was sitting on the ground
in front of a *mida*. She was rolling long strings of dough with her fingers
and, with a quick movement of her thumb and index finger, pinching off
little pieces of *hlalem*,[9] which fell like sad tears. Her child was sleeping on
a mattress near her. When she saw me hesitating in front of her door, she
stopped her work, stood up, and came toward me with one hand on her
hip as if to support her body. "You've come. I knew you would need help
one day, I saw it in your eyes."

I suddenly felt afraid of her. I wanted to go back home. What if she
was a witch who would do me harm? I took a step back, but she stopped
me with her arm.

"Why are you trying to leave? Don't be afraid of me. I'll help you. Sit
down and tell me your story."

The little room had only a wicker mat on the ground, two cushions
covered in tattered cloth, a mattress, and a *kanoun* in the corner with

---

8   Traditional garment worn by peasant or Berber women. A long striped piece of
fabric that covers the whole body, fastened at the waist with a belt and at the shoulders with ties.

9   Dried pasta in an elongated teardrop shape, used in the soup of the same name.

some clay pots. There were bits of *hlalem* spread out on the *mida* to dry.
The *dégasa* would most likely be selling it at the market or from door to
door. The child was sleeping peacefully without a care in the world.

"What is your name, my daughter?" she asked, taking me by the hand
and motioning to me to sit.

"Fatma."

"Fatma, like Fatma Ezzahra, *Masha'Allah*,[10] *Masha'Allah*, the name of
the daughter of our *sidna*,[11] *Alaihi Assalat wa Salam*.[12]

Those words reassured me. She had called on the Prophet and praised
him. She would not do me harm.

"Your eyes tell me everything. I see far, very far, farther than other
people. There is a sadness in you. What has happened? I will help you, do
not be afraid, tell me, *ya* Fatma."

And as if I had known her and shared my secrets with her for years,
I told her the story without fear or embarrassment. My cousin Rafika's
wedding, the night I had been overpowered by Am Chedli and how he
had entered me without my understanding what was happening. She
became the second person, after Farida, to know. Strangely, I felt better. I
found her presence reassuring. Her eyes were piercing but her touch was
soft and gentle, and the words she chose so well calmed me when I felt
completely shaken.

When I was finished, she gave a long sigh. "What a sad story, my
daughter! That man continues to live as if nothing happened. He sees his
friends, he fills his belly, he goes about his business as if everything were
normal. But you're here before me, lost forever, stained by him."

Her words made me cry. I wept in front of this stranger, this woman
I called a *dégasa*, whom my family would certainly not trust and would
chase away if she came to our door. But this woman had understood my
suffering.

She stood up and went to the corner of the room where the *kanoun*
was, squatted down, and looked for something in a basket. She came
back with some leaves and black seeds, which she wrapped in a piece of
newspaper and held out to me, saying, "Here's something to cleanse you

---

10 Praise be to God.
11 Our master, in the Tunisian dialect, used here to refer to the Prophet Mohamed.
12 Blessings and peace be upon him: formula of respect when Muslims refer to the
Prophet Mohamed.

of the filth that man left inside you. You boil some water with one little leaf and seven black seeds, and then you drink the water every morning when you wake up. You do that for seven days and you'll see, all the dirty blood will flow away and you'll be clean again." She placed her hand on my shoulder. "You'll see, don't worry, everything will be all right. God does not abandon his weak servants. One day this man will pay for his actions. You will find happiness. One day it will come looking for you."

These mysterious words made me curious and I wanted to ask her questions and learn more. But her child woke up crying; he wanted his mother's breast. She picked him up and took out her large brown breast, and the child grasped it eagerly and began to suck greedily.

I took a small coin from my bosom. It was all the money I had. I had received it on the Eid and never spent it. "Here, this is for you. I don't have anything else to give you."

She took the money and looked at me with a radiant smile. "Go home, and may Allah open his doors for you, my daughter."

Her child, his hunger somewhat satisfied, let go of her breast and turned his head toward me, gave me a long look, and took his mother's nipple in his mouth once more and continued drinking.

I returned home. Everyone was still napping.

The *dégasa* hadn't lied. I did exactly what she had told me, and after seven days, the blood flowed out of me like I'd never seen. There were clots the size of chickpeas in it. At first, I was frightened, but after a few days, I felt better. The traces of Am Chedli had been flushed away in the *douira*, into the sewers where they belonged, with the shit and the rats. I slowly regained the freshness I had before that night. The *dégasa* had saved my life.

Chapter 17

Monsieur Giuliano

The construction of the stable was progressing nicely. Kamel Ben Mahmoud had gotten the loan after difficult negotiations with the bank. He told me he'd had to put up the other tracts of land his family owned in order to obtain enough money to cover the construction. I signed a ten-year lease with him for a yearly rent of a thousand francs, and in return, I'll be able to work the land, feed my cows, and make my cheese. The lease also states that I can live in the little house on the land, and we'll soon be moving there. I have to start tilling the soil and planting crops for fodder, and continue building the stable in order to carry out my plan.

Recent weeks have been very hard for me and the rest of the family. The death of old Fabio took us all by surprise. I don't know yet if I was relieved or sad. Relieved at the passing of this man who had made me suffer so much throughout my youth. Who had never made me feel loved as a son. But still, I was sad that I'd never see him again. He would often sit on his wooden chair in front of the building, his eyes bright, watching the people of the neighbourhood, greeting acquaintances, talking with them, sometimes raising his voice to scold the kids playing around him.

Old Fabio didn't have a happy life, and he had done his best to ruin mine. After my mother died, Maria, my Uncle Claudio's wife, took care of us. Like all the women in the building, she was constantly washing and mending clothes and cooking for the family. My father was always angry, at life, at other people, at my mother, and especially at me. He wanted me to become a mason like him and Uncle Claudio. But I never learned the trade. My hands weren't made for laying stones one on top of the other, trimming them, and binding them with mortar. I simply didn't have an eye for judging if the stones were properly aligned and the corners square. And every time I failed at a task he assigned me, he would reprimand me and even beat me with his belt, and send me home.

Luckily there was my Uncle Claudio. He was the one who found me the job with Emilio, the cheese vendor at the Marché Central. When I apprenticed with him, my life got better. I quickly took to the odour of the milk, which smelled of cows and sheep and hay. I learned to manipulate the wheels of Sicilian cheese gently, as if I were carrying a baby. And he showed me how to prepare ricotta with love and care so as not to waste any milk.

❧

The day of old Fabio's burial, it rained. It was the sky that was crying instead of me. Not a tear fell from my eyes. I was unhappy to see my father go, but something in me was finally rid of the fear, the humiliation, the shame he'd subjected me to at every opportunity. And it was that something that rejoiced at his going. I was reborn the day we laid old Fabio in the ground, and I began to learn to be happy. He was buried in Borgel Cemetery, on Esplanade Gambetta, which runs along the Lake of Tunis. The cemetery was once reserved for the Jews of the city, but a few years ago, an adjoining piece of land was added for Christians, and the French began to bury their dead there.

My Uncle Claudio wanted to give my father a proper funeral. He insisted that he be buried in that new cemetery and not in the old one in Bab El Khadra, which had become overcrowded and dilapidated by the weather over the years. I recalled my father in his coffin, his face ashen, a bit twisted, not well shaven. He was dressed in his best suit, the navy blue one he wore to go to mass on Sunday and put away religiously afterwards in the tall mirrored wardrobe in his bedroom. His black shoes, which he had polished dozens of times in the hope that they would shine a little more, were now faded, like the rest of his clothing.

I stood beside my uncle without moving, without a gesture or a word, gazing out into the desolate space, empty in spots, with some new graves and tombstones. The employee of the funeral parlour had hardly thrown the last shovelful of earth on the grave when I wanted to leave the place and the memory of my father and the misery I had experienced with him. But I had to wait and walk solemnly with my uncle, his friends, and the neighbours from our building. All those poor Sicilians who sweated blood every day to feed their families, dreaming of better days for themselves and their children.

But everything is going to change with my new endeavour. Lorena and Graziella have packed our things in two old suitcases and the two wooden trunks in which we stored our winter clothes in summer and our summer clothes in winter. I gave everything old Fabio owned to my Uncle Claudio. He didn't have much: some worn clothes, a wooden table and a chair, the one he would sit in outside our front door to watch the passersby. Lorena had found three gold coins in one of the pockets of his blue suit. I assumed they were his entire savings. Three gold coins, the reward for all those years of hard work. I thought of the stones he had cut over the years and joined with mortar and sand, of the days he had spent in the sun using stone and plaster to finish the masonry work he was so skilled at. He had put everything he had into it all his life. I didn't want to take those coins. I gave them to my Uncle Claudio. He was the one who deserved them, he and his wife, Maria. They had never let us down, never an insult or a mean look, not the slightest complaint about all those years we lived crammed together like sardines in the two-room apartment in La Goleta. The money old Fabio had saved over the years, one centime at a time, one franc after the other, should go to his brother Claudio, who had protected and guided all of us.

In a few days, Lorena and Graziella will pack up our few pots and pans, plates, glasses, and spoons in a box I brought back from the Marché Central, and we'll leave to go live in the house in Jedeida. We'll live there and continue work on the stable and the adjoining room that will be used for making the cheese. We'll soon start working together and forgetting old Fabio and the dark years in La Goleta.

Chapter 18

Farida

The baby was moving within me. It was stretching and giving little kicks, and I could feel my belly becoming hard as stone on one side and then suddenly relaxing again and becoming a little balloon. Kamel was being nicer, but as soon as things didn't go as he wished, a meal that wasn't to his liking, a comment on the quality of the fruits and vegetables he purchased, the truce would be over. He would shout insults and storm out of the room. Just as well! I felt so much better when he wasn't with me. I would read my brother Habib's books or spend the time with Fatma. Being pregnant made me hate going into the kitchen even more. The smell of food nauseated me. My stomach would turn and I would rush out to vomit. I would often make do with potato ragout, which I cooked much better now, or *broudo*, a vegetable I considered the ideal dish for using up the rotten carrots, bruised potatoes, and shrivelled onions Kamel bought to save money.

Sometimes I regretted not having spent more time in the kitchen with my mother. I would timidly ask Fatma to reveal the secrets of some of her recipes, but I still ended up ruining them. I told myself it was time I became a good wife. But my regrets would quickly disappear as soon as Kamel, in a rage over some dish I had made, would put on his *jebba* and leave. "You'll never be a good cook!" he would shout, his eyes flashing with rage.

"And when will you understand that it takes good ingredients to make tasty dishes, not wilted, stunted, puny old vegetables or olive oil full of black residue or meat that's nothing but fat? You would do better to spend your money on the baby and me rather than on your mistresses."

He stared at me for a moment. An eternity. I thought he was going to raise his hand to me, to give me a hard, burning slap. I stood without fear, my eyes defiant, my belly protruding with new roundness. But he didn't do anything.

I heard him muttering on the patio on his way to the door. "Yes, my mistresses . . . at least they know how to take care of me. They know how to treat me like a man. While you, *Lella* Farida, what do you know how to do? Oh, yes, I know. You know how to talk. Words, words, words . . . so talk, then, and may the wind blow your words away."

His voice came to me softly, like the sound of raindrops on the roof on a winter day. For a moment, I was taken aback by my sudden boldness, but also disconcerted, wondering how I could continue to live with this man whose child I was carrying. Gradually my heartbeats slowed down and my breathing became calm. Kamel's shadow faded.

My reading transported me far away, to the country that invaded us a little more every day with its airplanes, tanks, and gendarmes, killing our men and seizing our wealth. I didn't know if I should hate that country or should love it, as Madame Lacroix often used to tell us at school. My father said I liked the French too much and they were turning my head with their blasphemous stories. Kamel detested the French because they controlled the whole country, and even the banker would humiliate him when he granted him a loan.

He was glad when we heard a few weeks ago that a German squadron had landed at El-Aouina, followed by thousands of soldiers. Kamel said that the Germans would finally get the French out and that they were nice to Arabs. I almost wanted to believe it, until the day our Jewish neighbour Thérèse Chemla, my mother's friend, came to see us after a long absence. She was shaking. She was fearful of them, as if she thought she might be kidnapped. She told us, almost in a whisper, that a friend of her father's, an important person in the Jewish community of Tunis, had been arrested and jailed by the Germans. And even after his release, he had been forced to report to the *Kommandantur* twice a day.

"What is that?" Aunt Hnani almost shouted, shocked at Thérèse's words.

"It's the headquarters of the German army. They've set up in the Hôtel Majestic."

I'd heard of the hotel. It was on Rue de Paris, in the centre of the modern section of Tunis. It had been built by the French, who held extravagant parties there. My father had spoken of it. "I'll take you there one day, Farida. You'll see, it's magnificent, like the buildings in your *gaouri* books." My father had laughed loudly. But he never took me there. Maybe he was trying to impress me, or maybe he simply forgot. And to think that it was now the place from which the Germans controlled our country. A place of joy that in a few hours had become a place of war. I shuddered.

Thérèse burst into tears, she was at her wits' end. "Just a few weeks ago, our chief rabbi, Haïm Bellaïche, was forced to post notices on all the streets of Tunis telling Jews between the ages of seventeen and fifty to be prepared for compulsory labour."

My aunts were both wiping away tears. I was barely controlling myself. And I had wanted to become a teacher like Thérèse. I saw her through a child's eyes as strong and invincible. And here she was in front of us, shattered, confused, humiliated. Could it be that our books and our reading served no useful purpose for us women and it was men's boots and guns that always had the last word?

I didn't know which way to turn. The Germans or the French, which of the two were "best" for us? Those who had come to protect us against ourselves, bringing the civilization of the Enlightenment while killing our men and stealing our land? Or those who had driven out our enemies while humiliating, killing, and imprisoning some of us in labour camps? And who was to say that after the Jews it wouldn't be our turn, the Arabs' turn?

And what about the language of those invaders, which I had learned at a young age and grown up with through my schoolbooks and the clippings from the *Dépêche tunisienne* that I devoured, and the books loaned to me by Habib or secretly borrowed from him and read in hiding? I adored that language, the rhythm of its words, the poetry of its prose, and its elegance, like fine lace. My reading transported me far from Kamel, it consoled me and allowed me to forget myself, and forget the blows and the quarrels, the French and the Germans and the war happening in front of our doors. To erase the unhappiness and replace it with an ephemeral happiness that lasted for a page or a quatrain.

A happiness like that I experienced when, as a child, I would sit beside my mother and she would quietly sew or do embroidery while I held a piece of fabric and a needle, imitating her and trying to sew a dress for my rag doll. Sometimes Ommi would gently chide me for sticking my fingers with the needle, which I always ended up losing, but my mother's smell, her caring gaze, her graceful gestures, her slender, delicate hands, everything about her, fascinated me and made me forget her occasional reproachful glances.

One day I will be like Ommi, a good mother to this child that will be born. I will give it love and tenderness. It will become a sensitive, educated person who will go to school and obtain a degree and earn a living through knowledge. I will be capable of any sacrifice so that my child will succeed in life. Nothing will stop me. Not Kamel's blows or my father's silent complicity with him, or the roaring of the airplanes at night, or the sound of boots in our street.

Chapter 19

Kamel

Tawfik Ben Mahmoud was born in the middle of Ramadan. In good health, strong and robust like me. May God protect him from the evil eye. I'll buy a *khomsa*[13] for him and tell Farida to pin it to his clothing so he'll always be protected. I wasn't sure if Farida knew how to take proper care of him. She often let him cry without giving him her breast. She said she didn't have enough milk and he might need a wet nurse. That Farida, with her demands and more demands! She had started, with her pregnancy and now the birth, to act like a princess. And my sister Fatma, who still hadn't found a husband, was always helping her.

I was sitting in front of Lamine's shop while he was at the carpenter's. His apprentice had told me he'd gone to order a new table for the barbershop. The old one was wobbly and about to collapse. But what a table it was! Always full of magic instruments, pliers for pulling teeth, brushes for beards, medium-size scissors for straight hair, smaller ones for the most manageable hair, and the smallest ones for moustaches and beards. The shaving brushes were lined up beside boxes of the soap Lamine used on his clients' faces, which left them with a fresh feeling that was further enhanced by a spray of cologne. I was waiting patiently for Lamine, who was taking a long time to get back.

Finally, I left for my meeting with Monsieur Leduc, manager of the Banque de France. I'd signed a loan agreement for ten thousand francs

---

13 Amulet in the form of a hand, also known as the Hand of Fatma

with him. Today I would receive the money and everything would be
settled. It hadn't been easy to secure the loan. First of all, I didn't always
understand what Monsieur Leduc was going on about. He had a colleague, Victor Smoula, who acted as interpreter when things got sticky.
Monsieur Leduc didn't like the idea of my putting up the house in Bab
Souika as collateral. He wanted something else, another property, one I
owned completely, since the house in Bab Souika was inherited from my
grandfather and had never been divided among his heirs.

But I explained to him as best I could that I didn't own anything in
my name and everything belonged to the family as a whole. Finally, with
the help of Smoula, who at times went beyond his role as interpreter
and came to the defence of my family and me, praising the business of
my uncle, who was the neighbourhood moneylender and who by himself owned five houses and five shops that he rented out—although he
had refused to give me a centime to build the stable on our land, claim-
ing that people were not paying him back anymore and business wasn't
good. I didn't understand everything Smoula said to Monsieur Leduc in
French, but from his intelligent look and animated gestures and his insistence, I knew he was saying good things about me and I sensed that the
Frenchman would change his mind.

I didn't like Monsieur Leduc, a scrawny man who always wore the
same brown suit and the same blue tie. He thought he was a somebody,
but I could have had him on the ground in an instant. His moustache, as
thin as the tail of a mouse in El Halfaouine, made him look like a beard-
less youth rather than an adult. If I'd been able to speak French fluently,
I could have put him in his place and not let him treat me like a beggar
living off the charity of a *gaouri*.

"The Germans are at our gates, the economic situation is dangerous,
I need more guarantees than usual." Smoula repeated to me in Arabic
what Monsieur Leduc had said in French. Leduc hardly looked at me, his
eyes were fixed on a French newspaper lying on his desk.

"I know, I know, I've heard about all that. What does he think I am,
an idiot? Tell him the stable will be used for producing cheese that
will be sold in the Marché Central. He has nothing to fear. Monsieur
Giuliano is a good worker. He'll pay me my rent and I'll be able to pay

the *cambialates*.[14] *Pas de problème*, Monsieur Leduc, *pas de problème.*" I said those last words in French to make sure that idiot Leduc understood me. Which he did. He gave me a quick smile. But then he looked uncertain again.

I continued, "At worst, Monsieur Leduc, I could borrow a little money from my uncle, Si Laroussi Ben Mahmoud, he owns five houses and five shops." I repeated the number five a few times, holding up five fingers, which was also to ward off the evil eye from our family. Smoula, a Tunisian Jew, understood exactly what I was up to, but Monsieur Leduc remained stone-faced.

Then, unexpectedly, he gave in. "All right, we'll sign the papers for the loan next week. Come see me here at the office, I'll be expecting you. Everything will be ready, including the money."

I recalled our meeting and his words as I walked through the lanes and alleys of Tunis. Some places reeked of the urine of the previous night's drunks, but soon the filth would be washed away with buckets of water. The great Mausoleum of Sidi Mahrez, the sultan of the medina, as my mother called him whenever she mentioned his name, adding her usual prayer, *Shah Allah, waliye Allah.*[15] Its ovoid cupolas fascinated me, and the pigeons that encircled them like grey necklaces made them more beautiful. Soon there would be swarms of beggars at the doors of Sidi Mahrez waiting for the offerings of food from wealthy families. An old maid who had gotten married, a troublesome husband who had died suddenly, there was always a good reason for a *nadhr*[16] at Sidi Mahrez. I'll take my son there before his circumcision to drink the holy water to protect him from the misfortunes of life.

Finally, I reached Souk El Attarine, where the perfume sellers were beginning to put their little vials out on wooden shelves: rose, amber, incense, jasmine, *fel*, geranium, the scents mingling and following me. I recognized one of the vendors and stopped to exchange a few words with him.

"*Mabrouk*, the new son! May God keep him and send you more and more. Don't forget me, Si Kamel, for the celebration of his circumcision."

---

14 Italian word for bills of exchange in payment of a debt.
15 Servant of God. Traditional formula used when invoking a saint.
16 Prayer or promise made in the name of a saint.

"*Insha'Allah, Insha'Allah,* you'll be the first one invited."

At a turn in the souk, the pale pink minaret of the Al-Zaytuna was visible, squat and rectangular. There were a lot of people. Women in white *safsaris* with young children staying close to them or older ones in *chechias* pushing and shoving each other, stopping now and then to take an almond held out by one of the dried fruit merchants. I imagined my son Tawfik wearing a vermillion *chechia* from Am Chedli on his head, walking beside me, proud of his forebears, enjoying the prosperity from the wealth we had preserved and the land we had protected.

I finally arrived under the arch of the Bab Bahr gate, with its crenellated parapet. My grandmother used to say that in the old days the sea came right up to the outskirts of the city. And that if it hadn't been for the constant prayers of our great saint Sidi Mahrez, the old city would have been swallowed up by the water. In front of me, Rue Jules-Ferry marked the beginning of the modern city, the city of the *Francisses*. I waited impatiently for the *tramfaille* to pass. Another diabolical invention of those *gaouris* who've taken over our country and ruined out city, killing us with their machines of death.

The adjacent buildings were still standing. The Port de France was crawling with people, all in European dress. Occasionally a burnoose, a *jebba*, a *chechia*, or a *safsari* made a timid appearance before being swamped by the tide of suits, coats, dresses, and hats.

When I arrived at the bank, I had only one thought: soon the money would be mine and I would do what I wanted with it.

Chapter 20

Habib

I've stopped going to the meetings of the patriots. I explained to Hedi that my place was elsewhere, in the world of words. He saw the struggle only in terms of action. While I sometimes glimpsed Bahi at Collège Sadiki, I avoided him, pretending to be too busy. The group, made up mainly of my friends or at least acquaintances, was no longer what it had been in the beginning. From a place where young activists met to reflect and discuss ways of fighting French colonialism, it had become a place of constant disagreement and power struggles between two factions, traditionalists and modernists. Not knowing which way to turn, nor which of the two groups was more correct, I preferred not to go at all and to contribute to my country's independence in other ways. I would use what I loved most: the power of words.

Besides, my friend Omar, who had returned from France after studying law there, had asked me to write a weekly column for the newspaper he'd founded, *La Voix du Tunisien*. Omar was older than I was, he must have been in his thirties. I had met him through my late cousin Jalloul, may God rest his soul. Both were graduates of Khaldunia, the first modern school in Tunisia, which provided non-Islamic education. Jalloul had dreamed of continuing his studies and returning to Collège Sadiki one day as a teacher, but sickness struck him down.

I still remembered when he would talk to me about his fascination with Mohamed Abduh, the great Egyptian reformer, who had come to Tunisia at the beginning of the century to teach a theology course.

Though diminished by sickness, Jalloul lit up when he expressed his admiration for that man who had sought to raise consciousness among Muslims and who saw his message harshly criticized by both Muslim and Westernized theologians.

"Can you imagine, Habib?! He dared to say in front of the sheiks of our esteemed Al-Zaytuna that faith was the engine of action and the light illuminating the path to truth." Jalloul repeated what his professors had said, those who had had the good fortune to attend Mohamed Abduh's lecture. He leaned back in his bed with a grimace, trying to forget the pain that was eating him from the inside. "He said it loud and clear, without fear of criticism or attacks. That is what we need. Comprehensive reform and a break from the old interpretations that have frozen us in time."

I listened to my cousin Jalloul with admiration for his love of knowledge and his compassion. Yes, his compassion. Because it was out of immense compassion that he studied day and night to become a teacher and help others free themselves from ignorance and misery.

"We will never be independent without education. But not just any education, Habib! Advanced education drawing from our rich, diverse Islamic culture and scientific subjects such as mathematics and natural sciences."

I silently agreed with Jalloul's words. If only he were still alive, he would know what advice to give me. Our new ruler, Si Moncef Bey, was a great nationalist. We had to support him in his mission to throw out the French. But how? How to go about it? "Armed struggle is the only thing that works in this world," my friend Hedi repeated constantly. I was not convinced. What if we went into the streets, in the cities and the countryside, and if we marched in all the public squares, climbed to the tops of the minarets, visited all the remote villages, knocked on the doors of middle-class houses and poor people's hovels and yelled loudly, very loudly, at the top of our lungs, impatiently, that our salvation could only come through education, and that a well-rounded mind is capable of doing anything, even resisting an invasion, whether military or cultural.

My theory made sense. Yes, I was confident. I believed firmly in it. So did Jalloul. We just had to put it into action. I would do it. I would throw myself heart and soul into that struggle through knowledge. I would teach the people—men and women—Arabic and French. The traditional and the modern. The old and the new. I would fight ignorance through poetic eloquence and the boldness of words. But first of all, I had to free myself from the grip of my father, who was dragging us all, day after day, into the dark depths of his greedy, sick soul, and from the stupidity of my cousin Kamel. That was how I would keep the memory of Jalloul alive. That was how I would help my sister Farida regain her freedom one day. That was how we would all be free one day. All of us.

Chapter 21

Kamel

I did something really crazy. I bought a house in La Marsa. I paid for it with part of the bank loan. The rest of the money went to building the stable, which was almost finished. I don't know what possessed me. The idea Samira had whispered in my ear almost as a joke had gradually taken root and stayed with me. Until the day my friend Lamine mentioned that house in La Marsa. It was near Kobbet Lahoue with its beautiful white dome, which had been built by one of the beys so that his family could swim in the sea. The house was owned by an old Frenchwoman, a widow, who wanted to sell it and go back to France.

"Make her a modest offer and the house will be yours. This is your chance, my friend, the old lady wants to go home, she has no one in Tunis anymore."

It was one of the customers at Lamine's barbershop who told him about the old Frenchwoman. She was a neighbour of childhood friends of his. The idea, which at first seemed far-fetched, stayed in my mind, haunting me every night, and it finally began to seem possible. And if I bought the house and set up my lovely Samira in it, we could finally enjoy life and, who knows, I could even marry her and make her my second wife. Farida was busy with Tawfik from morning to night. I couldn't even touch her anymore. I had thought she was lazy, but she'd turned out to be a mother hen. She didn't sleep day or night, she spent all her time nursing him or helping him learn to walk. She would walk him around the patio, reciting nursery rhymes. *"Dadache, kbir ou ach, jab kfaifa bil michmach."*[17]

Farida had literally stolen my Tawfik from me. She even read him stories in French. The woman was crazy. I couldn't stand her anymore. Tawfik was growing, and he was handsome. But he didn't seem to care much for me. When I picked him up, he would burst into tears as if I were about to murder him, so I would hand him back to his mother. She continued to insult me and demand extravagant things. "We need pistachio nuts, almonds, and walnuts for the *assida*."[18]

Didn't she know everything was rationed? Sugar, rice, oil, flour. And there she was, asking for pistachio nuts and almonds! You'd think she hadn't heard the deafening noise of the German bombers. Was she living in a different world, or what? And my sister Fatma who helped her like a servant. She did everything for her. Even the *assida*, she was the one who ended up making it. I didn't buy the pistachio nuts, only a few walnuts. That was enough. The *assida* was delicious. I wasn't surprised, my sister was good with her hands.

But we weren't able to find her a husband. The other day, I heard that Sadok Bel Kadi was looking for a wife. He was nearly sixty, my father's age. I could suggest Fatma to him. I'll talk to my father and my uncle. What could be better? A husband who's rich, from a good family, and a widower. A bit old, maybe, but that's not a problem. What's important is that he be a man and that he accept my sister, that little hussy, who sneaked out of the house and made dresses for herself that only went down to her knees. With him, she'd do whatever she wanted, even walk around naked if he let her. But he'd keep her from getting out of line.

I went to see the house in La Marsa. A real gem. And the asking price wasn't exorbitant. The Frenchwoman was asking three thousand francs, a bargain. I couldn't let it slip through my fingers. A house for a *Francisse*, with a modern toilet you sat on like a chair, unlike our *douiria*, where you had to squat and be careful not to fall in or get your ass bitten by a sewer rat. From the veranda of the house, I could see the sparkling white dome of the building with its pilings, the waves tickling its toes. There was even a bathtub,

---

17 Run, run, one day he'll grow up and bring me a basket of apricots. (Author's translation)
18 Custard made from Aleppo pine nuts, milk, and sugar.

where Samira would wash my body with her soft hands. She would rub me like a *tayeb*[19] in a hammam until all the dead skin fell from the horsehair glove like scales from a fish, and then give me a massage on the bed. And the little garden where I could plant a lemon tree or a bergamot orange tree and some pots of mint to make good mint tea. I'd be a bey in my kingdom with Samira my *beya* at my side. No, I had to buy it. I would buy it.

My Uncle Laroussi won't suspect anything. The bank loan was in my name. I received the money and counted it with my own hands. With that money I paid the old Frenchwoman. She seemed pretty harmless. Too old, too eager to go back to her native city. My uncle won't know anything, I'll pay back the loan with the rent from the land. It will all work out.

When I brought Samira to my new house, she was amazed. She kissed me on the mouth and I wanted never to let her go. "*Ya* Kamel, it's the most beautiful gift of my life. I adore you. I'll never leave you." She kissed me again, on my right cheek this time, and I wanted to take her to the bedroom.

"But I have a very small favour to ask you . . . " She hesitated, looking at me with those eyes that drove me wild. "When will this house be in my name? You see, *ya azizi*, I'm a woman alone, with no father or mother. And if something bad happened to you, may God protect you, I would be thrown out by your family and your heirs."

Samira was absolutely right. What would happen if I suddenly died? The house would go to my father and my uncle. My uncle already owned five houses and five shops. My son Tawfik was too young, and Farida would take advantage of it to increase her power over him. But if I put the house in Samira's name, nobody would know about it. And after all, Samira was almost my wife. She loved me too much to hurt me or leave me.

"So, what do you say? I, Samira, your faithful servant night and day, who will wash your feet and give you massages and make your favourite couscous with lamb's head and raisins. What do you say?"

"I'll go to the notary tomorrow and you'll have your house."

Samira pressed her body against mine. I was in heaven. Life was smiling on me. And Samira was smiling too, her most beautiful smile. For once I would be able forget the house in Bab Souika, with that ingrate Farida ignoring me, my father always busy with his lessons at Al-Zaytuna, my uncle religiously counting his pennies, and my cousin Habib with his nose buried in his books, which will one day bury him alive.

---

19 Man who gives massages in a hammam for men.

Chapter 22

Farida

Kamel hardly ever came to the house anymore. He must have been with one of his mistresses, I was sure. The rare times I confronted him, he was evasive. His *jebbas* smelled of the woman's perfume. A heavy, suffocating perfume. I wondered how she could love a man like Kamel, who loved only himself. On the rare occasions when I found him generous and loving, it was with his son Tawfik. He would pick him up and twirl him in the air. But as soon as Tawfik started to wail, Kamel would lose patience and the child would tremble with fear. Kamel spent a small fortune buying him shoes at Chez Carlo. He wanted to dress Tawfik like a miniature version of himself. But for some reason unknown to me, Tawfik never liked those clothes. He would even take the little red *chechia* off his head and throw it on the ground. And although I tied his *sirwal* at his waist, it would fall down around his ankles and he would end up tripping. And Kamel would lose his temper and accuse me of coddling his son, and storm out of the house.

And when he suddenly reappeared, he'd say he was busy with the work on the stable for the new Italian tenant, Monsieur Giuliano. The difference this time was that Baba no longer believed Kamel's stories. He suspected him of plotting something dangerous. I could see it in my father's eyes when Kamel was telling him that the stable was almost finished, that Monsieur Giuliano had bought his cows and that the production of Sicilian cheese and ricotta was going well.

"Monsieur Giuliano has promised to give me a bit of his ricotta to taste. I'm dreaming of a ricotta tajine[20] that melts in your mouth."

My father was still examining his register. He was going over it with a fine-toothed comb. That big book in which he noted the names of his debtors, their addresses, the sums loaned, the dates of the loans, and the type of collateral provided: the deed of a house, ruby earrings, a few pieces of gold. He noted everything in tables drawn in ink using a wooden ruler. Everything was carefully written in impeccable order. When Kamel finished his sentence, my father looked up from the register and asked, "Yes indeed, *Insha'Allah*! My daughter Farida will make us a nice ricotta tajine . . . but tell me, my son Kamel, you've never said exactly how much the bank loaned you for the stable. I have no record of it in my papers. We need to have a receipt, a document, a contract as proof. Because you know very well that those damn Frenchmen could always play a dirty trick to get us to reimburse more money than we agreed to."

Tawfik was playing at my feet, pulling a little pot on a string every which way. The sound of the pot on the tiles was annoying.

Kamel spun around to face Tawfik, his face red, his eyes blazing. And pointing his index finger at me, said, "Tell your son to stop that, or else . . . "

Tawfik, absorbed in playing, started at Kamel's violent tone of voice, dropped the string, and rushed to take refuge with me, burying his head in my lap. He was holding back a sob.

Baba got up, his right eye wandering. The conversation was over. "Don't get angry over nothing, Kamel. Children play with all sorts of things. Isn't that so, Tawfik, my dear grandson?"

Baba stroked Tawfik's hair. The boy was still trembling like a frightened little bird. He gradually calmed down, looking at Baba with a fearful gaze and a timid smile. Kamel's reaction was typical, he was impulsive and impatient and he wouldn't let anyone interrupt him or change his plans. But this time was different. Something in my father's eyes told me he was not going to let himself be taken in by Kamel's stories. There was a thought running through his head, barely perceptible but nevertheless making itself felt. Slowly but surely. I felt a ray of hope within me, soothing the pain I'd been feeling since my marriage, a pain that only Tawfik's existence made tolerable.

I had stopped pleading with Baba, who until then had been like an

---

20 A sort of crustless quiche containing pieces of chicken or lamb as well as several kinds of cheese.

impenetrable fortress protecting Kamel, and at the same time his own fortune. Now, cracks had become visible. Now Kamel no longer had his trust.

A few days after that incident with Kamel, Tawfik, and the old pot, my father called me to his room and closed the door. I sat down in silence, not knowing what to expect.

"Is it true Kamel has a mistress?"

I blushed. I hadn't expected such a question from my father.

He continued, "You know, Farida, women and business don't go together. It's one or the other. But the two together are a disaster. You can lose your fortune, you can lose everything."

I was dumbfounded. I didn't know what to answer. I didn't know what Baba was getting at.

"I'm more and more convinced that Kamel is playing a dangerous game. I'll soon know for sure. I'll put an end to it. *Insha'Allah*. As long as it's not too late."

His words gave me courage. I took a chance. "Baba, I want a divorce from Kamel. God keep you, please accept . . . "

He rose suddenly. His eyes were vacant. I'd never seen him like this. A man betrayed, ravaged by suspicions.

"Everything in its time. The fruit isn't ripe yet, Farida. We mustn't be too quick to pick it. Your *mektoub*[21] is still with Kamel."

He put on his burnoose, opened the door, and rushed out onto the patio. It was cold outside. Through the window, I could see the lemon tree, denuded and battered by the winds. Spring was slow in coming. I resigned myself to waiting for it.

21 Destiny.

Chapter 23

Habib

I passed the baccalaureate exam, an honour that only my sister Farida and I could appreciate. She with her shining smile and the sweet kiss she placed on my cheek when I told her, and I by preparing to go away to work as an Arabic professor in the *lycée* in Bizerte, in the north of the country, which was occupied by the Germans because of its strategic port.

My aunts Zohra and Hnani spent most of their time at the home of their cousin Daddou. Although they came to visit us from time to time, their role with us was over. Farida was married and had a child. Even Fatma was going to leave. It appears that a husband had been found for her. My father's business was not going well. He didn't say much. But it was enough to see him sitting in his little office in Bab Souika alone, twiddling his thumbs, waiting for clients, who were few and far between. People no longer lined up outside his office to borrow money from him. The war had wiped out everything, both people and fortunes. His face gloomy, Baba would wait in silence for someone to come and provide him with collateral and go away relieved, with the money in his pocket. Baba waited like a hunter on the lookout for prey, his breathing slow, his eyes staring at an invisible point in the distance. But the prey didn't come. Instead, there were German soldiers patrolling the streets. Sometimes they would laugh with the Arabs without either really understanding the other, eyeing each other while trying to appear as friends. Temporary friends, united by hatred for their common enemy, the French.

In the evening, it was a different story. The German soldiers would knock on the doors of the houses in search of traitors, collaborators with the French, *kaouda*, as they were called. Hedi had told me that German soldiers had broken down the door of one of their neighbours in the middle of the night. They had searched everywhere. Even the basket hanging on the wall containing the leftovers of the dinner from the night before. A German soldier had stuck his hand in it, thinking there could be a weapon, a knife or even a bomb. But his hand came out red, dripping with tomato sauce, with little pieces of green, viscous okra. The women of the household, frightened by the stolid presence of the Germans, had burst out laughing, and the Germans were not pleased. They left empty-handed and disappointed. Perhaps Hedi's neighbour was embellishing the story when he told him about it. A way of feeling strong in the face of the invaders, regardless of whether they were nasty or nice, Frenchmen or Germans.

One thing was certain, when the Allies came back to Tunis and the Germans were pushed out, there was euphoria. All the Europeans in Tunis came out to welcome them as victors, with open arms. French and English and even Jewish Tunisians went out into the streets, singing and honking their horns to show their gratitude. The Arabs, afraid, hid away in their houses. They knew that the revenge of the French would soon come crashing down on them. When you're small, you always ended up on the wrong side.

When I learned that Si Moncef Bey had been pressed by France and its allies to abdicate, I was totally disillusioned. Hedi wept with despair. I felt like doing the same, but I couldn't manage it. They had taken from the bey the only power he had seen fit to use. "The prince of the poor," the "nationalist king," had been deposed. Now, the path of exile awaited him.

Feeling more and more humiliated, I persevered with my reading, channelling my rage into my studies. Thus I was able to pass my exams. Many times, I just wanted to give up. I flirted with dropping out. What was the use of education when you weren't even master in your own house? However, I hung onto two images that never left me: the smile of my Uncle Jalloul, who appeared to me in my dreams, and the photograph of Si Moncef Bey, his humiliated expression, on his exile to Pau, in France.

When I told Farida I was leaving for Bizerte, she gave me a piercing look and said, "You're abandoning me again."

At first, I didn't realize what she was alluding to. But I soon understood that she was talking about Kamel, her disastrous marriage, and her miserable life in our house.

"I'll come back to see you, Farida. As long as I'm here, in the shadow of Baba, I'll never be able to grow."

"And me, Habib, what about me? I'm lost forever. I'm being crushed by Kamel and by Baba."

"I'll write to you. I'll keep you informed. I'll tell you about my classes, about Bizerte, the sea, the students. I'll never forget you, Farida."

She was crying softly. My nephew Tawfik was sitting beside her. Seeing his mother's tears, he followed suit and started crying too.

I was distraught. There was nothing in my books that told me what to do with human distress. How to deal with it? How to wipe it from the eyes of women and children?

Poetry. Yes, poetry. "I will write you poems, Farida. You will never forget me."

She stopped short and so did Tawfik. They were soulmates. They shared everything. The same joys and the same despair.

Chapter 24

Graziella

When I opened the stable door, I found my father's lifeless body. I had gone, as usual, to help him milk the cows. I really liked our new life on the farm. It was certainly better than our life in La Goleta, with the screaming children, the smell of rotting fish wafting up from the Lake of Tunis in the summer heat, the fights and curses and insults that shattered the silence of our evenings and chilled my blood. I would help my mother from morning to night, washing the floor, dusting the furniture, scouring the cooking pots, it never ended. When I stopped for a minute, my mother would send me to my Aunt Maria's place. "She helped us a lot, so we have to help her now that she's old." So I would go over and clean her kitchen and take in the wash that had been out all day on the lines between our building and the one opposite, trying to keep the neighbour from getting angry and making a scene if I pulled it too much to our side. When night came and I laid my head on my pillow, I would feel all my muscles aching. At the farm in Jedeida, everything was good. The scent of the earth, especially in the mornings after the first rains of autumn. It reminded me of the aroma of bread fresh from the oven. The cows that smelled of new grass, and the warm milk we drew from their pink udders, and the rhythmic sound of the milking that soothed me like a lullaby. Their liquid gaze, as if they were saying thank you to us.

My mother also felt better here, although she sometimes missed the noise of the city. Here, everything was calm. The crowing of the roosters at dawn and the lowing of the cows at dusk were like soft caresses to our ears. The only thing bothering us was that some Arab workers would sometimes throw stones at our windows or our door. My father would go outside, a rifle on his shoulder, his eyes nervous and his stance wide, ready for an attack. But there would be no one there, only the muffled sound of footsteps running through the wheat fields. The work on the stable was not yet finished when we began to produce little wheels of Sicilian cheese, which our family would eat. And the ricotta was a tremendous success. I would contemplate those beautiful white curds in the metal strainers that drained the whey drop by drop. They were like bouquets of flowers in perforated vases. And when I cut off a piece of the cheese, it would quiver in my fingers. It would melt in my mouth, leaving a taste that reminded me of the smell of the cows and the fresh grass of Jdeida. A treat that would magically lift me to the heavens.

I found his bloody body lying face down. I began to shout, "Mama, Mama, come quickly, something horrible has happened!"

My mother was in the room where we kept the large utensils for making the cheese. There was a big stove in the middle of the room, where we would heat the fresh milk in big pots before acidifying it with vinegar to curdle it. On the counter, there were sieves, funnels, ladles, and muslin cloths. My mother was doing her morning rounds to make sure everything was immaculate, from the big cans filled with milk to the strainers holding the still-quivering cheese.

Sometimes Arab peasants would come to buy milk from us, bringing an earthenware jar or a metal pot. My father would look at the coin handed to him and put it in his pocket. Often, when it was an old woman or a little girl buying the milk, he didn't want to take anything. "Here, it's for you, it's *balaash*, gratis!" The women would leave uttering a string of blessings and kind words that left my father with a satisfied smile. No more now, he was lying on the floor in a pool of blood.

My mother came running, wearing the work apron she took off only at night. Seeing my father on the floor, she started moaning. "What happened, Mio Dio, what happened? I just left him for a few minutes, just to take back the cans and . . . " She fell to her knees, holding my father's head, and turned him on his back to see his face and check if he was breathing. "Thank the Madonna, he's still breathing . . . he's still alive!"

I was crying, and the fact that my father was still breathing was hardly reassuring. My Papa, the person I loved most in the world, was lying on the floor in a pool of blood that was spreading more and more. I took off at a run to the house of the closest Arabs to get help, any kind of help. The most important thing was to get help for my father.

It took hours until help finally came—French gendarmes, a country doctor who lived close by, and an Arab who said he was a nurse. My father had lost too much blood. The wound that was now visible under his torn white shirt formed a red belt on his abdomen. The doctor examined him. His verdict came quickly. "The wound is fatal. He won't survive."

My mother didn't want to believe it. "Who would want to kill my poor Luigi? He's the gentlest soul in the world. He's an angel." She started sobbing and so did I.

The French gendarmes did not want us to spend the night in the house. "Come, ladies, a crime has been committed. We have to investigate and find the criminal, who is still at large."

My mother didn't answer. She was sitting beside my father. She didn't want to leave.

The gendarmes were beginning to lose patience, and one of them sighed loudly. "Madame, please understand me. This place is dangerous now for you and your daughter. We have to find the culprit. Don't you have family, friends? You must go stay with them. At least for a few days, until we find whoever committed this heinous crime. In the meantime, the victim will have to be buried. I imagine there's someone who can help you with the funeral preparations."

My mother gave a heart-rending shriek that left everyone shaken. I put my arms around her and we clung to each other.

The doctor concluded that the deep knife wound in his left side was the cause of death. He drove us to La Goleta in his car. It was a long, silent, bumpy ride. My mother was sitting in the front seat and I was in the back. I was starting to recognize places when the car took the road to La Goleta. My heart was heavy. I didn't want to go back there. We were returning to the battlefield of my childhood, this time without my father.

As soon as the car stopped in front of our old building, it was surrounded by an army of boisterous children, one holding the door with his hand, another examining the rear lights, a very small one trying in vain to open the hood. Then someone spoke my name and my mother's name. "Signora Lorena and Signorina Graziella are back."

We got out of the car, still shaken by the tragedy. In the space of a few hours, our lives had been turned upside-down. My father's remains had been taken to the morgue in the Tunis hospital. My mother looked lost and I followed her like her shadow. My Great-uncle Claudio came running to the car with his shirt creased and buttoned crooked and the belt of his pants barely fastened. Seeing him, my mother, who had been calm during the drive, started to cry again. "Zio Claudio, Zio Claudio, I don't understand what happened, il mio Luigi . . . he's been killed."

The doctor had gone to stand a little to the side of the crowd that was now forming around us. He was smoking a cigarette.

"How can that be? No, I can't believe my ears. How can Luigi be dead? I saw him two days ago. He still had a little finishing work to do on the stable roof. Everything was fine, he was getting ready to sell his ricotta at the Marché Central in Tunis next week . . . "

"That's true, Zio Claudio, it's true, but an evil person took his life. We don't know who, yet. The French carabinieri have promised to find him. They have to find the criminal and he has to be killed . . . "

There was a murmur of approval in the crowd. I agreed, whoever killed my father must be killed. An eye for an eye. I didn't want to forgive. I no longer had a father.

It took the French gendarmes a week to find the monster. He was an Arab. His name was Romdane Jlassi. My Great-uncle Claudio told us he was the former tenant, who had been evicted by the owner, Kamel Ben Mahmoud, the man my father did business with.

My mother and I were again living with my Great-uncle Claudio. Fate had taken us back to La Goleta. My mother wailed constantly. She didn't want to go back to the farm. Everything would have to be sold— the cows, the pots, the coal stove, the cans, the strainers. Everything. Absolutely everything. "Who would buy those cows? Everyone will think they're cursed. They would only bring bad luck."

Kamel Ben Mahmoud came to see us one day after my father's burial. He was visibly shaken by the death of my father. He kept wiping his forehead and his eyes. But for him, at least, the loss was material. He had only lost his money. "That kelb Romdane Jlassi. I knew he was a scoundrel," he shouted. "He wanted to take revenge on me by killing poor Monsieur Giuliano. He wanted to get rid of Monsieur Luigi and he killed him on my land to frighten people so that they would no longer rent from me. If he were in front of me now, I would spit on him."

And I would scratch his eyes out. I would plunge my fingers and my nails into his flesh and tear out his soul. Unfortunately, nothing could bring my father back. Neither the death of his killer nor the little bit of money we would get from selling the cows and the cheesemaking equipment. La Goleta had cast a spell on us. It had taken revenge on us for leaving. It wanted to keep its poor Sicilians inside its dark, rotten belly. It wanted us for itself, for always.

Chapter 25

Fatma

Sadok Bel Kadi became my husband. My father and my brother wanted to punish me by choosing an old man for me. But they had no idea. They saved my life. They didn't know that another old man had already destroyed my life by raping me on a bench in the vestibule of his house. They didn't know that their respectable friend Am Chedli had made me "undesirable" to any young man who might ask for my hand. But it was different with Si Sadok. I told him everything on my wedding day and he immediately believed me. Not the slightest doubt in his eyes, not one hurtful word. He took me in his arms and held me for a long time. He gave me love, the love Am Chedli had taken away.

That night I remembered the words of the *dégasa* and I said to myself that she was absolutely right. God would never abandon me. When my father said Si Sadok would be a good match for me, I didn't say anything. I wasn't sure. I knew he was old. A man from an important family, whose wife had died. He had sons who were already married. How could I accept such humiliation?

My cousin Farida said, "Don't accept, he's old."

Again, I didn't say anything. Normally so talkative and often spontaneous, this time I couldn't afford to make a mistake, and I wanted to let my heart decide, and it decided that Si Sadok would be a good husband for me. I wouldn't have to prove anything to him. He wanted a companion and I was ready to be that to him.

Right after I married and left home to go live with Si Sadok, things started to go wrong. We were struck by a series of disasters, one after another. At the beginning I didn't know anything. Nobody told me anything. I was getting used to my new life in that lovely house in the heart of the medina, with a patio on the roof where I would hang out the wash and admire the view of the city. Si Sadok was not fussy or demanding. All he asked was that I make him a cup of coffee after every meal. We would sit together on the green sofa in the sitting room, a tray on the table with two steaming cups of coffee, one for him and one for me. He would talk to me about his day, the people he'd met, who asked him questions about the shares of an inheritance in their family, divorce, births, and marriages. Rich and poor would come to him for his opinions on everything. I learned from him, and for the first time in my life, I regretted that I hadn't been able to finish school like my cousin Farida.

Fortunately, she would come visit me, always with Tawfik. She would spend the whole day at my house before going back to her "hell." During one visit, she described the situation at her house after the Italian tenant, Monsieur Giuliano, was found dead, killed by the former tenant, Romdane Jlassi. "Kamel has lost all the money he invested in that business," she said. "Nobody would want that cursed stable."

"And what does my Uncle Laroussi say?"

"I've never seen him as angry as he was the day Kamel told him of Monsieur Giuliano's death. He's been in a rage since then. Worse, he accuses Kamel of lying to him about the amount of the loan."

"Is it true Kamel lied to him?"

"I believe my father. He knows his money better than anyone. He counts it again and again every day. But as you know, Baba gave Kamel too much power over us, starting with me."

She was right. Farida was trapped in that marriage that darkened her days. Her only ray of light was Tawfik.

"The good thing in all this is that Kamel has gotten off my back. He doesn't argue with me anymore. It's my father he argues with, morning and night. My father says he's a liar and Kamel answers that if not for his hard work, the land would long ago have been stolen by the peasants. Oh, Fatma, if only I could close my eyes and forget all this misfortune, our house and these endless arguments. But tell me about your life and your husband."

She came to me to forget, and my insistent questions only reminded her of her sorrows. But how could I ignore what was going on in my childhood home, where I had grown up, where I lived until the day I left to go live with Si Sadok? And what would become of my mother and father and my brothers if the conflict between my brother Kamel and my Uncle Laroussi didn't get resolved?

In fact, as the months passed, I learned through my mother's and Farida's visits that things had gotten worse, and that what had started with the death of a tenant had led to my Uncle Laroussi's discovery that Kamel had indeed lied to him about the amount of the loan. Actually, my brother had borrowed twenty thousand francs, only half of which had been used to build the stable. With the rest, he had bought a house in La Marsa and had put it in the name of his mistress, a certain Samira, a prostitute on Rue Zarkoune.

"Just think, he beats me for a potato ragout that turns out badly, and then he goes and spends the night with a prostitute. Even worse, that girl now possesses a house in her own name in La Marsa. My mother dreamed of that her whole life. And I, the *bahloula*[22] who believed my father when he told me he'd buy one for me . . . a mirage, I was hanging on to a mirage. All I can do now is complain. My dear Fatma, guess who's the rich man and who the poor man, who's the fool and who the clever one, who the respectable one and who the contemptible one in this story? The whore from Rue Zarkoune made a mockery of us, our fortune, and our good name. Poverty took revenge on greed and stupidity."

I had never seen Farida like this. Furious and sad. And I too was appalled that my brother had squandered the family's money to please his mistress. And to think that he criticized me for wearing a dress that only went to my knees!

Farida continued while Tawfik played in the courtyard, "Worse, Kamel mortgaged our family home behind Baba's back. Now, unless the bank receives regular payments, our house will be seized and sold."

I was starting to feel faint. "Can't Uncle Laroussi help us at least keep the family home and reimburse the bank?"

"I don't know, Fatma. Life in that house has become unbearable. At least you're happy with Si Sadok. You've managed to get away. All I want is a divorce. I don't know if my father will change his mind now that he's

---

22 Naïve or simpleminded.

angry with Kamel. But I'm afraid. All this has weakened him. He has heart trouble. Kamel betrayed him. My father only discovered what was going on when it was too late. I don't know if the people at the bank will give us a period of grace, time to settle the *cambialates* that are piling up."

I found it hard to understand the news, which I only got in bits and pieces during Farida's visits. I was happy in my new life. Si Sadok treated me like a princess and I treated him equally well, cooking a new dish for him every day. But at the same time, I sensed that the situation was beyond me and that my family's financial affairs had taken a dangerous turn. It was as if too much good fortune for me could only lead to misfortune for them.

I finally learned that our house had been saved. Just barely. My Uncle Laroussi had to sell off two of the houses he owned. After the bank was reimbursed, he no longer permitted Kamel to have anything to do with managing the land. Kamel refused to accept that humiliation, and the arguments continued, making life horrible in the Bab Souika house. I often thought of my cousin and her little boy. They were like hostages. Escaping Kamel's control, they had fallen into my uncle's clutches. When would God finally set them free?

Chapter 26

Farida

Dear Habib,

At last I am free! Yesterday I went to the courthouse on Place de la Kasbah. How often have I made that trip? Some ten times, or twenty? I've lost count. I waited in the courtroom for the judge's verdict, which had been a long time coming. I had been waiting to finally hold his written decision in my hands and read the whole thing. Like a first drink of water after a long day of fasting. I had been waiting for the day when those words elegantly written by the hand of a man on official stationary bearing the seal of justice would finally quench my thirst. My thirst for the freedom that had been taken from me more than ten years ago, on the day of my marriage to Kamel.

And that freedom came to me when I could hardly believe I would ever find it. When I could no longer tolerate Kamel's constant ranting. Nor believe my father's promises that everything would turn out all right. Nor put faith in the so-called hearings, which no one attended except me and the porter of the courthouse. And at those times of despair, I would think of you. Of the years of our childhood, which was so short, especially after Ommi's early death.

I would think of our daily walk in Rue El Kaadine, through Place Bab Souika to Rue du Pacha. You would accompany me, saying that you were protecting me, but in fact, you allowed me to do anything. To run a little, to stop for a second to tie the ribbon on my braid that had come undone. And I never told on you either. Your awkward movements, the teasing of the other boys, who would bump into you and pretend they hadn't seen you. We protected each other.

Then Baba wouldn't let me continue going to school. But it was different for you. You were a man. You were free, at least more than I was. I had to free myself. First from Kamel, then from Baba. It was a long battle, but I did it. I was helped by destiny, but especially by books. The books I would steal from your room taught me that there's an end to everything, even unhappiness. My unhappiness ended when the judgment was handed down, the divorce final, and Kamel gone. I don't know where he is now, perhaps in Samira's house with her. Perhaps with some other woman. Frankly, I don't want to know. It's better that way.

I regained my freedom when my father fell ill. Didn't you use to quote a famous verse by an Arab poet who lived in America? I forget his name, you'll tell it to me the next time you write. "Fate is my ally; destiny, my travelling mate."[23]

Yes, poets are never wrong. Once I was resentful of you. When you didn't support me in opposing Baba about my marriage. If you were not a poet, you could have overcome him. But you preferred words to physical force. And then you went away. I forgive you, because you followed your dreams. Because you didn't try to become a man like Baba or Kamel. You accepted your destiny while shaping it. But it was my destiny that shaped me. It took too long to understand my suffering. At times, that destiny gave me moments of respite. Respite when everything was sombre. When everything had become dark and I wanted only one thing. To go away and find the light again.

You told me you didn't like your new life as a teacher in Bizerte very much. You wrote that it was cold and damp there. The north wind crept into your bones and your students were too poor to learn. They quickly left the lycée to go to work. But since your transfer to Sousse, you've been reborn like clover in the spring. The sunny city, the view of the sea from the balcony of your building, and especially, the fort in the old city where you liked to sit in one of the cafés and watch the passersby and write. You said the fort made you feel protected. There was something exceptional about that fort. A magical protection like that of an oyster holding its pearl. Protection from intrusive looks, arrogant French soldiers, or just human stupidity.

Oh, my dear brother, what I wouldn't give to visit you and see with my own eyes your little earthly paradise! The last time you wrote, you spoke of your brilliant and ambitious students who wanted to go study in France after they graduated. How you discussed poetry and literature with them for hours and hours after class. How you introduced them to works of Arabic and French literature. How they devoured your knowledge down to the last crumb. And you also

---

23 From "Peace of Mind" by Mikhail Naimy, translated by Mounah A Khouri and Hamid Algar.

wanted to do a graduate degree in Arabic literature. I have no doubt that you'll succeed in that.

Come see us during the winter break. Fatma sends her regards. She says that this time, she'll find you the right wife.

Your sister,
Farida

Chapter 27

Tawfik

It was a year or two before the great return of *Zaim*[24] Bourguiba to Tunis. I must have been eleven or twelve. The blood of youth flowed strong and powerful in my veins, beating like a drum on the day of the Eid. I could feel myself becoming a man. My body was changing. There was a ferment within me that wanted to burst out, but something held it back. Ever since I'd opened my eyes to the world, I had seen my mother and father arguing. At first, I didn't really understand what was going on, but over time, I saw the blows raining down on my mother and heard her cries of distress, and when she began to confront him, I prayed fervently that my father would go away. These scenes were endlessly repeated in front of my eyes when I was a child, unable to do anything to stop them.

It's a good thing my mother was able to comfort me with nice stories that chased away the bad ones that filled my nightmares with tears and anxiety. My father frightened me. Sometimes, when he was in a good mood, he'd ask my mother to dress me in my nicest *jebba*, the one he'd bought me especially for the Eid when I was seven. A beige *jebba* made of raw silk, with a matching *sirwal*, shirt, and jacket, all hand-embroidered in nice patterns, with buttons like orange blossom buds. My father would show me off to his friends, the merchants in Souk El Attarine, like a rare piece of art. On a morning visit, I'd be the pet of all those older gentlemen, who would sometimes give me a shiny coin, a mint, or just a pat on the cheek. But aside from these times of relative calm, my father was

---

24 Leader.

quick-tempered and violent.

I spent most of my time between school and my mother. At the start of every term, she would walk me as far as the blue door of my school. She was the one who talked to my teachers, never my father. She helped me with my homework and asked how I was doing. A *safsari* hastily thrown over her head, her face uncovered, nothing stopped her, not the offended looks of some passersby at seeing a woman walking in the streets of the medina with her face uncovered nor the words whispered behind her back by some members of our family. Farida couldn't have cared less. Only one thing was important to her: my report card at the end of the school year.

When my grandfather would no longer allow my father to manage our land, there was nearly a complete break between them, but after a few years things settled down and my father started renting out the land again. The stable built by Monsieur Giuliano had fallen into ruin. Nobody wanted to rent it. The sons of Romdane Jlassi took over from their father, who had been condemned to death by the colonial justice system. One less Arab, those who administered French justice must secretly have thought. Our land was now untouchable except by the Jlassi family, who had taken its revenge against my father by continuing to rent it at the ridiculously low price of a hundred francs a year. In the absence of other tenants, they had imposed their conditions and increased their power. Our whole family suffered. My grandfather lost his standing as the neighbourhood moneylender. People had gotten wind of Kamel's misadventures and mismanagement and had slowly stopped going to my grandfather. And when they did go to him, they insisted on less collateral and sometimes even none at all. Finally, nobody came to his little office in Bab Souika. He returned to the house, looking annoyed, his right hand on his heart as if he was looking for something in his jacket. When the old man saw me, he would open his arms and I'd let him hug me. My life and my mother's life gravitated around him.

I remembered the days when my mother's cousin Fatma would come visit with her children, from the toddler in her arms to the eldest, who was a few years younger than I. We'd play in the courtyard of our house while my mother and her cousin spent hours and hours talking. They would fall silent as soon as my father appeared. That was when Fatma would call her sons, saying it was late and they had to go home. Her husband was seriously ill at the time, and one day my mother told me he had died and Fatma had nowhere to live. Her husband's sons had inherited everything and they hadn't given her a share of his house. That's how Fatma and her children came to live with us, on the upper floor, where her parents already lived.

At school, more and more of the children were talking about independence for Tunisia, saying we would soon have our own country with no French gendarmes. We would discuss these things in secret at recess, not in front of our teachers, who were all Frenchmen except for the ones teaching Arabic and the Quran. I dreamed of France, and of my country's independence and also my own, no longer under my father's yoke. I was not spared his violence. When he was arguing with my mother and I went near them, I'd feel his blows on my back like a hammer breaking my bones or a violent wind pushing me into a void. My mother would place herself between us and put her arms around me to protect me. But Farida didn't have Kamel's physical strength. She would get beaten instead of me. I lived torn between violence and fear.

Until, one day, my body rebelled. A strange feeling of power took hold of me and I resisted my father's blows. And that was the beginning of the end. My father had never expected that little Tawfik, the nice little toy he showed off in the streets of the medina, would one day become an adolescent capable of using words to answer him back and his fists to defend himself. The little bird had taken flight for the first time. My father was stunned by my audacity. He had always seen me as a little boy clinging to his mother's skirts. He would make jokes about my lack of physical strength and my uncertain future. My sudden defiance put an end to his despotism. I became a threat to his territory, and one day he left the house. Not just for a few days, as he was in the habit of doing, but this time for good.

My mother started to speak of divorce, and my grandfather, who wasn't strong and no longer had a financial arrangement with Kamel, finally stopped opposing it. After ten years of suffering, my mother became a divorcee.

◦◦

When *Zaim* Bourguiba returned to Tunis a hero, everyone wanted to go out and see him. Everyone but my mother. She stayed in our courtyard sitting on a wooden stool, a big laundry basin between her knees, washing our clothes. She had started smoking, I didn't know how, and there was a cigarette between her lips. She had a big cake of green soap in one hand and an item of clothing in the other. Her cousin Fatma, who had returned to our house, did the cooking, and my mother did the laundry. On the day of Bourguiba's return, even Fatma and the children went to wait for the *Zaim* in the main square of Bab Souika. Bourguiba had brought independence back to the Tunisian people, he had succeeded where so many before him had failed. My Uncle Habib had said it wasn't true that Bourguiba was the *combattant suprême*. Well before him, there had been other fighters just as intelligent and courageous. Si Moncef Bey had been one, but unfortunately he was exiled by the French and came back to Tunis in a coffin.

"I want to go see Bourguiba."

She continued scrubbing, her mind elsewhere.

"My friends, my cousins, everyone is at Place Bab Souika. You can hear the crowd from here."

She fixed her eyes on me. "Go if you want. I'm staying here. Men that are too powerful scare me."

Farida was like that, strange and unpredictable.

I went. Some of my friends who belonged to the Tunisian boy scouts were already there, forming a human buffer to hold back the excited crowd. I joined them. We waited for hours. People were elbowing each other and greeting old friends. Lost children were screaming, looking for their mothers. Women in *safsaris*, some with their faces hidden, some with their faces uncovered, and some with their hair loose, were smiling without fear. When the majestic procession finally appeared, everyone was euphoric. We were surrounded by the ululations of the women, the shouting of the children, and the singing of the patriots. The *Zaim*'s procession advanced slowly toward us, heading from the port of La Goulette to Place Bab Souika. It was preceded by dromedaries decorated with brightly coloured pompons, on which were mounted dark-skinned Bedouins from the desert, their heads wrapped in turbans, carrying rifles and firing into the air. For once, the sound of bullets was a sign of joy. They were followed by other Bedouins, on horses, just as flamboyantly decorated. There were young men on bicycles and others simply walking.

I saw him with my own eyes. It was the *Zaim*, his back straight, his chest thrust out, dressed in white, stepping out of a convertible with one arm raised to acknowledge us. I shouted our liberator's name with all my strength, "Vive Bourguiba!" Along with the jubilant crowd, I celebrated the return of this man who had successfully negotiated with the French to take us on the road to independence. But in my mind, as a young man, I was also celebrating my father's exit from our lives and the return to a life that I hoped would now be calm and peaceful.

LE BELVÉDÈRE

1964-1994

It was a dream, a pale dream
Not without sweetness,
Where, in your inhabited tomb
I saw your form rising . . .

O season of the Unforgettable,
Knees brushing the tombs,
Fingers groping the Impalpable
And hopes in tatters . . . !

MAY ZIADEH (1886-1941),
Fleurs de Rêve (Dream Flowers)

Chapter 1

Leila

My mother left our home a few weeks after my first birthday. Left without a trace. A shadow swallowed up by the forest. Footsteps sinking into quicksand. No note or phone number scribbled on a scrap of paper. No kiss on my cheek or tender touch to melt my heart. None of that. One day, my mother was there, and the next day, nothing. She called my father a week later to tell him not to try to find her, that she would never come back and live with him. She had made her decision and no one could change her mind.

It was then that my grandmother Farida came to live with us. She became the mother I no longer had, while remaining the mother of Tawfik, my father. But apart from the two of us, there were other things that counted in her life: books, newspapers, and the radio. My grandmother loved me well enough, but she didn't always know how to look after me. She found things like giving me a bath, changing my clothes, or preparing a meal tedious; they bored her to death. In fact, she really didn't know how to manage things. My grandmother was never a real housewife, although she stayed in the house her entire life. Her life was elsewhere. Her life was in books and stories, literature and words. When I began to talk and understand, she would sit with me for hours, reading and telling me stories. Stories from books and others that were invented, probably written in her head without her ever being able to share them with anyone but me.

If I interrupted her to say I was hungry while she was reading to me, her eyes, calm and gentle until then, would suddenly become angry. "Can you tell your stomach to wait a bit until I finish the story and we find out if the heroine conquers the *ghoul*[1] and returns to her family?" My eyes wide, my belly screaming hunger, I would listen to the story until she was finished, and then we would go to the kitchen. Often she would open the fridge and stand motionless for a moment as if looking for a meal that existed only in her imagination. "Okay, we'll make a shakshuka," she would say, taking a few eggs, two peppers, an onion and three tomatoes from the fridge.

"With merguez?" I would ask hopefully. I loved those little sausages.

"And where do you expect me to find merguez? Your father doesn't buy much these days. We only have a few pieces of chicken left over from last night—a thigh and two wings."

Disappointed and resigned, I would accept my grandmother's explanations and eat whatever she made without much enthusiasm.

My grandmother didn't talk much about my mother. I was the one who insisted she tell me about her. She never said bad things about her. She always had tender words for her. Words that were like the fragrance of the jasmine she gathered every summer morning and that scented the air on our hot evenings. "She left because she realized that she wanted to be something other than a good wife and a good mother." Those words came out of her mouth as naturally as can be, as if I were not the little girl who had been abandoned by that mother, and as if she herself were not the mother of the poor husband who had been abandoned. With the years, I learned to repeat her words without tears pouring from my eyes like water from a fountain. But at that time, my mother was in my child's imagination a horrible witch.

"But she abandoned me, don't you understand? A-ban-doned."

"Who's been telling you this nonsense, Leila?" she asked, exasperated, a cigarette between her lips, her ears straining to hear her little radio as she fumbled with the dial to adjust the frequency.

"The girls at school. They always say the same thing. That my mother didn't love me, and that's why she left."

Farida put down her cigarette in the ashtray on the dresser. I stayed where I was, in the blue armchair facing her bed. It was where I sat

---

1   Female vampire in Arabic folklore.

whenever I came to her room. That chair with the little hole in it that kept growing as I stuck my finger in it while I listened to Farida telling me stories. It was one of the rare times that I saw her angry, almost in a rage.

"You can tell those little pests to shut up, or else I'll come to the school with you and I'll shut their mouths for them. Those little girls are repeating nonsense from their mothers. Don't believe them. Do you hear me, Leila? Don't believe them! Their mothers are liars and hypocrites. Maybe they, too, once wanted to leave their husbands, to go away and not come back. But they couldn't do it. Your mother, Jouda, did it. At least she had the courage. There, that's all there is to it."

She hesitated a moment, as if she wanted to say more. Something more serious. Something about her own life that would reassure me about mine or that would make what my mother had done less terrible in my eyes. But she said nothing. She calmly picked up her cigarette, frowned and turned to the radio that didn't always stay on the right frequency.

I continued to turn my finger in the little hole in the chair, a smile on my lips. Farida knew how to reassure me, especially regarding my mother. But that was when I was little. Since then, she has stopped smoking, and I don't ask questions about my mother anymore.

Chapter 2

Habib

Dear Farida,

As promised, I'm still writing letters to you. Sometimes in my darkest moments, I've considered stopping. I wondered what was the point of writing to you when I never had the courage to confront my father and convince him not to marry you to Kamel. But Kamel finally left, thanks to your patience, and to fate, which gave you a little help.

Those dark moments often came in the night. When sleep would dissipate and I'd find myself haunted by old images of my life. The only remedy would be to get up and let my wife sleep. When I passed Nourreddin's bedroom, I'd want to go in and kiss his forehead. Seeing him growing up peacefully would calm my anxiety for a moment. Then I would sit down at my little table and start to write. A poem. A story. Another poem. A letter to you. Words have been my release from my torments. I would forget the political machinations of the other teachers, who would do anything to climb the rungs of power and become principal in a lycée, or regional director in another part of the country. Even if it meant lying, even if it meant demolishing their colleagues, even if it meant hurting me.

I don't want to worry you, Farida. Or to play the victim. But it's the truth. Day after day, I have been discovering that many people around me are malicious. The ones who smile at me in the morning in the staff room are the most vicious, they malign me to the principal. They say that they are better qualified than I to receive some promotion. That I'm not ambitious and that, in any case, my poetry matters more to me than anything else. I'm inventing nothing. Those words were reported to me by the principal himself, one of my former students in

Bizerte, my first teaching position.

All those teachers come to the school in their cars imported from abroad and newly acquired at great cost. With no regard for our young country that is still developing. With no regard for the currency that costs our national budget a lot, money that comes out of our coffers to fill those of France, Germany, or Italy. Whereas I always come to work by bicycle. I annoy them. Some of them find me ridiculous. Some say I'm crazy. Think of it, Farida, all that gratuitous nastiness!

At home, things aren't going well. My wife feels I spend far too much time on my studies and my students, and that I am not taking proper care of her. She, too, wants a car. "What's the point of being a teacher when you can't even buy a car?" That's her favourite comment. I did buy her a colour television. But apparently it wasn't enough. If it weren't for Noureddin, who is still young, I would already have left. Fatma chose me a wife who was pretty, but unfortunately she is not suited to me. She's too traditional and she has a viper's tongue. However, I have to admit she's a good cook and she has given me a beautiful, intelligent boy.

I don't know how long I can hang on, but I can see that the end of the relationship is fast approaching. And it's precisely that near-certainty that has made me think of you. You who for so long endured the pain of living with someone you didn't love, someone who was hurting you. It seems I'm always too late. All these years to understand the depth of your unhappiness. Forgive me, dear sister.

Habib

Chapter 3

Leila

I met my mother one December day. My mother, the woman I had seen only in the photos my father kept in a big white leather bag, where old photographs shared the space with birth certificates and the postcards Farida had sent him when he was studying in France. The woman who came to meet me didn't look at all like my mother. There was a wedding picture that I almost never looked at and another one of my mother holding me in her arms. She wasn't looking at the photographer, who was probably my father, but rather at me, a baby a few months old. Although her gaze was tender, I interpreted it many times as a look of anger. Anger for having given birth to me, anger because she no longer wanted to live with that man who was my father. Her long hair was loose around her face. She was wearing a checked dress that I found ugly, but Farida said my father had given it to my mother when they were engaged and had paid a lot for it. I liked neither the dress nor my mother's long hair. The only thing I liked in the photo was her fingers holding mine, something I often longed for during my childhood. That was my mental image of my mother. The woman who came and met me in front of my school was completely different. A woman with short hair, and a determined but gentle look. A grey wool coat, velvet pants, and brown knee-length boots.

She was standing in front of the street vendors with their displays of candies, chewing gum, sugar-coated almonds, and pink cotton candy, and the children jostling after a day spent writing compositions and doing mathematics under the strict rules dictated by our teachers. In the midst of that familiar confusion, children often were able to convince their parents to buy them treats. "I want that one . . . no, no, the blue one . . . yes that one!" Sometimes a child would hesitate, holding the treat and smelling it like a flower, then return it to the vendor who was waiting to be paid and was beginning to lose patience. "Can I have the little licorice stick instead?" Some children went away happy, with the candy already in their mouths, moving it from cheek to cheek, but others looked sad, having gotten nothing for lack of money or an accommodating parent. Others were crying or screaming because their parent had grabbed them by the arm and dragged them away.

When I was ten years old, in grade four, my father stopped coming to pick me up at school. I began to go home on my own or with one of the women who lived on our street. And that was when my mother came back into my life. She walked over to me, touched my hair with her hand, and smiled at me: "Leila, my daughter, you've grown so much!"

I didn't really understand what that woman who had appeared out of nowhere was saying to me. I pulled away roughly from her hand. When I was small, Farida had filled my head with stories of little girls being kidnapped by wicked strangers in front of their school. But my mother didn't seem offended by my sudden movement. She continued, speaking softly, "Leila, listen carefully, I'm your mother. I'm Jouda. It's true you don't know me. It's true I disappeared from your life almost ten years ago, but I'm your mother and I want to see you again."

It was quite a shock. I'd never expected to see my mother again in such an ordinary setting. Gradually recovering, I went with her to a nearby park, walking in silence. From time to time, I would turn my head to look at this woman who said she was my mother. I wanted to catch a glimpse of her face without her seeing me. But each time, she would catch me looking at her, and our eyes would meet and she would smile.

"Are you afraid of me?" she asked.

"Yes, a little. Maybe you're with a gang waiting in the park and you're going to kidnap me, like in the story Farida said she heard on the radio the other day. She told me a dozen times that I was not to talk to strangers."

My mother's eyes lit up when she heard the name Farida from my lips. "Is Farida still faithful to her old loves . . . her radio and her cigarettes?"

"No, no more cigarettes. She stopped smoking. And she doesn't cough anymore. Well, just a bit. Only in the morning when she wakes up. Anyway, not like before."

"Swear to me that she stopped smoking, I can't believe it."

"I swear it on my father's head."

My mother's eyes, which had been smiling, clouded over. She continued walking beside me in silence. We arrived at the park. The trees were bare. There was a little pond with a bronze statue of a dolphin in the middle, which I would look at while I was crossing the park on my way home. In the spring and summer, the dolphin standing almost upright on a pedestal was surrounded by fountains that made it look like it was leaping out of the water. It often reminded me of myself, alone in life. But I had people around me who wanted to make me happy. When the weather was nice, I would contemplate the statue, the leafy trees, the fresh grass, and watch the people strolling, the children running back and forth. I would often sit on a wooden bench in front of the pond and count the passersby. I would dream of my mother, of what she was doing, of what we could do if she ever came to live with us. The books she would read to me, the dishes she would cook, the jokes we would tell each other, laughing together. And when it was cold and grey, I would watch the leaves floating on the water, the pond reduced to a few puddles with the fountains shut off, and the people bundled up in their coats hurrying home.

We found a spot on my usual bench. The one where lovers had carved hearts with arrows going in one side and out the other, with blood dripping in the middle, and almost all the letters in the alphabet. The grass was dry and the mud stuck to our shoes, leaving little clods that fell off like fish scales.

My mother spoke first. "Do you like this garden?" Now I could see that I looked like her. We had the same hazel eyes and the same eyebrows, long and curved, meeting in the middle like palm fronds.

"More in the spring or summer. In the winter, there's nothing to see."

"You're right. You know, you talk like an adult, my little Leila, not a ten-year-old girl."

I said nothing. I wondered why she was surprised that I spoke like a lady. Had she forgotten that I had been raised by my grandmother and that she, my mother, had abandoned me nine years ago?

"Why aren't you saying anything, my dear?"

She put her arms around me, and this time I let her. I wanted to make up for everything I'd missed all those years. My mother's arms were soft and supple. I let myself be cuddled by that woman I had only known for a few minutes. My head was close to her heart and I could hear its regular beating like a distant dream. Tears slowly welled up in my eyes. I held them back, but they were more determined than I was. I was crying. So was my mother, because with her left hand, she pulled a handkerchief from her bag and wiped her nose. I don't remember how long we stayed sitting on that lovers' bench with me leaning against my mother's chest and her arms around me and her head against mine.

"I'm really sorry, my dear. I abandoned you. Yes, I went away and left you. But believe me, I had no choice. I had to leave. I had to finish my studies and become a teacher."

I didn't really understand what she was talking about. I preferred her to say nothing and continue stroking my hair.

"You see, my dear, I never wanted to get married. I wanted to finish my studies. But after my father's death, my mother really wanted me to marry your father. She told me I'd be happy with him and that I'd have everything I wanted. But that wasn't true. Only a few months after my marriage, I realized that all I wanted in life was to finish my studies and become a teacher."

I looked at the motionless dolphin. There were no jets of water or rays of sunshine or birds coming to perch on its back to drink a few drops and take off again. The dolphin was alone and abandoned. And so was I.

"And why didn't you come and see me before, after one or two or three years? It took you nine years. Nine years to come to my school and tell me you're my mother."

She was also looking at the dolphin. But I didn't know if she was thinking the same thing I was. Her tears were flowing like water from a faucet someone had forgotten to turn off.

"I was afraid to come back and see you. I was afraid that when I saw you again, my heart would falter and I wouldn't be able to leave you. I was afraid I would no longer want to continue my studies, but just want to hold you in my arms and take care of you. To smell your smell that hasn't left me since your birth. If I'd returned in those early years, I never would have been able to finish my studies and become independent."

My bitterness was too great to be mollified by a few words.

"And now, have you come back for good? You won't leave me again?"

That was all I wanted to know. To know that my mother's hands would not leave me again, that her arms would hold me tight and that I could keep listening to her words even though I was not too sure I could believe them.

"Of course, we'll see each other again, every day if you wish. You'll be able to come to my house whenever you want. I'll arrange with Tawfik that you can come to my house. You'll see, you'll forget everything."

She spoke my father's name, the name of the man who had once been her husband. The man she had perhaps loved for two years, and had left forever. She spoke his name in an insignificant, ordinary way, the way someone would say "pass me the bread" or "give me a glass of water." My father, her husband, Farida's son, had become a minor detail, a name said without trembling, without shivers, without remembering all those years of waiting, of despair, of tears and sadness. My mother was like that. She knew how to find the words to survive.

Chapter 4

Jouda

After I saw my daughter Leila again, my life was no longer the same. How could I have lived all those years without seeing her, smelling her, touching her? And yet, I survived. Where did I find the strength to break free from that marriage and leave, giving up my own daughter? I've never been able to understand my action. But I did it and I took responsibility for it. I accepted the consequences of that painful separation. There were some who said I was hard-hearted and merciless. I put up with the callous, brutal words, the hateful looks and the constant gossip of people around me. I had no regrets. Leila will always resent me a little, but perhaps one day she'll forgive me. The day she becomes a mother, she'll understand my terrible crazy act, the act of an unworthy mother. In becoming a mother, maybe she will be able to finally let go of that fear, that barely veiled fear that was still in her eyes when she greeted me on her visits. That moment of silence that occurred every time we watched a film together and there was a scene with a mother and her children. That wall of resistance that had been built up between us, brick by brick, in the nine years of my absence, and that I was never able to tear down. I constantly kicked at it in the hope of seeing it crumble, but the resistance prevailed. It clung there, defiant, almost triumphant at the sight of my futile efforts. When she gives birth and sees her baby for the first time, she'll be able to understand and forgive me, and free herself from that fear.

The first time I saw Leila, I immediately realized that I had to finish school and get a job. In the hospital, when they put my daughter on my breast and our flesh touched, I felt that the bond between us would never be destroyed and that it was for her that I would leave that marriage, so that I could come back stronger, more determined, better prepared.

A few weeks after marrying Tawfik, I realized I was not ready for marriage. Tawfik was good, kind, and attentive, but that wasn't what I wanted in life. I wanted to become a teacher, and Tawfik didn't encourage me at all. He wanted a wife and children, and I was looking for something else. I got married to please my mother. She was suffering a lot after the death of my father and thought that my marriage would bring her the peace she yearned for. I soon realized that it was a serious mistake. I realized that taking care of my husband and my house was smothering me. I couldn't breathe, I felt as if I didn't have enough air. Every day I felt the snare close more tightly around my neck. In the meantime, Leila arrived. Sweet, adorable, and full of life. I almost changed my mind. I almost returned to the quiet life of a housewife cooking her husband's favourite dishes and waiting patiently for him to come home from work. I almost became like my mother, my aunts, and my grandmother. But I stood firm. Each time I held Leila in my arms or put her in the stroller to go for a walk, I felt maternal love get the better of me. I felt my heart failing. I was going to stay for her. I was going to give up my dreams. Each time I saw Leila enchanted by a cat crossing the street or pointing at a bird in the sky or a passing car, stammering incomprehensible words, I would go back to my original idea: to leave. To leave before it was too late. Before maternal love took me hostage and the years went by and I found myself with two or three children, pacified by the years, trapped by destiny. A defeated Jouda facing a satisfied Tawfik.

When I told my mother of my intention to leave my husband and abandon Leila, she thought at first that I had gone mad. "You're going to destroy your life and your daughter's life to do what? To become a teacher? Are you crazy or what?"

"I'm not destroying anyone's life. On the contrary, if I stay I'll be destroying my own life."

She looked at me with her deep, dark eyes. "It's those books that are giving you these crazy ideas, isn't it? And the people around us, what are they going to think of you? That you've abandoned your daughter, that you've left your husband for another man, that you're a bad mother."

"They'll think whatever they like. I want to finish my studies. I want to get my diploma and go to teacher's college. It's important to me. You have to understand."

Seeing me so determined, my mother tried another tactic. "Why don't you talk about it with Tawfik? Maybe he'll agree to help you finish your studies and become a teacher. Anything's possible, isn't it? Why couldn't you find a solution without a break-up or a divorce or rumours or a bad reputation?"

No one understood me, not even my mother. The minute I opened my mouth, they would scowl and give me dark looks. "Why go to school? Aren't you happy with Tawfik?" "But you have everything girls your age dream of—an apartment, an adorable baby. You don't even have your mother-in-law living with you, so why do you want to leave your husband?" "She wants to become a liberated woman, poor thing; the books have made her a bit cuckoo." "And her daughter, the poor child is only one year old and she wants to leave her to go to school. What will she do with a diploma? Is it worth more than a child? God help her poor mother, Jouda is a lost daughter!"

That was all they would say, that was all they would understand, and that was all they would see. They would never understand my thirst for learning. They wouldn't understand my need for an independent life. In their world, they couldn't conceive of a woman dreaming of anything other than getting married and having children. It was to avoid all those nasty looks, all those useless words, and all those hypocritical sighs that I calmly took my things and left. I went to the home of Farida, my mother-in-law.

When I took my things, I didn't know exactly where I would go. I knew I wanted to leave and not come back, but I had no idea where I would live. Go back to my mother's house or rent a small room or stay with a friend? I was in a fog. It was clear in my mind that I wanted to get out of that house where I felt I was being swallowed up a little more each day, but the details of my new life after the end of the marriage were vague.

The person who came spontaneously to my mind was Farida. We had always had an unusual relationship. Even when she came with Tawfik to ask my mother for my hand, I wasn't able to read her eyes. One moment she would seem warm and good-humoured, and a few moments later, she would become silent, distant, and cold.

Farida lived in an old house with an inner courtyard, on the edge of the working-class neighbourhood El Halfaouine. A house she had inherited from her father. Tawfik had told me that his grandfather was very fond of his daughter, who had been divorced quite young and never remarried. Before dying, he willed her a small house so that she would have a roof over her head without having to pay rent. It was in front of that house that I found myself, with Leila in her stroller and a bag in my hand containing some clothes.

Farida opened the door. She was wearing a dressing gown and her white hair fell loose around her face. A cigarette in one hand and a book in the other. Her eyes immediately focused on the stroller, where Leila was sleeping. "*Marhaba, marhaba,* welcome, welcome! Look who's come to visit me: my granddaughter and her mother. Come in! Don't just stand there in front of the door!"

"Thank you, *Nana!*" I called her *Nana,* as all girls from good families called their mothers-in-law as a sign of respect but also to please their husbands. I left the stroller and the bag in the foyer, a dark room that had once been used for guests to wait in before they were received in the sitting room. I picked Leila up; she was still asleep. Farida put out her half-smoked cigarette and threw it into a pot of geraniums in the middle of the interior patio. We took the stairs to her room.

Downstairs, in addition to the patio, there was a room that was used as the sitting room for guests and a kitchen. Upstairs, there was a spacious bedroom, where Farida spent her days. She would read, listen to the radio, smoke, and take naps. She rarely cooked, but there was always a box of anise cookies in her cupboard, a piece of cheese she would nibble on, and oranges, dates, or pomegranates according to the season. That day, she had oranges. I put Leila down on the bed, covered her, and came back to sit down on the red and ochre velvet sofa. Farida handed me an orange. The room, as usual, was untidy, but it was an untidiness that perfectly suited Farida and her life. They went together, hand in hand.

Farida didn't understand the reason for my visit. Usually I came with Tawfik. She stared at me and then looked from me to Leila and back again. "*Insha'Allah,* you're not angry at Tawfik," she said.

I stammered, groping for words. I didn't know how to tell her of my decision. "Tawfik hasn't done anything to me. Actually, I don't know. Maybe it's because he hasn't done anything that I'm unhappy. What am I saying? I'm just babbling. *Nana*, I don't want this marriage anymore. My life can't go on like this."

Farida stood up and started pacing the room like a prisoner in a cell. From the far wall, where her bed was, past the table strewn with books she used as a desk in the middle of the room, to the other end, where a wooden wardrobe occupied a large part of the space. Her face darkened. Without many words, she had understood the gravity of the situation. "Leave for where? To go back to your mother's?"

"If she'll take me, for a few months at least, long enough to get a grip on myself and register as an independent student for a diploma."

"You want to study for a diploma? Really? What a great idea!"

I couldn't tell if her tone was serious or sarcastic. She didn't ask about her son's future, about Leila, about the family I was going to destroy. After a few seconds, all she was interested in was the diploma.

"I also wanted to finish my studies, like my brother Habib. But my father didn't want me to. 'Education is for men. Women have husbands to take care of them,' he would repeat. That was what he always said if I talked to him about my studies."

I hadn't known this. Tawfik hadn't told me any of it. I knew that Farida loved books and that she was one of those rare women her age who knew how to read and write, but I hadn't known that she, too, had once dreamed of finishing her studies.

"In fact, I wanted to become a teacher like Thérèse, our neighbour. My Aunt Hnani, God bless her soul, told me many times that Muslim women didn't go to work. They had better things to do: take care of the home and raise their children!"

Leila woke up crying, which put an end to our conversation. Farida went over and picked her up, and Leila, surprised to see her grandmother, stopped bawling. "She's grown a lot since the last time I saw her. She looks like both of you, you and Tawfik."

I said nothing. I saw Leila in her arms, looking at her with a hint of a smile. Farida, who seemed quite unworried, was comforted by the innocent gaze of her granddaughter. I felt like taking my things and running away. Leaving Leila with her grandmother and going far away. Far from the suffocation, far from the judgments, far from the daily humdrum that was dragging me down, devouring part of my soul every day. Suddenly Leila started to cry again.

"She's hungry. Do you have a bottle?"

"Yes, and I have pablum and hot water in the thermos."

I went to get them from the bag downstairs, while Farida tried to get Leila to be patient. She sang her a little children's ditty, "*Taïta, Taïta, Taïta, Baba jab houïta.*"[2]

Leila's cries changed into nervous little giggles. I hurried to prepare her bottle. A few minutes later, Leila was again lying on Farida's bed, her head slightly raised on a little cushion, holding the bottle in her chubby fingers. I was going to miss the familiar soft sounds of her drinking from her bottle.

Farida looked at her again, then turned to me. "We didn't have powdered milk or baby bottles in my day. You had to find another woman to nurse the baby, a wetnurse or a cousin or sister who was also nursing and who could breastfeed your child too. Today, women are spoiled, you can do anything . . . and without tiring yourselves out." She came over and sat down on the chair facing me. "What do you want to do? Go away? Leave Tawfik? Go back to school? Work?" She stared intently at me. Her barrage of questions didn't give me a chance to think or find answers.

Farida understood my confusion. Farida understood everything. "So many times, I wanted to get away, to leave Tawfik with his father and go. But my father would never have forgiven me. 'You read too many *gaouri* books,' he always accused me. In the end, I listened to him, and my life became what you see in this room. Almost a recluse. Between these four walls and the stairs that lead to the kitchen and outside. It's my father's fault. He destroyed my life by trying to protect me. Protect me from what? From books, from men, from fate, from love, from freedom? I don't know. But one thing is certain, he never protected me from Kamel, my husband, who beat me."

Leila continued drinking her milk without worrying about our conversation. I couldn't believe my ears. Farida, whom I had never been able to understand, was revealing her past to me. She suddenly burst out laughing. Leila stopped for a moment, surprised, then started feeding impassively again.

"Life is very funny. Yes, so funny. Where I failed, my daughter-in-law could soon succeed. How ironic!" She guffawed as if someone had just

---

2   Taïta [name of a Jewish girl], Papa brought a fish. (Author's translation)

told her the funniest joke she'd ever heard. "I really feel like lighting a cigarette. It's a rare moment in my life. I absolutely need a cigarette. But, I can't. I won't do it, for Leila's sake. She's so young, I don't want to poison her lungs with that filth."

I just sat there. Looking foolish. Farida understood everything, when nobody else did. She guessed my feelings, understood my dilemma, knew that it was a question of life or death for me. I couldn't hold back the tears. They flowed down my cheeks.

"Leave Leila with me and go away. Go study, work, learn. I'll take care of her and Tawfik."

She went over to the window, which looked out on a tiny alley. The sun transformed her white hair into a silver crown. Her eyes were sparkling. She rubbed her hands together to forget her desire for a cigarette. I glanced at Leila. The empty baby bottle was lying beside her. She turned onto her belly, then slid cautiously to the floor. Gripping the edge of the bed, she took a few small steps. Her life would go on, and so would mine.

I quietly picked up my bag and went over to Leila and kissed her. She continued happily discovering the things in the room. Farida, still looking lost, followed me with her eyes without saying a word. She had told me everything. She was still thinking about her life. I took her hand. She held mine for a moment and then, looking outside, said, "Leave. I'm giving you your chance, the chance I never had, the chance that was taken from me."

Her words came to me like an echo as I rushed down the stairs, my eyes still filled with tears, my heart aching, my ears filled with Leila's babbling.

Chapter 5

Farida

I lost my head the day I let Jouda go away and start a new life. I let her go, leaving me with a one-year-old baby in my arms. How could I have done that? What would Tawfik say? How could he raise a baby girl without a mother? Couldn't I have reasoned with Jouda, begged her to stay? Offered to help her at home or talk to Tawfik and maybe find a compromise that would be acceptable to everyone? But I didn't do any of that. I let her slip away as I had wanted to do thirty years ago but did not manage to. I saw myself in Jouda. The sadness in her face, the fear in her eyes, and the same mother's divided heart. I was a young woman thirty years ago. I was the Jouda who was not permitted to follow her dreams. Who was confined in a place where she felt like a stranger. Yet my son Tawfik was not like my husband Kamel. At least I succeeded in making him an educated man. For me, there was also my domination by my father. Who never let me finish school. Who married me off to my cousin Kamel. Who wouldn't let me leave Kamel or start a new life with another man.

Was it possible that in my mind I was trying to take revenge on Kamel, and on my father and my aunts Hnani and Zohra? All of them had kept me in the grip of abuse and tradition. They all tried so hard to maintain the old habits that they didn't see the times changing.

What got into me? I let Jouda do what she wanted. I left the door open for her to leave freely, with no conditions and no promise to come back. And what about Leila? What will become of her? Who will raise her with her mother gone, her father working? I watched her exploring the room, tottering and stumbling and picking herself up, her little hands holding on to the leg of a chair or the edge of a wardrobe, unaware of the drama that would mark her childhood and the gravity of the action taken by her mother and approved by her grandmother.

I went around in circles in my room, keeping one eye on Leila, my mind tormented by what had taken place with Jouda. I was living between two worlds. The old one that had swallowed up my whole family and the new one that was dawning, with all its hope for a better life. Between the world in which I'd had to bow to tradition and the one in which I encouraged Jouda to choose her own path. Wasn't I, the mother, the grandmother, the one who should be upholding the traditions, safeguarding our heritage, keeping things in place? I didn't do that. Worse, I helped Jouda walk out and slam the door. I was her accomplice. In an act of ultimate revenge or an impulse approaching madness, I destroyed my son's marriage.

Chapter 6

Tawfik

That day, my mother called me at the office. She rarely called, because she didn't have a phone. We usually saw each other once a week. I visited her every Sunday, sometimes with Jouda and Leila, sometimes by myself. I left home early in the morning, when the building was still sleeping. The dark entry hall, where there were usually children making a racket, jumping around, rushing in from the street panting after running too hard, was quiet. I crossed the usual streets. I knew almost all the houses in the neighbourhood. The one with the lemon tree leaning over the fence, from which I would sometimes grab a few lemons. The owner, Monsieur Ben Mrad, was an old friend, he worked at the Banque Centrale. He never complained about those innocent thefts; in fact he encouraged them. Whenever we met and talked about politics and the weather, he'd end the conversation by insisting I come more often to gather lemons from his garden. A little farther on, the Lahmar family home, a beautiful large house in the colonial style, guarded by a big German shepherd that would bark like mad every time someone passed. On Sunday mornings, everything was quiet, even the dog.

I arrived at Place Pasteur. The benches were empty. The paths of polished white stone stretched ahead of me like elegant satin ribbons floating from the back of a dress. The trees, pruned to perfection, tenderly protected the paths from sudden rainfalls or long sunny summer days. I loved this place. To me it was like the gateway to Tunis, leading gradually into the noise and chaos of the city, with its crowded buses, lines of cars, and motorcycles weaving between them like little lizards trying to find a refuge in that crazy jungle. Sometimes on my Sunday walk I would sit down on one of the benches and take advantage of the unaccustomed silence to listen to the singing of the birds, who were happy to wake up and find themselves the only ones there.

I continued my walk on Avenue de la Liberté. The stores were closed on Sunday, with the exception of a few groceries that were almost always open. I turned onto Avenue des États-Unis d'Amérique. The buildings were like the one where I lived, only more imposing and better maintained. The shutters were still closed. Soon they would be open to welcome the sun drenching the city. Ahead of me, the gate to the Parc du Belvédère, the one leading to the zoo, was wide open. The cries of pelicans and exotic birds shattered the fragile calm.

At the end of Avenue Taieb Mhiri, I walked to Bab El Khadra, another gate, this one to the medina. Two arches supported by the walls of the Barrek Jmel Mosque. I went through the one on the east side and walked toward the market, which had been open since the wee hours of the morning. Farmers from around Tunis were displaying their fruits and vegetables, and fish vendors their red mullets, grey mullets, and little sardines, all covered with ice to keep them fresh. Above the displays, makeshift awnings, faded, patched tarpaulins suspended from wooden frames, protected the vendors and their merchandise from inclement weather. The streets were wet from the melting ice and the buckets of water poured on the sidewalks. They had to give an impression of cleanliness to the place, what with the crushed spinach, orange leaves, and squashed grapes mixed with the spittle of the vendors, who were hawking their products at the top of their lungs, stopping only to clear their throats and spit or take a sip of water.

I would never have imagined what my mother was going to tell me when she called me at the office that day.

"Tawfik, you're still at the office?"

"Yes, I have some work to finish."

There was something strange in her tone of voice. I wondered what it could be. Was she sick? Angry? Anxious? "Are you not well?"

"No, no, I'm fine. But could you come see me before you go home? I have something important to tell you."

"Where are you calling from?"

"From the grocery next door, Am Ali. The one where I buy bread."

"Oh, I see. You're sure you're all right?"

"Yes, yes. I'll be expecting you."

I don't know how I managed to concentrate and finish my work after my mother's call. What could she have to tell me? A sudden illness, need of money, an unexpected death in the family? All the possibilities ran through my mind, but none seemed plausible. But I couldn't leave the office, I had a report to finish for the director of my department.

When I got to my mother's house, how surprised I was to see my little Leila! Cheerful as always, she held out her arms to me and I immediately picked her up. My head was spinning. I wondered what was the meaning of her unexpected presence.

"Where's Jouda?" I asked, looking around as if she might come out of a corner any minute.

"Come sit here," my mother said, gesturing to the place beside her on the sofa.

I obeyed without any questions. The worried look in her eyes promised nothing good. I put Leila down on the floor and she immediately began to whimper, but stopped as soon as she discovered her toy near the foot of the sofa. She grabbed it and put it in her mouth.

My mother looked sad and fearful. She was holding an unlit cigarette, a reflex that gave her the impression that she was smoking and calmed her a little. I could feel her trembling beside me.

"Jouda is gone. She's not coming back."

In a fraction of a second, I saw my whole world crumble. My marriage, my daughter, my life. Everything disappeared, erased, buried by a few words from my mother's mouth. *Jouda is gone. She's not coming back.* At first I didn't understand whether my mother was joking or serious. I didn't know if she was in full possession of her faculties or if something bad had happened to her. I was in shock. "Gone? Gone where? Why? When?"

My mother looked at me with the eyes of a ghost, expressionless. As if she was very far away. Some other place in time, some other world that she knew and understood, where only she could live. I was about to lose patience. Leila was still playing with her toy. She would put it in her mouth and nibble on it, and then take it out with a disgusted expression.

"She's gone . . . because she couldn't take her life anymore: housekeeping, cooking, caring for Leila, doing laundry, scrubbing floors, washing diapers, hanging clothes . . . every day, the same thing, day after day, over and over. Do you think you could do the same thing over and over, day after day?"

"But she never complained. If she had talked about it, we could have gotten a cleaning woman, someone to help her."

My comment seemed to annoy my mother. She dropped her cigarette on the floor without even seeming to notice. "It's not only that, Tawfik, it's the fact that she never finished school. She wants to grow, to see the world. Do you understand?"

I didn't understand this crazy behaviour. Jouda had betrayed me. She had betrayed our child, our relationship. I didn't know if I could ever forgive her for this childish, impulsive act. "And Leila, how will she grow up without a mother? Who will take care of her?"

"What about me?" she answered quickly, as if she had already thought about it. "I'll come to you and take care of Leila. And afterwards, we'll see . . ."

I didn't say anything. What was she up to? Why was she trying to justify Jouda's crazy behaviour? Had she forgotten that I was her son? My mother was the one who had always supported me. I was the apple of her eye, as she never tired of telling everyone, the little boy for whom she had sacrificed her youth, her whole life, to see him finally become a man, educated and married. Now she was betraying me, letting me down as she had never done before. I had lost not only Jouda, but Farida as well.

"But she can't do that. She didn't even request a divorce. There's not even a reason for divorce. What judge would grant such a request? She'll come back, you'll see. It was a tantrum, a sudden impulse. She'll come back in a few days. A few weeks. If not for me, she'll do it for our daughter, for Leila."

Leila started on hearing her name, and turned to us. She gave me a dazzling smile that almost made me forget my misfortune. I opened my arms. "Come, sweetie, give your papa a kiss."

Unaware of what was happening, she made her way toward me, holding on to the edge of the sofa. The feeling of her arms around my neck, her smell of milk and lavender soap were like balm for a wound that would keep bleeding for the rest of my life.

Chapter 7

Jouda

I left my daughter with my mother-in-law and almost ran out of the house. I was afraid Farida would change her mind and come and catch me on the stairs or in front of the corner grocery store with Leila in her arms, to tell me it would be better if I came back, took my daughter, and returned home to my husband.

I left Bab Laassal, the area where Farida lived, and walked along the street leading to Bab El Khadra. I passed the *lycée* of the same name. A few taxis honked feebly to get my attention, but I pretended not to see them. I let them go by and quickened my pace. I was in a hurry to get to Habib Thameur Bus Station. There was a big garden there, the "lovers' garden," where couples would go to hide from disapproving eyes and hold hands and exchange a few furtive kisses in the shadows under the palm trees. My mother had told me that it had once been a Jewish cemetery, and that after Independence the land had been expropriated by the municipality of Tunis to be turned into a large garden in the middle of the city. A few bodies had been exhumed at the time and put in coffins to be reburied in the other cemetery, Borgel Cemetery. Today, there was nothing to remind passersby of that history. The place was a refuge for couples, unconcerned that beneath their feet or the benches they sat on with their fingers interlaced and their heads touching, there perhaps still remained a skull, a femur, or a shoulder blade, forgotten by some, left in peace by others.

Beside the park was the main bus station, from which I wanted to travel to the home of a friend of my mother's. No question of going to my mother's house. I knew she would do everything she could to make me return home. I knew she would never accept my decision. And, above all, I knew that Tawfik would come to her house to try to dissuade me, to beg me, to cajole me and take me back home with him.

At Naima's house, I was sure I would be protected and welcomed. Naima had never married. I didn't know why. My mother said she had waited too long and missed the boat. She also said that Naima was no great beauty and that she should have accepted the first man to ask for her hand without conditions or hesitation. But apparently Naima didn't pay attention to the opinions of those around her. She did everything a woman shouldn't do. She hesitated, set too many conditions, waited too long, and, especially, continued her studies to finally become a teacher. She was the one who helped me with my homework when I was in primary school. She lived with her mother, not far from our house. I could go there on foot. Since her mother's death, Naima had been living alone in an old building with the paint flaking off like dry skin. Her apartment was on the second floor. As soon as you entered the building, you were struck by the smell of the urine of the stray cats that took advantage of the fact that the door was always open.

I recalled, when I was young and timid, climbing the stairs to her apartment and knocking on her door. Naima would open the door and rescue me from that acrid, nauseating smell. Her apartment always smelled of incense. My mother said it was to keep away the *jinn* and their evil spells, but Naima said it was to remember her late mother, who burned it as an antidote to the stench in the foyer. I didn't know which one to believe, but it was that same smell that hit me full in the face when I got to her place after taking the number 6 bus from Habib Thameur Station.

Naima insisted that I call her by her first name without *tata* or *tante* or any of those frills, as she used to say. "I'm not that old!" she would repeat every time I slipped and added a *tata* by reflex. I would laugh and promise never to do it again and, of course, I always did.

That day, seeing me at the door looking downcast, my eyes red, she exclaimed, "Jouda, what happened? You look so upset!"

I couldn't say a word. She asked me in and I sat down in her sitting room in the spot where I used to sit as a child when I came for help with grammar, composition, or dictation. "What do you want to do when you grow up?" she would ask me while I sucked the end of my pen and hesitated between the imperfect and the past perfect.

"My mother wants me to marry a rich man because we don't have money anymore."

"That's what your mother would like, but you, Jouda, what do you want to be? A doctor, a lawyer, a teacher, a nurse, an engineer, a writer, a hairdresser? What is it you want?"

It took me years to be able to answer that question. It took me a breakup and a wound that would never heal. But at the time, I didn't know what to say. I hesitated, unsure how to answer Naima's question. "I don't know. Maybe a teacher in a school, like you."

Naima would look at me, a smile on her lips and a quizzical expression in her eyes—was it pity or curiosity, love or simply lack of understanding? But ultimately, the meaning of her gaze did not much matter; she always ended up helping me finish my homework, and I passed my exams. But then one day my mother decided that I should stop going to school, that I needed a good husband, because she couldn't make ends meet. My father's death had left her no choice; marriage was required. No time for sorrow. It was time for action. I had to be married.

I was thinking about all that while Naima continued looking at me with the same quizzical expression. "But really, Jouda, what's the matter?"

She brought me a glass of water, which she held out with a trembling hand. I accepted it, took a sip, and put the glass down on the little wrought iron table with its white and blue ceramic tiles.

"I've left my home, I've left Tawfik. Leila is with Farida. I want to finish my studies. I want to become a teacher like you, *Tata* Naima." How I was able to come out with that barrage of words without choking, without fear of having a heart attack or being struck down by divine lightning, I have no idea. But I managed to do it.

Naima was stunned by the news. "You acted without thinking . . . on the spur of the moment. You can't do that to your daughter."

But that's all I'd been doing, *thinking*. Thinking of Leila, of her future, of her well-being, of the life she would have without me. Why did even Naima not understand me? "That's just it, I'm doing it for my daughter. I have to leave that marriage that is suffocating me and that doesn't give any meaning to my life. I thought a lot before making that decision, and my heart is bleeding and will always bleed until I can see my dear

Leila again. But I have no choice. If I stay, I'll die. Please understand me, Naima, I—will—die."

I had never seen Naima like that. Usually, I was the student and she was the teacher. The person I listened to in respectful silence, whose words I ate up without speaking. But that day, that fateful day, that day when my life tumbled from stability to the unknown, from respectability to shame, from certainty to doubt, everything changed. Naima's face was transformed. Now it was Naima who was listening and I who was talking.

When she finally regained her composure, all she said was, "Are you sure of your decision? Are you sure you couldn't find a better solution?"

I nodded, and she said nothing more.

She was the one who supported me when everyone rejected me. She helped me get into teachers' college. She reassured me when at times I wanted to drop everything and go back to Tawfik so that I could see Leila again. Naima and Farida were the ones who gave me what I needed most: the possibility of choosing, choosing instead of submitting and putting up with things.

Chapter 8

Tawfik

She went away without a word, without a murmur, without even a last glance. She went away without leaving a trace, or almost. Actually, I knew where she was, or rather, I thought I knew, but I never went to look for her. I didn't want a woman who didn't want me. And I had so foolishly and naïvely thought Jouda was the woman I could create a family with, the woman who would be with me to the end of her days. I was an idiot. Yes, an idiot, to think that Jouda loved me and loved our daughter and that she was happy with me. I never saw it coming, it hit me right in the face, leaving me permanently traumatised. I hadn't been able to read in Jouda's eyes that she was not happy. I acted like a man from another time, perhaps like my father, who wanted a wife at home to take care of him, prepare little dishes for him, raise his children, and surround him with love. But what am I saying? No, I'm not like my father. I'm not illiterate like him. Farida made me an educated man, a reasonable man, who doesn't abuse his power and doesn't do harm to others. But now my wife, with whom I lived for two years, had left me because she wanted something else in life. I always thought she was happy, or at least, I never wondered whether she was. Things seemed normal to me. But apparently Jouda had other dreams, desires I hadn't imagined. A need for freedom and independence. Farida told me that the other day, the day she gave me the terrible news.

I didn't understand Farida's reaction. Many times when she was talking, I felt she was taking Jouda's side, that she somehow wanted her to go, to leave me, to abandon our daughter. I knew my mother well enough to be able to discern a certain subtle complicity with the woman who had ruined my life. Farida didn't tell me that outright. But her eyes, her hands, her face, her manner all suggested that she had given her approval for Jouda to leave. Oh, Farida! You too, my mother, the other love of my life, you too let me down. By encouraging my wife to abandon me. Opening the door for the mother of my daughter and saying to her, "Go, enjoy your youth, I'll take care of the rest."

Farida had nonchalantly said, "Don't worry, I'll take care of Leila." While it was a relief to know that Farida would come live with us and take care of my little girl, Leila needed a mother, not only a grand-mother. In addition, Farida was getting old. I found her more and more absent-minded, sometimes even confused. How would she manage every day with a little girl and demanding responsibilities? And the cigarettes, those damn cigarettes she was constantly smoking, what would she do when she was with Leila? Luckily there was the courtyard. My mother never smoked in her bedroom, only outside, sitting on the wooden bench by the lemon tree. Or sometimes, during the midsummer heat, on a mat-tress against the wall, absorbed in a book.

After my father left to live with his mistress, Farida had more freedom. There was only my grandfather, who was sick, living in the house with us. Farida took care of him. My mother's cousin Fatma and her children had moved out and gone to live in one of the new neighbourhoods of the city. Not everyone was happy with the country's independence. For our family, things got worse.

I had endured my father's beatings with increasing resentment as my body grew and developed, until I was as tall as he was. One day, I fought back, and it ended our relationship. I had intervened to protect my mother from his violence, and as usual, he tried to strike me. I ducked his blow, and then, instead of doing nothing, I responded by grabbing his hand to stop him from hitting me. I don't know what got into me that day. Probably the rage had been brewing in my guts, running through my veins, beating in my heart.

My father didn't leave immediately. After I stood up to him, he started to shout. "You're going to hit your father now? Your father who raised you? Who spared no expense to make a man of you? But you're not a man, you're a mule. Not a horse. Not even a donkey. A mule, sterile, incapable of giving life, only good for carrying things. That's what you are."

Farida tried to push my father away, but he shoved her with both arms. I couldn't stand to look at him, and I spat out words I'd never have thought myself capable of saying: "If you're a man, come here. Kill me or else I'll kill you!"

I thought he was going to kill me. I thought he would go into the kitchen and rummage in the clutter on my mother's counter for a knife, and that he would come and take my life and put an end to the mule that I was. But he remained silent, turned on his heel, and left the house.

We didn't speak after that, and only rarely saw each other. Until a few weeks before his death, when I learned that he was sick and his mistress had left him, I went to see him. A son's love is incomprehensible. Impatient, thankless, but above all, unpredictable. I felt the need to go see that man who had sired me, who had given me life, the man I had loved as a father but hated as an enemy.

The *oukala*[3] where he was living was in a pitiful state. There was filth everywhere, dripping down the walls, coating the ground. I felt like leaving and letting him end his days alone in this foul place. After all, he had preferred the company of a prostitute to that of my mother. His obsession with money and his ignorance of what was happening around him had led him to this dead end. There were clothes on a clothesline in the middle of the patio and a trickle of soapy water on the ground. He was in one of the rooms surrounding the patio. Each room had a striped curtain in place of a door. I lifted the curtain and entered. A nauseating smell filled my nostrils. He was lying on a makeshift bed in the dark. His crumpled grey linen *jebba* lay in a corner, and his impeccable shiny Italian shoes beside it contrasted with the bleak surroundings and the pervasive atmosphere of death.

"You've come, Tawfik. I knew it, my heart sensed it. A child never rejects his father. A young bird never flies far from the nest."

I didn't know how he had recognized me. By my hesitant footsteps, the sound of my regular breathing? I remained silent, revolted by the smell of the place but also appalled by my father's changed appearance. There was no longer any trace of his arrogance, his hard expression, his piercing gaze. I was facing a man with a limp body and an evasive gaze. Tears streamed down his face, which was almost unrecognizable, worn by sickness and solitude.

---

3   Old inn where poor people lived in rented rooms.

"You are my son, never forget that. I spent ten gold coins for the celebration of your circumcision. Unheard of in our lane. I was the envy of
all the important families of Tunis . . . " he paused for a moment, trying
to find the words, "you understand, all the important families of Tunis."

I wanted to cover my ears. I had heard those words dozens of times.
I had no recollection of that event whose extravagance and opulence he
had constantly boasted about. Times had changed and my father was still
stuck in the past. Nothing could arouse him from his mental torpor or
raise him from abject poverty or cure his encroaching disease, not even
death, which was stalking him.

I approached him with heavy steps. The stench was overwhelming.
"You can't stay in this place. Come to our house." I hadn't expected these
words to come out of my mouth. Where would I take him? To my mother's house? To a hospital?

My father's life ended two weeks after he left the *oukala*. He came to
live in the downstairs bedroom of the house Farida had inherited from
her father. She lived upstairs. When I told her my father was not well and
I was going to bring him to the house, she at first didn't believe me. Then
she said, "He'll always be your father. Do as you wish."

For two weeks, a nurse came to change my father's clothes and feed
him. He was already at death's door. He breathed his last in my presence. My mother, who lived on the floor above, never came to see him.
She acted as if he didn't exist, just as she always had, even when she was
married to him. Until the end, she managed to ignore this man who had
ruined her life but—the ultimate irony—had given her time to devote to
her two passions: reading and her son.

Chapter 9

Leila

When my mother reappeared in my life, everything changed. At least in the first few years after her return. With time, I got used to her and to that new life, buffeted between two worlds, the world of my father and grandmother, and that of my mother. Two opposing worlds. I would dive into one, then resurface to breathe the air in big gulps before diving into the other. My mother's return was like a birthday present I had wished for. I was proud that I was finally like all the other girls, that I had a father and a mother. I wanted to exhibit my mother, to show her off so that I could hear people say "Oh! Your mother is so beautiful. We didn't know her!" Pride filled my heart and spread through my body. I wanted to show everyone, the teachers at my school, the neighbours, and even people in the street, that woman who had not seen me grow up for the first nine years of my life. I loved hearing them say the words that would wipe away the comments people used to make under their breath, the whispers behind my back, and the buzz of rumours about me as a daughter who had been abandoned. With my mother now back in my life, I put the past behind me. The woman who had given birth to me existed, and she had finally come back. I didn't know if my mother was aware of what I was feeling, but she seemed accepting and even pleased by all the happiness suddenly radiating from my whole being.

At first, my father didn't want my mother to come back into my life. "Why now?" he asked when I told him that she had come to see me at school.

I didn't know what to answer. I would have liked to defend her. To tell him that she had missed me. That she'd had no choice! That she was too busy all those years, studying and looking for work, trying to stand on her own two feet! In short, all the reasons I repeated hundreds of times in my head, in the dark before falling asleep at night. But no words came out of my mouth. I was dumbstruck whenever my father mentioned my mother.

My father continued reading his newspaper. In the distance, Farida's radio was playing softly. I could hear the voice of the news reader. It must have been toward the end of the afternoon. Suddenly, my father put his newspaper down on the small table. The specks of dust sparkled in the day's last rays of sunshine. I followed them with my eyes.

"Now that you're almost a young lady, after my mother and I have done all the work, she's remembered you!"

I no longer heard the voice on the radio. Farida must have turned it off. I thought about my mother's hair. I would have like to stroke it, to make it into a little braid, holding one strand, then another, then another. And her slender white hands whose fingernails with their rounded shape reminded me of my own. If she had been with us, she would have put her hands on my shoulders or on my cheeks, and I would have felt loved. I could have smelled her and that would have soothed me. I stood as straight as a frail little pine tree in the north wind.

"She has no right to come and bother you. I won't allow it. I'll go see a lawyer. I'm going to put a stop to this charade." My father stood up.

He was about to go to the kitchen to get a glass of water, as he always did when he was agitated. To quench his anger, to forget. But he found himself face to face with Farida. She was in her slippers, an ill-fitting dressing gown over her shoulders. Her hair white and limp. Her face the meeting of past and present.

"Jouda came to see you at school?"

I suddenly regained my strength, my wits and my voice: "Yes, she came to see me after school and walked with me to the door of our building." I held my breath.

"What good news! At least, Leila will be able to see her mother again. She really needs it."

Like a scared little rabbit, I went to my grandmother. I wanted press my body against hers. To feel her warmth, to hear her speak, to touch her clothing. Everything about her reassured me. She neutralized my father's rigidity, which was growing with time like a second skin.

Farida's words dissuaded him from saying more. He didn't do anything to prevent the "charade."

That was how my mother slipped into my life again just as she had run away from it years before. With astonishing ease. One day she had left, and one day she had returned.

My mother didn't live far from my school. She had rented a little studio apartment in an urban labyrinth, between two former garages, one of them converted into a dry cleaner's shop and the other into a video store, both attached to a three-storey house, the top floor of which was still under construction, half covered with a layer of grey cement and the other half bare, with the red brick exposed. It was the kind of modest neighbourhood Farida would call working-class. These areas, which were called *hay naguez*, had been constructed illegally, without authorization, but with gentrification, some had become almost respectable. Farida made a face while pronouncing those words. It was all she had left to express her status as a fallen bourgeoise with her back to the wall in a society that had changed and in which she had become a living social vestige.

We were not rich. But Farida still gave me the impression that we were, or at least that we had once been. Her way of talking, her choice of words, her mocking little smile, her erect posture in spite of the years. Farida was not a haughty woman, but everything about her indicated that she had once known affluence.

My mother's house, or rather the tiny room she rented, belonged to a man who according to the gossip was too friendly with people in government. Si Khmaies was his name, and he was from that new social class that some people, with a certain disdain, called *nouzouh*. My mother had told me during one of my increasingly frequent visits that Si Khmaies had been a penniless young man from some backward village who had come to Tunis looking for work. He found a job as a clerk in a grocery store on the street where her house was now. His dynamism, his intelligence, and especially his *zhar*, luck—my mother emphasized this—had permitted him to become the manager of the grocery store and to marry the grocer's daughter Latifa. Si Khmaies and *Lella* Latifa were the owners of the house where my mother lived.

"They're all right. They rented me their studio apartment, although they knew I'm a divorcee. They've never asked me for anything except the rent." After saying those words, which became a sort of slogan as if she were beginning a solemn ceremony, my mother continued, "But, you know, everyone talked about his double life as the official tattletale for the city councillor of the neighbourhood. Nothing escaped Si Khmaies. The comings and goings of the neighbours. The new car one had bought, the new floor being built by another. Where the money came from and where it went. And especially, their political opinions. A neighbour told me one day that if someone told a joke against President Bourguiba, Si Khmaies would report it to the councillor, who would report it the mayor, who would report it to the Minister of the Interior. But as God is my witness, he has never done me any harm!"

At the time, I was obsessed with my mother. Her face, the stories she told me, her tidy room, which contrasted with Farida's perpetual chaos. It all fascinated me. I wouldn't ask any questions. I would lie down on her bed, which was impeccably made, and breathe in the smell of the clean sheets. I always left it messy when I got up. She would stand a few metres from me in front of the portable stove, her neck bent, stirring a chocolate pudding she was making for me. The sound of bubbles popping on its velvety surface would make me almost tremble with joy. A little bookshelf holding a few books and old knick-knacks, a plastic table covered with a tablecloth, where students' notebooks would be piled up one week and disappear the next. That was all my mother owned.

My father didn't mention my escapades with my mother. And I didn't say a word. I learned to hide my joys from him as well as my sorrows.

It was my grandmother I confided in. At first, I sensed that she was a little jealous of that second mother who had suddenly come to lure me out of her circle of kindness.

"Did she become a teacher?" she asked, the first time I talked about her.

"Yes, a French teacher, at Victor Hugo private school."

Farida looked at me in amazement.

"Are you sure, Leila? It's a very good school. Only people with connections can get positions there."

"Or the ones who are very good."

She looked at me as if she was wondering how I could have come up with such a retort.

"I don't doubt that Jouda is an intelligent woman. I was just asking."

She fell silent. I wanted to know more about her reaction.

"But my mother isn't rich, you know. She takes the bus. They're building a subway not far from her house, she told me."

Farida's face remained expressionless. My mother's poverty didn't worry her much, nor the bus she took, nor the subway that would be built. She was only interested in the school. Suddenly she said, "You know, Leila, I always wanted to become a teacher. I could have become one. I had the ability, but my father didn't want me to. He let my brother, Habib, continue his studies and he married me off."

She sat down. She had almost forgotten the peas she was shelling in a bowl on the kitchen counter. I already regretted my glib words. I didn't want to see her sad. Our conversation had taken an unpleasant turn.

"What are we going to eat tonight?"

"Lamb stew with peas . . . I'll probably add a few potatoes."

I said nothing. I didn't like lamb, and why would she mix peas with potatoes? I almost complained, but I stopped myself.

"Bring your French notebook, I'll give you dictation. You have to get ready for your exams. I think you're spending too much time with your mother these days and you're not doing enough homework."

I wanted to talk back, to defend myself, but I obeyed. I could never say no to Farida. In fact, who could?

Chapter 10

Jouda

I lived with Naima for years. At the beginning, my mother came to see me. She threatened me: "Return to your husband or you won't be my daughter anymore."

I remained silent. I was not going to return to Tawfik.

Then she tried to convince Naima. She begged her, "Naima, talk to her. Tell her she can't destroy her life and the lives of her daughter and her husband. Make her see reason."

Naima, speaking through clenched teeth, answered firmly, "She's not a little girl anymore. Jouda is a woman who wants to make choices. Let her choose. She's the one who'll have to live with the consequences."

My mother was not pleased with Naima's answer. She stood up and made a last appeal: "Naima, now you're talking like people on TV. But the consequences . . . you know, it's my daughter and little Leila who will take the consequences . . . the things people are going to say. This is not a story that's happening to somebody else. This is our reality, our flesh and blood," she said, striking her chest with her fist to emphasize the words *flesh* and *blood*.

Naima didn't bat an eye. She lowered her head.

I went to my room to avoid my mother's accusing gaze, which could have made me change my mind. I really didn't know what to do anymore.

Then it was Tawfik's turn to plead with me to return home: "Jouda, you have to come back. If you won't do it for me, do it for Leila, our daughter."

I almost agreed. I almost returned to the status quo, to simple things. To Leila's intoxicating smell.

Naima left us alone. Tawfik was still the same. The impeccable shirt, the brown pants, the well-trimmed moustache. And the eyes that were colder than ever. But he really wanted me to return home.

"But if I do, I won't be able to finish my education and become a teacher and work," I said.

"Where do you get these ideas? Why do you need to work? I earn a good living. You lack for nothing. And frankly, how would you be able to study while taking care of a one-year-old daughter?"

My hands were clammy. I knew he would never understand my desire to get out of the house, to break out of that prison that was swallowing me up a little more every day. "But, I need to do things besides cleaning, cooking, and changing diapers."

"We'll find a cleaning woman. You should have told me. I would have gotten you one already. Everything can be resolved. Things can go back to normal."

What "normal" was he talking about? The normal order of the house: pots neatly lined up on the kitchen shelves, beds carefully made, his clothes ironed and hung up in the wardrobe without a crease or wrinkle, or the normal image of me in his head, seen through his prism, as a sweet, loving wife and perfect mother? The normal family he never experienced as a child and that he wanted to have, even if it meant confusion and madness for me?

"I don't need a cleaning woman. I need to breathe and live my life. I need light . . . "

He looked at me in bewilderment. He couldn't believe the words I'd dared to speak. His ears rejected them, he couldn't take them in. "What light and what life are you talking about? Don't tell me you really believe those stories about women's liberation. All that is just theory. It's only good in books. In reality, those ideas lead to the destruction and loss of the family. If that's the case, you shouldn't have married me and had a child. You should have stayed with your mother and continued your education. You can't have everything in life."

"You know very well it was my mother who wanted me to get married. I wanted to continue my studies. I love Leila. But with her birth, I realized that my life has taken another direction and if I don't pursue my

dream of a career now, I never will. I realized that this was not the life I
had dreamed of. I don't want to lie to myself or to you. I want something
else, something other than the life you're offering me."

Tawfik took those last words very badly. His pride was wounded. His
eyes were no longer merely cold, now they were filled with bitterness.
His lower lip was trembling. He stood up abruptly, put his hands in his
pockets, and said, "Too bad for you."

I opened my mouth, but nothing came out. I couldn't say anything.
It was obvious neither of us was going to back down. We would go our
separate ways.

Naima came and found me disheartened by that confrontation. "So,
what have you decided?"

"Nothing. Absolutely nothing. I'm staying here, that's all I know for
now."

Naima had no children. She acted like a teacher with people, a little
detached but always very willing to help. But that wasn't the way she was
with me that day. Her eyes were full of tenderness and her arms were open,
ready to receive me. I didn't hesitate a second, I threw myself into that sanc-
tuary and clung to that last bit of hope. The faces of Farida, my mother,
and Tawfik flashed past my eyes like fleeting shadows. Only the image of
Leila remained clearly imprinted. I clung desperately to that image.

My life was not easy afterward. Had it not been for Naima's help, I never
would have been able to become a teacher, to realize my dream despite the
loneliness and constant guilt of having abandoned my daughter. *Abandoned*
her: I, too, began to use that word. I claimed it for myself. It became
my destiny. Isn't *abandoning* her child the worst thing a mother can do?
No comparison with a mere divorce or even a mother's natural death. To
allow that part of herself to live, to smile, to cry, to grow with somebody
else. Without being able to visit her, to hold her hand, to wipe her cheek,
without being able to hold her to my breast or sleep beside her. My mother
said that was what I had wanted, and that I had made my choice between
being a mother and a teacher. Tawfik, my ex-husband, said in front of the
judge who granted our divorce that he would never forgive my disgrace-
ful, purely selfish act, and that in his eyes, I was an ungrateful wife and
an unworthy mother. He never understood me and he never will. It was
Naima who convinced me that I had to choose my place in life.

The judge granted me the right to visit on weekends and during vacations. I did not exercise that right, because I was afraid. I was too afraid. Afraid of wavering if I saw my daughter again without being able to take her to live with me. Afraid that my yearning to be with her again would be too much for me and would make me hesitate. Afraid that my determination would falter at the sight of her and I would go back to live with Tawfik and never be able to continue my education. Everyone demanded that I choose or else was convinced that I had already made my choice.

In reality, I never had any choice in my life; I quite simply put up with things. Put up with my mother's poverty, which pushed me into marriage. Put up with the indifference of my husband, who always thought he was doing the right thing but who never asked himself whether or not I was happy. And even when I chose to leave Tawfik, I put up with the loss of my daughter. I put up with the accusing looks of my friends, of my family, and of society for abandoning my daughter. I wasn't given the least chance to explain myself. But in the midst of all the turmoil, something in me resisted and refused to bow down. I locked my heart, the heart of a mother, I shut it up deep inside so as not to hear it beating, so it wouldn't explode from too much sorrow. I left my daughter because I had no choice. I left my daughter the better to be able to come back to her.

Chapter 11

Leila

Ever since I opened my eyes on the world, Farida has been living with us. Sometimes she would go spend a few days with her cousin Fatma or, very rarely, her brother, Habib. Of the two, she preferred Fatma. When she visited Fatma, she always came back happy and exhilarated. She would bring me back little presents, a skirt or a dress Fatma had made or honey cakes, but mainly, lots of stories. After a short visit to her brother, she would come back silent, glum, a scowl on her face.

When Farida was away from the house, I would feel abandoned once again. Her absence weighed heavily on me and on our whole household, which felt like an inn without an innkeeper. Sometimes I would imagine I heard her voice or even saw her crossing the hall from her room to the kitchen, walking slowly in slippers, as if she were pushing a pebble with her toe. I had to stop myself from talking to her.

Since Farida had quit smoking, a dozen years ago now, it was the radio that kept her company. Often I would go into her room and find her sitting on her bed, legs crossed, holding the radio to her ear. She wanted to listen to everything, the songs, poetry, news, and, especially, the radio plays and stories that were run and rerun every evening, which she listened to as if she were hearing them for the first time.

In the morning, once she'd finished breakfast, she would turn on the radio and go into the bathroom to wash her clothes. She didn't like the washing machine much. She also wanted to kill time which, with age, weighed on her more and more. She would fill the blue plastic tub and put in her underpants from the day before, a shirt or a sweater. She would let them float on the water a few moments, swollen with air like balloons, and then lean over and plunge her hands into the water and start rubbing them with a piece of green soap. Sometimes, in the middle of her chore, she would stand up, go to her room and rest on the bed a while, long enough to listen to a morning song on the radio, and then she would return to the bathroom and continue with the washing. Then she'd go out the French doors of her room to the veranda and hang her dripping clothes on the line in the sun, which was nearing its zenith.

Sometimes she'd stay outside for a while. I would often see her from the French doors in the dining room, which led to the same veranda. She would slowly go down the two steps, softly placing one foot in front of the other, and walk around the garden. I would see her touch the leaves on the trees as if she were greeting them or telling them a story. In the summer, she would stand there for a moment gathering jasmine flowers. She would wrap the little flowers, mauve when they were still closed and white when they opened, in her handkerchief, and in the evening, their scent would fill our house, reaching as far as my bedroom.

My father divided his time between the sitting room and the garden. When he got tired of one, he would go to the other. There was nothing special about our garden. A band of rocky soil around our suburban house. For years it had been neglected. Then one day my father began planting shrubs, and then trees, and finally a barrier of cypress trees against the winter wind from the northwest. Summer was the time of jasmine, delighting us with its sweet fragrance in the stifling heat that settled on our house for months. The garden was a bit wild, like an untamed animal. Since my mother had come back into my life, my father spent almost all his time in the garden. It became his refuge. I would see him from the window of my room, turning over the earth, breaking up big clumps of clay with the back of his shovel, digging a hole to plant a shrub that was waiting to be rooted, watering the dry earth and leaving pools of muddy water that would be quickly absorbed by the thirsty ground. When he got tired, he would come back into the sitting room. I would hear the door creak, then his heavy footsteps, then a thump like the sound of a bundle being thrown on the floor. It was him collapsing into his chair. He would read his newspaper for hours on end. As if the words and photos were multiplying and the articles getting longer as his eyes perused the pages. The ink would leave stains on his fingers.

Sometimes Farida would call to him from the kitchen to tell him we were out of milk or that he absolutely had to buy two baguettes for dinner. With a resigned look, he would put on his coat with its frayed collar and go out to get the milk or bread.

We hadn't always lived in that house. For years, we lived in the Belvédère apartment as we called it, after the name of the neighbourhood. It's there that I was born, it's there that my mother left us, and it's there that I lived until my father one day said he could no longer live in that neighbourhood filled with *haftarich* and that we would have to buy a house in the new suburb.

"What are *haftarich*?" I asked Farida, careful to pronounce the word, which I found so sophisticated that it made me feel a year older.

"They're people who are penniless, the poorest of the poor . . . people who have no money and no education."

I was a little disappointed with that explanation. I'd been expecting her to say it was a new kind of insect I didn't know the name of that was starting to infest the neighbourhood. I didn't think my father was talking about people like us.

Farida didn't want to sell her house in the Bab Laassal neighbourhood. It had been empty since she came to live with us. No one ever went there except my father from time to time, to check that the door was still solidly shut and no one had broken it down to move in or to take the furniture that was held prisoner by time and dust.

"Why don't you want to sell your house?" I asked her while watching TV, as I did every day after school until she started nagging me to do my homework.

Farida was not in a good mood. Her radio had been refusing to work for days and she didn't much like TV. She thought the images would destroy my imagination. "Because my father gave it to me. It's the only thing I have left to remember my former life."

I still didn't understand how memories could make you happy. Mine always made me sad. "But haven't you always told me your father didn't want you to get an education, and that made you unhappy?"

She looked at me and I pretended to be watching TV.

"You're right, Leila, you're perfectly right, but sometimes it's the people we love the most who hurt us the most. In spite of everything, I still love my father and I don't want to sell the house he gave me."

"But you could still love it in your heart. What do you need the walls and roof for?"

She didn't answer. She left me to watch TV and went to her room.

A few weeks later, we were at the table eating a chicken couscous Farida had made, the only dish she did well. She poured herself a glass of buttermilk and I could see the butterfat floating in it. Farida loved it, especially with couscous, but it turned my stomach. "I'm going to sell the Bab Laassal house," she stated simply.

She was in a happy mood. My father had brought her radio back from the repair shop and she had returned to her daily routine of songs, news broadcasts, and the voices of the announcers.

My father could hardly believe it. "But you loved it so much—and all your memories? You said you wouldn't give away your life for money."

"My memories are in my heart. I don't need old stones to protect them . . ."

She gave me a little wink that I didn't understand.

That evening, sitting on my bed in the dark, I heard my father solemnly announce to Farida that with the money from the sale of the Belvédère apartment and the old Bab Laassal house, we would finally be able to buy a house in a new suburb and leave this neighbourhood full of *haftarich* and their brats.

Chapter 12

Farida

Twenty years. It has taken Habib twenty years to finish his translation of the Quran. He sent me a copy. I was proud of him. I kept it on my night table for weeks. I haven't read it all. It will take me months and months, but I'll do it. What fantastic work, what courage, for my brother to finally achieve his wildest dream!

When he told his students and colleagues of the idea, nobody took him seriously. Translating a work from Arabic into French was no small task, especially when it was a sacred text. Everything was complicated.

"Can one really translate the word of God?" Hedi, one of his best friends, had asked. He thought Habib was making a mistake.

Habib was saddened by such comments. He told me so once when I was visiting him. But he never gave up. He worked tirelessly until the idea became a reality. Habib was not particularly pious or observant, but he told me he hoped the translation of the Quran would "allow people to learn about each other, and end hatred based on religion." His project, which had begun as a personal challenge, became something he wanted to pass on as a kind of universal legacy. A poet's legacy.

He had started working on it after returning from Sousse. He had bought a small apartment and had just gotten married again, for the third time. Another of Fatma's finds. Perhaps she should have become his wife when she was still young and innocent, and Habib still fearful and hesitant? But what did I know, it could have been a disaster, like my marriage. At least he was finally happy with his third wife. And his children from the previous marriages would come visit him. I didn't much like this latest wife. She always made me feel unwelcome. And to think that I had come to see my brother, the only one in the family who had been able to go to Collège Sadiki.

Habib was not lucky in love or in politics. All his friends and acquaintances were given important positions in the government after Independence. Starting with Bahi, who was appointed prime minister by President Bourguiba. Even Hedi, from whom my brother was inseparable, who had started his career as a mere secretary of an embassy, held various diplomatic positions in international organizations. Honours and privileges Habib didn't really want, but from which, I was convinced, he had nevertheless been excluded. He had never said anything to me about it. But I read the news and listened to the radio. I didn't miss a thing. In one of his letters from Sousse, he had told me a student of his was going to be appointed minister of education. I sensed some bitterness, or at least the disappointment of a patriot who had never been recognized for his literary work. While he had a literary program on the radio, gave lectures, and was even appreciated by French writers, it seemed that the government had its eye on him and was keeping him as far as possible from political power. Was it because he hadn't been active in Destour or because he wasn't very assertive and gave the impression that he didn't have enough drive for politics? I didn't really know. Still, his exclusion from the political arena, whether deliberate or not, while his friends and students were sought after, had allowed Habib to throw himself heart and soul into translating the Quran.

"We needed a translation that would capture the poetry of the Arabic language and, especially, of the Quran, but without changing the spirit of the original message," he once explained, his eyes shining, while his wife watched us intently out of the corner of her eye.

"And what do you say to those who criticize your idea? Can the word of God be imitated?" I asked, using the same word Hedi had, as Habib had told me in a letter.

"I don't tamper with the sacred text, I try to bring out its poetic quality. Here's an example, Farida. Take the word *Janna*. That word has been translated by some as 'paradise.' Which is not wrong. But I think I'll use 'garden,' it's more faithful to the original and more descriptive, more evocative for the reader, don't you find?"

His wife had gone out onto the balcony and we were alone. I don't know why, but the past suddenly came back to me. What a pity I couldn't become a teacher. Maybe I would have written a book, a novel or a children's story . . . But it seems fate had other plans for me.

"Tell me frankly what you think, Farida, isn't 'garden' more evocative? It evokes greenery, abundance, fruits, water, tranquility. You look a bit lost. Do you disagree?"

"No, on the contrary, that's a remarkable idea! I'm really glad for you, Habib. After all those years of doubt and searching."

He smiled. He wanted to continue, but his wife was calling to him from the balcony.

Chapter 13

Leila

After a few attempts to put a stop to my weekly visits with my mother, my father understood that he couldn't keep me from seeing her and that, on the contrary, the visits were doing me good and drawing me out of the shyness that had clung to me since the first years of my life.

My mother was different from my grandmother. She didn't constantly give me dictations and she sometimes read books to me. Once in a while, she helped me with my homework. Most of the time, we did other things. She would make my favourite dishes or we would go shopping. At that time, a new shopping centre had just opened in a wealthy suburb of Tunis. Everyone at my school was talking about it. Shopping centres were a novelty. I was dying to go there. My mother promised to take me there on the bus. I had never taken the bus before. I went to school on foot or my father drove me in his car, and of course, there were taxis with Farida from time to time. Taking the bus was like diving into the sea for the first time. I remember the people who got on, they seemed different from the ones I met in the street on the way to school. They looked unhappy, they were sour-tempered, they had waxy complexions and muttered incomprehensible words that sounded like swearing. The bus was dirty, with cigarette butts on the floor and chewing gum stuck to the backs of the seats. And it smelled bad.

But as soon as I was on the bus with my mother sitting beside me, I'd forget this strange new world and launch into a rambling conversations with her. She would talk about her work, which she loved, about her students, the ones she liked the most and the ones who gave her a hard time, but especially about cooking and fashion. Things that barely existed in Farida's world. To Farida, cooking was a necessary evil, a chore she did reluctantly. To my mother, cooking was an art, a constant quest for aromas and flavours. Whenever I went to see her, I would find a new dish waiting for me. A culinary discovery that transported me, delighted me with its delicate flavours and bright colours. While my mother used a variety of spices to create a range of flavours, from lemony to sweet and sour, to peppery or even floral, Farida would say that too much spice gave you ulcers.

And when there were no new dishes to tempt me, there were the amazing clothes I would look at in the magazine *Burda*, which my mother bought every month. My mother didn't sew, but together we would look at the dresses, divided skirts, coats, and pants. The feminine world my mother transported me to was magical, joyful, fascinating, and full of colours and shapes. The new shopping centre was my favourite place for outings with my mother. We would look at the windows of the fashionable ladies' wear shops. The mannequins reminded me of the poses of the models in *Burda*. My mother never bought anything. She would feel the fabrics between her thumb and index finger and hold the dresses up to her body, looking in the mirror and asking for my opinion.

At the end of each adventure, we would go to Pizza Fiori and order two pizzas, one for her and one for me. The owner was a Tunisian who had lived in Italy and had just opened the pizzeria.

"I heard from some of my colleagues that he made his fortune as a drug dealer in Sicily," she told me one day.

I must have been fourteen and it had not been long since I'd first heard of drugs. I felt like an adult hearing my mother speak that serious word. "Is it true?"

She shrugged, looking cynical. "Yes, maybe, but his pizza is the best."

I said nothing. My mouth was full, I was savouring the crust, a bit moist in the middle and crisp on the edges, the mozzarella cheese melting blissfully in my mouth.

She stared at me for a moment as if she wanted to share a terrible secret with me. "It's water buffalo mozzarella. The real thing, the kind sold in balls swimming in whey."

In my mind, I compared that new flavour with the pieces of dried-up cheese sitting in the back of our fridge that would end up in the garbage when they got too hard to be eaten or even grated. "What's a water buffalo?"

She looked at me for a moment, surprised by my question, and then laughed. "You know, I love you, Leila, because you're so innocent. I see myself in you when I was your age. Above all, don't do what I did. Don't get married too early." She hesitated for a moment and added, "If you do, it will be a disaster."

It was one of the rare times when my mother mentioned her marriage to my father. Suddenly the pizza lost its flavour. Everything lost its flavour. It all became monotonous. I no longer wanted to know what a water buffalo was. It didn't really matter, and anyway, Farida could tell me.

Chapter 14

Tawfik

I hardly noticed the years passing anymore. I no longer blamed my mother, or Jouda, or anyone. I let time heal the wounds. The only thing that gave me any real consolation was the firm belief that the *mektoub* between Jouda and me was over, that regardless of what I once thought, we were not destined for each another. Some couples realize this after a few months, others after years, and most, never.

Our divorce was relatively easy. A bit like a putsch in which I suddenly found I'd been removed. Jouda didn't want me anymore. She had quietly revolted. Here in Tunis, when we speak of things like this, we say they were "woven in the jasmine." Exactly as had occurred when Zine El Abidine Ben Ali took over as president of the Republic from Bourguiba, who had once been hailed with pomp and ceremony as the *combattant suprême*. Quietly, with no spilling of blood, no rifles or machine guns. One day, Bourguiba was the country's strong man, and the next, he was declared senile, incapable of managing the country's affairs, and confined to his room, replaced by his prime minister, a career police officer. "Change within continuity" was how the newspapers described his taking power, which was no less brutal and barbaric than killing the man with a bullet to the head.

I, too, was killed. Not by a bullet, but by Jouda's words, a knife that kept being turned in the wound, deeper and deeper. Yes, Jouda's words cut into my flesh and reduced me nearly to nothing. They left me completely exposed. The last time I saw her, she said, "I want something else,

something other than the life you're offering me." As if I made her eat the
bread of adversity and drink the water of affliction. I thought I was doing
something good in sparing Jouda the life my mother and I had endured.
That wasn't what she wanted, she was looking for something else. She
dreamed of freedom and independence, she said. She had become like the
girls in France, the ones I studied with at Sciences Po in Bordeaux. But at
least the girls there knew what they wanted to do in life. They didn't marry,
they had boyfriends. They didn't have children, they took the pill.

෧෨

May 1968 in Bordeaux. I nearly packed my bags and scurried back to
Tunis. I had a few courses to finish when the strikes paralyzed everything. At first, I enjoyed this new adventure. I enthusiastically attended
the general assemblies of the students. I listened to the trade unionists'
impassioned speeches about the oppression of the proletariat and I
dreamed of the same thing for Tunis. Sometimes, when I felt the tension mounting between the cops and the students and it looked like
there would be a skirmish, I'd slip away and rush back to the apartment
I shared with two other Tunisian students. We'd go to ground like rab-
bits, each in his own room, in fear of being caught and beaten up by the
police. Being Arabs, we had to keep an especially low profile.

Farida sent me letters, and I sent her postcards with pretty pictures.
Of the Palais Rohan, the Bordeaux City Hall, and its majestic fountain.
The stone bridge across the Garonne, with its seventeen arches and
masonry vaults. And, of course, Bordeaux Cathedral, with its spires like
two swords pointing up into the sky. Farida wrote that it reminded her
of Saint Louis Cathedral in Carthage. I didn't agree, but I decided not to
say anything. I wrote about banalities and forgot about the essentials: the
people who were injured, the blood running down their faces, the blows
of truncheons that fell indiscriminately on backs and skulls. Yet I knew
that Farida was aware of what was happening in France at this time.
I knew she read the papers and listened to the radio. But I had a little
boy's reflex of wanting to protect her. I didn't tell her how afraid I was
of classes being cancelled and my degree left pending and, who knows,
maybe never granted? When I had the opportunity to take my final
exams in June, I jumped at it. I studied day and night. I thought of Farida,

of my grandfather in his sickbed, and of the money doled out to me. Nobody knew how the chaos engulfing France would end, and I wanted to get away from it. Thank God, I passed all my exams. Some students refused to take theirs, preferring to wait until September, and a lot failed outright. The minute I saw my name on the list of students who had passed, I decided to go home. I missed Farida, and Tunis too. Bordeaux was a beautiful city, with its clean streets and its well-maintained buildings. The Place du Marché on Sundays, the bouquets of freshly cut tulips, the burning hot coffee sipped while sitting lazily on the terrace watching the passersby. The things that had made me happy in my first months and years in this city no longer meant anything to me. All I wanted now was to go home to work for my country and take part in its development.

I dreamed of a new Tunisia. Partly modelled on France. The France that we sometimes idolized, but also sometimes hated. From my grandfather, who despised the very sight of the French gendarmes and the sounds of their boots and their rifles, to my father, who accused the French bank of cheating him, stealing his property when he couldn't repay his debt, and even to Farida, who, while she adored the French language and its writers and poets, could never get rid of the bitter taste the French presence left in her mouth. "If only the French had not gone up and down our streets humiliating our men and ogling our women, my father might have let me finish school, he might not have been so intransigent, and things would have been different."

Unfortunately, the departure of the French was not as simple as everyone had thought it would be. The country had been infantilized by the years of occupation. Nothing worked without the French. New roads and hospitals and schools needed to be built, but the Tunisians, proud of their new-found freedom, quickly realized they lacked the skills to manage this country that now belonged to them. Worse, they now had to call on the French for help in building that new Tunisia.

In my youthful idealism, I, too, wanted to contribute. My head was full of ideas. I thought I was capable of anything. Eradicating poverty and ignorance and establishing order like that which I had experienced in Bordeaux. Unfortunately, nothing like that was possible. Tunisia was still talking baby talk, while I wanted it to speak eloquent words of wisdom.

My return to Tunis was marked with a family celebration. My Aunt Fatma prepared all the delicious dishes and pastries for that wonderful feast. My Uncle Habib, whom I hadn't seen since I left for France, was seated beside me. "What do you plan to do now that you have your degree?" he asked me quietly, his mouth full of lamb tajine, his hand reaching over to the basket for a slice of Aunt Fatma's semolina bread.

"Work for the government of Tunisia." I answered, raising my voice on the last word. When he failed to react, I felt my childish ambition go up a notch. "Work for the Ministry of Finance . . . regulating imports by businesses, supporting our local industries, seeing that public money is well spent . . . "

Habib took another mouthful of the tajine. His salt-and-pepper hair hadn't lost its sheen, although he was now retired from teaching at the *lycée*. Farida had told me he had begun a translation of the Quran. "The inimitable Quran," she had said, exactly as he had written in one of his letters to her.

I sensed that my excitement bothered him a bit, as he himself was usually so stolid.

"And you want to do all that, by yourself, in how much time?"

The table had been cleared and we had moved into my grandfather's sitting room. Despite his illness, my grandfather was making an effort to be present for his guests. He weak eyes went back and forth between me and Uncle Habib. From the window, I could see Farida in the patio serving mint tea to the women.

Uncle Habib was holding his glass of tea. He had the long, slender fingers of a pianist. He was looking at me as if I were an extra-terrestrial.

I wanted to reassure him. "I won't be alone. Friends and colleagues will be working with me. We'll lift Tunisia up to new heights of progress. We'll all do it together. You'll see."

A little sip of tea, then another, longer one. Then a moment of silence that lasted an eternity. "My dear Tawfik, I've chosen a solitary path, the path of poetry. Some people see it as the most difficult one, but I see it as the easiest. I don't know. Politics and administrative work are worthy, even noble. But to be successful, you mustn't be inflexible, like an oak tree . . . " He smiled, cleared his throat, and continued, "And you mustn't be like an olive tree . . . too many ideals, too many roots. You have to be able to say yes when your heart wants to say no, and to say no when your head insists on saying yes. I'm sure you know what I mean, don't you? Forget the olive tree of our ancestors, forget the oak tree of the French,

forget all that. Follow the example of the poor and oppressed, the colonized people of this world. Become a reed."

One of the guests, an old acquaintance of his, came over and sat down
beside him. Uncle Habib turned to him and apparently forgot about me.
I was offended. I had always found him a little strange, but now, I remember thinking, he was getting old too quickly.

How disillusioned I was, years later, when I had become a civil servant
in the rapidly developing Tunisian public administration and I understood
what Uncle Habib was getting at. Nepotism and corruption were rampant.
I understood that I didn't have a clan or a clique to protect me against strong
winds. I reluctantly accepted that I was a slender reed. Yet I had wanted to
be the olive tree Uncle Habib had spoken of. Upright, solid, proud. Uncle
Habib, the poet, the solitary man, had early in life quietly found his place in
the forest of men. It took me some time to find mine.

Chapter 15

Leila

When I was sixteen, I began to feel smothered by the visits with my mother. I was no longer the shy little girl desperately seeking her mother. Nor was I the little girl who showed off her mother to the other girls in her school. And I was no longer that girl who was impressed by everything her mother told her or did for her. I had become suspicious, mistrustful, and, above all, rebellious.

It all began with my father. Again and again, I would challenge his coldness that, while he didn't say much, expressed his bitterness and resentment. Often I would say, almost screaming, that I wanted him to talk to me, to ask my opinion, and often, he would just give me a weary, inscrutable look. I wanted to hear his version of my mother's departure. "Why didn't you try to stop her?" "Why didn't you help her finish her studies?" "Why did you let her go so easily?"

And each time, it was the same. He would answer like an automaton, devoid of emotion, leaving me wanting, seething with rage. "I tried, but she wouldn't hear of it." "She insisted on working when we had enough money to live comfortably." "And why was it so easy for her to leave you?" That last question felt like a knife at my throat. Disconsolate, I finally stopped my desperate questioning.

Around the same time, the visits with my mother were becoming a source of conflict for me, with more and more painful questions. "Why did you abandon me so easily?" "Why couldn't you find a compromise with my father?" "Were your studies and your work more important than me?"

My mother would answer all my questions, my many questions that were always the same. No words quenched my thirst, no answer satisfied my hunger.

"There was no compromise possible with your father. To him it was either the family or nothing. He never understood my desire to become an educated, independent woman. He never understood that the tasks that I had to do day in, day out were poisoning my life. He never sensed or understood my suffering. He thought he would make me happy by bringing home money."

"And what about me?" I kept reminding her. "Didn't you think about *my* suffering during all those years?"

I went from victim to tormentor. From a sweet little girl to an embittered one. I spared no one. I tormented everyone.

In response to my mean words, my mother would just curl up, her knees to her chin, her head down. Only the shudders of her slender body told me that she was still alive. Seeing her that way, I would regret my harsh words, but a week later, I would do it again. There was no end to my questioning.

Those were dark years. I found peace only with Farida. My mother's return had left her half rejected, half abandoned. But she didn't let anything show. There was always her radio or the newspaper my father brought daily from the office, which she would read from the front page to the classified ads, including the obituaries and horoscopes. The only section she skipped was the sports. Everything else she devoured. She no longer gave me dictations, but we would talk about books and poetry.

"My brother Habib was a poet, you know, Leila, a great poet. He knew the big names in Tunisian literature."

"I know . . . you've told me many times."

"Yes, but a poet should never be forgotten. A brother, perhaps . . ."

Her words piqued my curiosity. "Why? Do you ever forget your brother?"

"A little, but I believe he's the one who forgot me."

"How?"

"His career took him far. Far from my father's clutches, far from the ignorance of Kamel, your grandfather, far from the decline of our family. But I stayed."

"You would have wanted him to help you?"

"Oh, yes, so much! But he was a sensitive, gentle man, he couldn't defy the power of my father, so he chose to leave. But for him, it was easier, he was a man, and that helped him. I was a daughter, and I stayed . . . "

"So in the end, he abandoned you, as my mother did me."

She looked at me for a moment with eyes that spoke volumes.

"Are you going back to your old ways?"

"Which ones?"

"Resenting your mother?"

"I don't know. I can't help it. I can't forget it, it keeps going around in my head, like the merry-go-round from my childhood."

"Listen to me, Leila. Your mother didn't abandon you. She went away to finish her education, and now she's back. She's here in your life now. You see her every week. Why are you still complaining?"

She looked for one of her books, opened it, and started to read:

Be wise, O my Woe, seek thy grievance to drown,
Thou didst call for the night, and behold it is here,
An atmosphere sombre, envelopes the town,
To some bringing peace and to others a care.

Whilst the manifold souls of the vile multitude,
'Neath the lash of enjoyment, that merciless sway,
Go plucking remorse from the menial brood,
From them far, O my grief, hold my hand, come this way.

Behold how they beckon, those years, long expired,
From Heaven, in faded apparel attired,
How Regret, smiling, foams on the waters like yeast;

Its arches of slumber the dying sun spreads,
And like a long winding-sheet dragged to the East,
Oh, hearken Beloved, how the Night softly treads!

She stopped short, looked at me for a long time and said, "Do you like that? Isn't it magnificent? It's from *Les Fleurs du mal*, by Charles Baudelaire. Habib was one of the first to translate him into Arabic. I'll never forget it."

No, it was not merely magnificent, it was quite simply magical. I didn't understand all of it, but the words solemnly intoned by Farida had an invisible power. It was as if she alone was able to replace my sorrows with little joys. Occasional simple joys that did me so much good. With her own words or those of others, Farida could take me out of the vicious circle in which I had gotten stuck in my adolescent years.

Chapter 16

Farida

My granddaughter Leila had just received her diploma. The most beautiful gift of my life, next to her father getting his. When she came to my room, waving her arms, her face glowing with joy, I immediately understood that she had crossed the finish line.

For me, however, her success would mean the beginning of the end. A little like when her father had gotten his degree and had decided to study in France. He had become a young man, capable of managing without me. Now she had become a young woman, ready to take her rightful place in society. While a baccalaureate is not the end of an education, it's still a stage completed, a diploma, something of an honour, which allows a person to make their own way in the world. This success was also a kind of loss for me. Leila no longer needed the stories I told or read to her when she came to my room, no longer needed my presence to reassure her when she came home from school and her father was still at work, no longer needed the food I prepared for her as best I could, which she sometimes devoured greedily and sometimes politely refused. She no longer needed any of that. I was not bemoaning my fate, though.

Taking care of my son had been a deliverance from the prison in which Kamel wanted to confine me: the kitchen and the bed. Raising Tawfik was the best way for me to escape the unhappiness of my situation. Until the day he no longer needed me. And even after he left for France, I would write to him and send him a little money, the crumbs my father, who was sick, gave me from time to time, which I saved for him. I did everything I could to remain useful and to help him.

When Jouda came to me with Leila in her stroller to tell me she was leaving, I decided to let her go and offered to help her by raising Leila. Tawfik never understood that. He thought I was taking Jouda's side against him. That wasn't so. I wanted Jouda to have her chance. And all in all, it didn't turn out to be a disaster. She was able to become what she wanted, and after a few years, to see her daughter again. They continued to build their relationship, swimming together in the sometimes calm, sometimes troubled waters of the sea we call life. And even better, Jouda will soon remarry and bury forever the few years of her marriage to my son. Leila suffered from her mother's leaving, but on balance, she too was able to overcome the obstacles. And now my dear Leila has her bac, which makes me so proud and happy.

There's still Tawfik. He lost everything: his wife and his life. He never wanted to remarry or accept the fact that his marriage had failed. Maybe that was his destiny. I couldn't do anything about it. Actually, I even benefited from it. Leila brought me out of the loneliness of my life after Tawfik's marriage. She became my reason for living, the ray of sunshine that has brightened my life since I came to live in this house.

All those years, I lived with the ghost of my father, his sickness, and his history. A powerful man who dominated other people, and who ended his life with the one he had oppressed the most, the one he believed he was protecting but whose life he destroyed. Destiny gave us the gift of one of its sweetest ironies. The person who should have fled from him was the very one who stayed with him until the end. Yes, that's true. I stayed when I could have left. I could have fled, distanced myself from him, after he had failed to protect me from Kamel, had not allowed me to choose the man I wanted, had kept me for himself, himself alone, until his last breath. In spite of everything, I stayed by his side. I had no choice. My brother Habib left and never returned. Even when he visited, he always seemed rushed . . . a class to give, a literary broadcast on the radio, or a dinner with his wife. He always had a good excuse for forgetting; I did not.

Only Fatma remained faithful—to our childhood, to our friendship, to the secret that bound us even more closely. And only God knows what she must have endured from that Chedli, who ended his days confined to his bed, unable to walk or move. Well, he got what he deserved, paralysis of half his body. Nobody wanted anything to do with him. Neither heaven nor earth. Not even his wife, Fatma's aunt; she only took care of him reluctantly. She waited patiently for his death, which was long in coming. And Fatma finally had a taste of happiness in marrying Si Sadok. But it seems she paid too high a price for it, having to go back to living with her parents after he died. She had become the burden no one wanted. Her father would have had her marry again, but she refused. Luckily, she was able to sew. She earned her living sewing dresses, skirts, and even trousseaux for brides. When my uncle, her father, died, she inherited some money, which allowed her to buy an apartment on Rue de Paris. How many times I went to visit her there! Her three sons were not good in school and I would help them with their lessons.

Fatma continued to receive clients in her little apartment. In time, and especially after Independence, she became one of the best-known dressmakers in Tunis. Society women, wives of ministers and heads of companies, came to Fatma, with her measuring tape around her neck and her greying hair. Ever since she made that first dress that had cost her so dearly, there was no style that daunted her. You just had to show her a photo or drawing from a fashion magazine, that's all it took.

"*Ya lella* Fatma, I'd like a suit like the one Jackie Kennedy wore," one of her clients said to her one day. Fatma described the scene, mimicking her client, the wife of an important executive of a company. "Who is this Jackie?" she had asked with a skeptical look. "The wife of the president of America," the client was quick to answer, showing her a photo torn from *Paris Match*. When she saw the suit and the elegant pose of the American first lady, Fatma answered with perfect candour, "There's no problem, my dear, I can make one the same or even nicer, but I must warn you, you don't have the same body as that Jackie." The client didn't seem offended by my cousin's impolite comment. She was only too delighted to have the famous suit.

Another Tunisia was coming into being. We were giving up our place to a class of newly rich people who had the means to buy themselves homes in the new suburbs and who sent their children to the best private schools, while the old bourgeoisie of Tunis continued to decline, eroded by its endless disagreements, unable to accept that the world had truly changed.

Fatma and I had just barely survived. I because of my education, which had always been my lifeline, and Fatma because of her capable hands and her outspokenness. We were vestiges of a bygone era.

Chapter 17

Leila

My Great-uncle Habib had just died. He'd been bedridden for months. He didn't really move anymore, except for his head and eyes. His wife would turn him from one side to the other with the help of a nurse. His flesh was bruising under the weight of his bones, it was opening up, it needed to breathe. I still remembered how sturdy his body was during my few visits to his house when I was a child. With age, it had become sickly, like the stunted trunk of a dying tree.

Farida went to the funeral reluctantly, as if she were being carried off to hell. Something was holding her back, and I didn't know exactly what. Perhaps fear of thinking about her own death, or of remembering that she once had a brother called Habib.

We took a taxi together, a *bibi*[4] as she always called them. She had put her *safsari* over her head and let the rest of the fabric float. She never hid her hair except when she went out of the house, which happened rarely. She was silent for most of the trip to her brother's apartment.

"Are you sad?" I asked.

She didn't answer. She had a faraway look, lost and confused. She seemed to have aged a lot in the last few years. At one point, she spoke as if to herself, without turning toward me, without any emotion. An automaton's voice, a survivor's voice.

"Habib was an intelligent man. He translated the Quran. He was on

---

4   Originally, Taxi Bébé; some Tunisians used the word *bibi* for the little red and white taxis that appeared on the streets of Tunis during the fifties and sixties.

the radio, had his own poetry program. He loved Arabic and French. We've lost a great man, may God rest his soul."

The driver, who was giving us furtive curious glances in his rear-view mirror, did not dare strike up a conversation. After Farida's little speech, he must have thought he was transporting two madwomen, an old granny talking to herself and a young girl who spoke only in snatches.

I knew my great-uncle had done a French translation of the Quran. I even had a copy. My father had given me the blue box with the two volumes and I kept it in my little bookcase with the books we bought each year at the Tunis Book Fair. I've even read some passages. It felt strange to read the holy book in French. The words followed one after the other without touching my heart. As if the Arabic gave them a solemnity that disappeared with the Roman letters.

"Here we are. Two dinars, five hundred millimes."

The driver's voice pulled me from my brief reverie. Farida was still sitting, her limp body leaning back against the cracked plastic seat of the *bibi*. I took the money from my purse and handed him the fare. He counted and recounted the money, still looking suspicious, and turned his head to my grandmother as if to tell her to get out of his taxi. She didn't even look at him, still absorbed in her own world of old age and death.

I opened the door and held out my hand to my grandmother who opened her eyes wide and said, "Are we here? I didn't even realize it. We're going to say goodbye to Habib one last time."

She leaned on my arm. I felt her entire weight. Farida, my paternal grandmother, who had brought my father into the world and had been living with us since I opened my eyes, was losing her balance.

Great-uncle Habib's apartment was full to bursting. It was a small apartment, with a bedroom that was barely big enough for a bed and a narrow sitting room. The door was wide open, and there was a row of chairs extending into the hallway. I knew most of the people present. Noureddin, Great-uncle Habib's oldest son, his daughter Sonia from his second marriage. The grandsons, granddaughters, cousins, and of course, Aunt Fatma, Farida's favourite cousin. As soon as she saw Farida, she stood up and made room for her. A slender woman with piercing eyes and a constant smile, although today she looked as sombre as a cloudy sky. The hair framing her face was straight and thick despite her age. She gave Farida a big hug.

"May God protect you, dear Farida, may God keep you for us!" As if she was suggesting that Farida's turn would be next.

Farida sat down without really looking at anyone. Her *safsari* had slipped off and was lying in a little white pile at her feet. She barely glanced at it. I picked it up, rolled it up haphazardly and stuffed it into one of the cupboards in the vestibule. From the bedroom, I could hear men chanting the Quran, one verse after the other, without a pause. A humming word machine that comforted people in their loss without their really understanding it. I thought about all those years Great-uncle Habib had spent studying the Quran. Reading, pausing, reflecting, translating one verse, then another, capturing the nuances, opening a dictionary, closing it, choosing one word, then another, then crossing it out and starting again. Today his body lay in the middle of the room covered with a white shroud, and around him those other men, strangers, their bodies swaying to the rhythm of the words coming from their mouths without love or poetry.

Farida stood up suddenly and turned to Fatma. "Where is he, I'd like to see him," she whispered.

"In his room. The *quora*[5] is reading over his soul."

Farida looked a little surprised, as if she had forgotten the death rituals. As if those rituals no longer meant anything to her and they only happened to others but never to her own relatives, least of all her own brother.

Great-uncle Habib's wife came over to Farida. The two old women hugged each other like two little girls. Death separated some people and brought others together. Those two women who had never been particularly friendly were now embracing, their eyes dry, their gazes distant, their pain infinite.

I was waiting for my father, who had promised to join us as soon as he left the office. Farida was behaving in an odd way. I had never seen her like that. At first, when she had gotten Fatma's call announcing her brother's death, I had the impression that she wasn't deeply affected. Then she took a lot of time getting ready, without really doing much. She put on a scarf, then took it off again, and then ran a comb through her snow-white hair a couple of times. She filled her bag with old dresses, then took them out one by one. Finally, when I told her the taxi was coming and we would

5   Men invited to the home of the deceased to chant verses from the Quran.

have to leave in a few minutes, she hurriedly put some dresses, a pair of socks and a nightgown back in. She walked very slowly, more slowly than usual, stopping at times, her hand on the wall in the hallway to maintain her balance. Before leaving her room, she took a last look at her radio. The radio was her life. She held that magic box to her ear from morning to night as if she wanted to miss nothing coming from it.

The smell of death hung in the air in Great-uncle Habib's bedroom. Farida and I were standing motionless by his stiff body and Fatma slipped between us. Her tears were flowing and she was sniffling. The opposite of Farida, who remained stoic. Her brother, her flesh and blood, was lying before her on a wooden plank on the floor, a lifeless body with only his face visible and his body hidden under a white linen cloth. His face was pale, his eyes closed, his lips dry and his skin blue.

Farida bent over the shrouded body, took him in her arms, and remained there for a moment in silence. Life embracing death. The sister embracing the brother. An image that would remain etched in my memory. I didn't know whether Farida loved her brother. But that image was strange. The eyes of my grandmother were closed as if to breathe in the smell of her brother one last time, with him already gone, lifeless, his eyes closed forever. There they were, suddenly close to one another. Cheek to cheek, nose touching nose, forehead against forehead. Suddenly she pulled away from him, whispered a few inaudible words and then, "I'm going to miss him."

Chapter 18

Jouda

I thought I would never find love. At the beginning when I married Tawfik, I told myself this was it. What a mistake! I was young and knew nothing about life. It was anything but love. I tried to lie to myself, to pretend I was happy. I wanted most of all to please my mother, and in spite of my reservations, I convinced myself that the marriage would make me happy. It was Tawfik who was happiest in that relationship. He had a wife who was young and beautiful, a little bit educated, but not enough to become troublesome. He was on top of the world. He wanted children. He wanted to give me everything. I continued to lie to myself when I learned that I was pregnant. This child will make me happy! Our relationship will become stronger! On the contrary, with Leila's birth, I felt that life in the home was giving me nothing, that I was not ready to spend my whole life cleaning, cooking, and raising children! I wanted to give a meaning to my life that I was only able to glimpse when I thought about the career I wished to have.

Tawfik never tried to understand. He shut himself up in his orderly world. So I made my decision. I lost my daughter and even the illusion of love.

But years later when I met Firas, things were different. I could stand on my own two feet, I didn't need a man to pay my mother's debts or buy me dresses and perfume. I needed a man to share my life. And that was Firas. I met him by chance while waiting at the post office to pay my electricity bill. We started to talk about the intolerable wait and the way the employees took their time serving us and treated us with contempt. He seemed calm, which I found reassuring. He talked about his mother, who lived with him and who was sick, and about his work at the Ministry of Justice, which he didn't much like but which brought him a paycheck at the end of the month. In short, a typical Tunisian, not too ambitious, but nice and good-natured. I didn't pay my bill that day, because when my turn came, the woman at the wicket decided it was time to close shop. Too bad for those of us waiting; they would have to come back the next day. I was ready to make a fuss. But Firas dissuaded me, saying it wasn't worth it and that, in any case, I would certainly be returning to pay another bill. His advice made me smile, it did me good to see someone make light of life's little difficulties with a sense of humour, which was something I'd lost since I'd been living alone. I took life too seriously, with my books, my notebooks, my work, and I didn't realize how that sapped my energy and my whole being.

In the meantime, life in Tunisia went on as usual, slowly and chaotically. Firas reminded me of that and I was almost surprised. As if I was realizing for the first time that life could be different. In the course of our conversation, I mentioned the name of the school where I worked, and I was surprised a few days later to see him waiting for me there at the end of the day. When I saw him, looking a little detached, wearing a suit, like most civil servants, clutching a newspaper under his arm, I felt a little pang of fear. A man was interested in me! The idea of starting to live life again where I'd left off when I broke up with Tawfik seemed incredible. I already had cramps in my stomach. But as soon as I began talking to him, my fears dissipated.

"I wanted to know if you finally paid that bill," he said, seeing my surprise.

I laughed nervously. "Not yet. I'm waiting for the water bill to come, and I'm going to pay them both at the same time."

He laughed with me. "Our lives are ruled by those visits to the post office, the city administration, the government ministries . . . the whole bureaucratic machine that leads us by the nose and holds us prisoner when we thought we were free."

I agreed with his remarks, but basically, I wondered why this stranger had ignored the risk in coming to meet me in front of my school when there was nothing between us. I was already thinking of the colleagues who would see me with him, and of my mother, who had started talking to me again and who always insisted that I should remarry. I even thought of Si Khmaies, my landlord. If he got wind of this meeting, he would ask me to leave the apartment. I could never forget that I was a divorcee. And if I did, people would remind me of it, with a word, a remark, or simply a look that put me in my place.

Firas guessed my thoughts. "I hope I'm not causing you any problems. My intentions are honest. I wanted to see you again and suggest we go for a coffee."

A man and a woman who didn't know each other going for coffee? It just wasn't done! At least not when I was married to Tawfik. Nowadays it was a little more common, but I was still on my guard. I agreed anyway. He told me about his life, his mother, and his work, and I told him about my divorce and my daughter, Leila. He wasn't shocked. He continued to talk to me normally. He even seemed curious about whether I saw my daughter.

During the whole period we were seeing each other, he never came to my place. We had an implicit understanding that there were limits that must never be crossed. My colleagues suspected something, and I was frank in saying that I was going out with Firas with a view to marrying him. I used those words to reassure myself and give myself a grace period, avoiding embarrassing questions and knowing looks.

No one wanted to give me time to test the raging waters I had barely escaped a decade ago. Regardless of my apprehensions, I was being pushed to leap back into them. I took the time I needed to become acclimatized, until the day Firas officially asked my mother for my hand. Everyone was happy for me, pleased that I was finally going to get married again. Everyone except my own daughter, Leila.

Chapter 19

Farida

My brother Habib is gone. He has died. I didn't want to believe it. Poets never die, and yet Habib was no longer with us. I said goodbye to him and the men came to take his body away in the hearse to bury him in Jellaz Cemetery. Not far from Ommi, Baba, and Kamel.

When Kamel finally left the house and my hope of getting a divorce was almost a reality, my father intruded into every corner of my life like a weed that colonizes every inch of a garden. He gave me money, but only when he felt like it,. And when I told him about Kaddour, he saw red. "You want to humiliate me in front of all the families of Tunisia? That's all I needed. You marrying a *goor*? As if there were no other men in Tunis."

I had met Kaddour when I was going to the courthouse almost daily to obtain my divorce papers. I was determined, because I felt Kamel would never let go of me and would keep me married against my will. My greatest fear was of becoming *ma'allaka*, like many women: neither married nor divorced, in a purgatory between two hells. Kaddour worked as a clerk in the court, he was in charge of the hearing room and kept an eye on people's comings and goings. Seeing me regularly, he came to recognize me. One day he gave me a smile and I returned it. There was something about him that appealed to me. Perhaps his kind face. I was wearing my *safsari*, but my face was uncovered. And once when I was leaving, he whispered a goodbye.

I was shocked. A man other than Kamel was interested in me. But he seemed nice. And after I'd waited in vain all morning to get the paper I wanted so badly, he ventured to speak to me. "*Ya lella*, I'm really sorry, but I'm sure the judge will be here tomorrow."

"*Y'ashik*, what's your name?" I was not afraid to talk to him. The kindness of his smile emboldened me.

"Kaddour, Kaddour Ben Mbarka." After that, he went with me as far as my house and I didn't stop him. I understood that he wanted to talk to me privately. I even let him into the vestibule.

The country had just been through a dark period. Jean de Hautecloque, who had put down the nationalist resistance in Syria and Lebanon, had been appointed French Resident General in Tunisia to apply the same methods against the nationalist aspirations of the Tunisians. There were riots, assassinations, and expulsions. People hardly left their homes. They were terrified.

My father's illness had begun to keep him in bed for entire days, and Tawfik was at school. Kaddour and I would talk in the dark like thieves, sitting on a *doukana*. I told him about my life and he told me about his. He was poor and lived in a small rented room. He smoked, and once he offered me a cigarette. That's the only thing I have from him. One day when he was leaving, he stole a kiss. I felt myself come back to life. I put my hand on his cheek. He held it there a moment and said, "I want to marry you, Farida. I know I'm not rich, but I've always gotten by. If you'll have me, I'll come and ask for your hand in marriage. Choose a day and I'll come talk to your father." My father's voice calling to me from his bedroom cut our conversation short.

For several months, I flirted with a dangerous dream. I naïvely thought I could marry Kaddour and finally live a love story like those of the heroines in the books that helped me survive. But my father did not want to meet Kaddour, much less accept him as son-in-law. He did everything in his power to keep me for himself. This time, his threat involved money and Tawfik's future.

Kaddour often came and knocked on our door. I did not answer. One time, my heart betrayed me and I opened the door to him. He slipped in and sat down on the *doukana*, the secret site of our tremulous love. "Why don't you open the door to me—you don't love me anymore?"

I blushed. I was becoming like my father. I no longer believed that such a man could be capable of love. He put his hand on my shoulder.

He bent his head toward my cheek and kissed it tenderly. His lips on my cheek. His skin against mine. A moment I wished would last forever. "I'm very busy. My father is sick. Tawfik is writing his exams. Things are not going well in my life."

"*Insha'Allah*, now that you have your divorce papers, I'll come and talk to your father. When we're married, you won't have to worry about all that anymore. I'll always be there for you." He hesitated for a moment before continuing, "And you'll be there for me too, won't you?"

I avoided his questioning eyes and forced myself to smile. There was no longer a place for words in this vestibule, the refuge of a love that had become impossible.

And that was that. I didn't open the door for him again. I would wait as his knocking on the solid wood became fainter and fainter. Carried away by the wind. Carried away by too much pain. Kaddour gradually realized that I would never be his wife.

I continued to smoke for years.

Chapter 20

Leila

My years at the University of Tunis were an initiation into life, real life. Before that, I lived surrounded by people who loved and protected me. In university, it was a different story. There were police cars and sometimes even military vehicles patrolling the campus. The regime claimed that it wanted to keep the country safe, but I was gripped with fear whenever I went through the big gate to the campus, where police officers checked our national identity cards. I would wait, my stomach in knots, while the policeman glanced quickly at me and then at the photo on my card before he finally let me continue on to the amphitheatres. Now and then, a girl wearing a scarf would not be allowed to enter the campus. "You have to look like the photo on your ID card," the policeman would tell her. Frightened, she would turn back without a word. Sometimes I would see girls wearing beach hats and long hippie skirts. I heard one of them say in response to a puzzled policeman that it was just her look, and the officer let her pass. I knew that, in fact, it was a subterfuge some girls used to get onto the campus without having to expose their hair. But except for those sporadic incidents, when I'd feel the tension quietly rising, there was nothing exciting happening on campus. General assemblies were forbidden except when they were organized by students from the Rassemblement Constitutionnel Démocratique, the new party of Zine El Abidine Ben Ali, the former soldier who was now president. Not many people attended these meetings; they were simply get-togethers of friends. Most of the clubs were really of no interest to me. Often they were run by boys who mostly wanted to drink and flirt with girls. For lack of activities on campus, I turned to the movie theatres. When it wasn't exam time, I would often go to the movies. There was an odd social situation on campus, a social divide that was palpable, even visible. The rich students socialized with the rich, and the poor with the poor. I could distinguish between them by their clothes and their attitudes. The former were flamboyant and dashing, the latter drab and unfashionable. I didn't feel I belonged in either camp.

"Are we rich or poor?" I asked Farida one day.

She was plucking out a few white hairs from her chin, holding her magnifying mirror in one hand and tweezers in the other. My question didn't seem to surprise her much. She continued trying to find the unruly hairs that were eluding her. Her vision was declining. "Why do you ask?"

I didn't want to reveal the real reason. The contradictory attitudes people around me had to money intrigued me. Some students flaunted their wealth and others hid their poverty. At home, my father always said that money corrupted, while for my mother it was the source of independence.

"Just like that, out of curiosity." I suddenly blushed. I wanted her to keep her eyes on her mirror.

"There was a time when my father was rich. Now we're like everyone else, we scrape by. You see, Leila, I was born in Bab Souika. I lived there my entire youth, at a time when middle-class and poor people lived side by side in the neighbourhood. Sidi Mahrez, the patron saint of Tunis, watched over everyone. Bourguiba decided otherwise. He tore down the old buildings and my father's office fell to the bulldozers. Bourguiba claimed he wanted a city without misery and without poverty. He ended up gutting the neighbourhood to build a horrible tunnel. Today, it's the neighbourhood of the wretched. The rich have gone elsewhere." Once again, she was beating around the bush. Her way of not answering.

"But what I mean is, are we, you and my father, are we rich or poor?"

She put down her mirror and laughed. She had lost interest in her hairs. "I don't need much. A radio, books, and a little food. I don't even need cigarettes anymore. But that's no longer the case for many people today. The rich have built themselves villas with swimming pools in the best areas. Many of them have never bought a book in their lives. And the poor have stayed in their slums. The government did them a favour, perhaps the only one: now they have water and electricity and their children go to school. They even go to university just as you do." Her hand went back to her chin in search of hairs.

She had given me a roundabout answer. Finally, I understood that the words *rich* and *poor* no longer had the same meaning today as in Farida's day. Then, the rich studied and the poor worked the land. Education was the key to social success. But not anymore. Business had replaced learning as the reason some people were wealthy and others poor.

Those questions arose from a passing curiosity. But it was my classes that really kept me awake. Reading and studying for exams took up all my time. I worked like a maniac. Maybe it was my way of avoiding thinking about my mother, who had remarried, leaving me once again with an immense feeling of abandonment, and my father, who was taking refuge in the garden, preferring the company of trees to mine. I had thought I'd find my place in the university and make some friends. But I was mistaken. The university showed me a fragmented society that lived in constant fear. Starting with the teachers who didn't dare discuss anything other than the course content, the administration that treated us like rowdy high school students who needed to be spied on and controlled at all costs, and the police officers who kept track of our comings and goings.

Sometimes I dreamed of getting out of that country and going to live somewhere else. To see what things were like in other places. But I was attached to my little life, with its ups and downs, and especially to Farida. I wouldn't leave her for anything in the world.

SANDY HILL

1995-1996

And a youth said, "Speak to us of Friendship."
And he answered, saying:
Your friend is your needs answered.
He is your field which you sow with love and reap with thanksgiving.
And he is your board and your fireside.
For you come to him with your hunger,
and you seek him for peace.
When your friend speaks his mind you fear
not the "nay" in your own mind, nor do you withhold the "ay."
And when he is silent your heart ceases not to listen to his heart;
For without words, in friendship, all thoughts, all desires, all expectations
are born and shared, with joy that is unacclaimed.

—KHALIL GIBRAN (1881-1931)

Chapter 1

Leila

It had been raining for hours. The sky was grey and my morale was at rock bottom. I was praying that the rain would stop, but the heavens were turning a deaf ear. The first time it had rained after my arrival in Ottawa, I'd found it odd. Not that I'd never seen rain before, but because it reminded me of Tunis in autumn. I dashed down the stairs, almost spraining my ankle, and went outside. I wasn't wearing boots or a raincoat, or even the winter hat Farida had sent me. She'd bought it in a second-hand clothing store with gloves that almost matched it, and mailed them to me. I'd recognized her handwriting immediately, it was that of a diligent student sitting with her back straight and her face sober, carefully forming the round Os and long stems of the Hs. I'd rushed out with my hair a mess, wearing the flannel pyjamas I'd bought on special at the Saint-Laurent Shopping Centre a few days after my arrival. The contact of the rain on my skin was like a first kiss. Cold but pleasant. Soft and surprising. I opened my mouth wide to the sky, trying to catch the drops on my tongue, to see if they tasted like the ones in Tunis. Sweet and sour at the same time. Fortunately there was no one in the street, only the glow of the streetlights that seemed to float in the darkness, making the rain sparkle like diamonds. Maybe some neighbours saw me from their windows, raised their eyebrow, smiled a bit, or mumbled a few words, wondering if the girl standing alone in the dark in pyjamas and bare feet was in full possession of her faculties. No matter, I felt better. The excitement had beaten out my sensible side. How could I see the rain falling for the first time in a new country and not be affected? Seeing the rain in a country where everything seemed so different gave me hope that my life would become normal again, as it had been in Tunis. I would have liked Farida to be with me. Or my mother, or even my father, even if he said nothing. But I had no one. Only silence was holding my hand, and only the northerly breeze caressed my cheeks.

It was my choice to accept the scholarship from the Francophonie and come to Ottawa. But did I really have a choice? I had to leave. Farida wanted me to go, to leave the family home and get out of this hole, as she now called Tunis. The city where she had been born, had lived, and had survived. For some time, she had been calling her birthplace "this hole." I didn't really understand what had happened to her. Her brother's death, her rapidly failing health, and her erratic memory, which wavered between lucidity and fog. Was old age overcoming Farida? I didn't even want to think about it.

"You've got to get yourself out of this hole. Your father will soon be retiring. He doesn't need to work for the money. Your mother has remarried. She has a new life. And I . . . I'll soon be gone."

I understood what she meant. I didn't want to hear her say the word. That word, which I hid in a very dark corner of my mind. I gently covered her mouth with my hand. I saw her eyes smile.

"Anyway, you have to leave before I go."

And then, like a ball on a soccer field, I left the "hole" and landed in this huge space. These long streets, these steel bridges that shook with the passing of every car or truck, these dismal buildings, and this hostile climate.

Farida had not thought about my new home. She'd thought only of the "hole." She'd thought of our house, where the paint was peeling and the garden was turning into a jungle. She'd thought of the dirty streets, the noise of the cars, and the garbage cans that stank like rotting corpses. She'd thought of her family members, who were dying one after the other, whose obituaries she read daily in *La Presse tunisienne*.

I would heard her talking loudly so that my father, sitting in the sitting room, could hear. "Well, Madame Zarrouk passed away last night. She'll be buried in Jellaz Cemetery. God bless her soul. She was married to one of my father's cousins on his mother's side. A judge, Si Tawfik Zarrouk. The funeral cortege will leave from her son's house this afternoon."

My father would say nothing. I didn't know if he'd heard her and was pretending to be dozing in his chair in front of the TV. He was not interested in death. No matter, Farida wanted to talk and no one could stop her, not even my father's silence.

Above all, she thought about my future. "In Canada, you'll finish your studies in literature, you'll make friends, and maybe you'll get married."

At the mention of marriage, I froze. "Who would want me, especially in Canada?"

"Why not, aren't there men there? Why wouldn't someone want to marry you? Have you forgotten that you have a university degree, and that in a few years you'll have another, and that you're the granddaughter of Farida Ben Mabrouk, one of the first Tunisian women to go to school?"

Farida was rambling, as usual. She was the living relic of another time. Antiquated, outmoded, misunderstood, ridiculed, and looked down on. Here in Canada, in Ottawa, in this neighbourhood of Sandy Hill, Farida would be a curiosity. A stranger among strangers. And yet, I felt her presence like a benevolent shadow. Her letters comforted me. They warmed my heart. Farida was slowly fading, I could sense it in her words. Her absence weighed heavily on me, more so than the absence of my mother during the early years of my childhood. But I accepted it because she was the one who had encouraged me to make that decision. And ultimately, I knew she was right.

The memory of my first days in Ottawa evaporated like a drop of water in the Sahara. A mirage, a sudden quick feeling of joy, then nothing at all. An airplane for the first time. The ocean, seen from the airplane window, an infinite expanse where blue mixed with white. Then the first sight of land, Labrador. And then Ottawa. The first city I saw after leaving the "hole." During my first few weeks here, the people administering the scholarship were with me constantly. They transported me, housed me, helped me get settled and start my classes at the university. Once registration was done, the forms filled out and signed, the cards issued, I found myself alone. Alone in my little apartment watching the street from the window. Another student was supposed to join me. From Morocco. Samiha was her name. But she never came. A change of heart at the last minute, plans cancelled for family reasons, administrative complications? I didn't know. Anything was possible, but the result was that I was living alone in that apartment, at least until the arrival of another scholarship recipient.

Fortunately, Farida's letters kept coming one after the other, as though she were constantly talking to me. Those letters kept me company. She told me about the neighbours. About the girl who slipped while washing the stairs and how they had put a pin in her tibia. About the corner grocer she suspected of collaborating with the police by reporting the gossip the "cleaning women" told him about the residents of the neighbourhood in exchange for free bottles of Coca-Cola. The man who didn't pay his bills. The one who was cheating on his wife with a colleague from work. The woman who left her husband to go live in Italy with a drug smuggler. The man who spent too much time in mosques.

I don't know if Farida herself believed all that nonsense. She got it from the neighbourhood women who came to visit with her or bring her something they had cooked. After the rumours and gossip, she told me about my father.

When he comes home from work, Tawfik changes his clothes and rushes out into the garden. He spends hours there. I watch him from the French window while I listen to the radio. He's like a crazy person. Like a person sentenced to hard labour, to spend his life breaking stones. He turns over the earth, breaks up the clumps of clay with his pick. Sometimes he bends down to pull a weed, then straightens up and looks at the wall as if he were seeing it for the first time. Then he takes out the hose and waters the trees. The garden is turning into a kind of jungle in which your father is becoming more and more ensnared. When he comes in, he eats or watches TV. Your mother is still a part of him. Her remarriage still bothers him. I hardly recognize the child I gave birth to, the one who always gave me the strength to fight. I don't feel like fighting anymore. Fighting for whom?

"For me, Farida! Fight for me now," I wanted so much to answer her, as if she were facing me, lying on her bed with her arms behind her head. Farida had to continue to fight, for me, Leila, her granddaughter. To overcome my loneliness, I would read and reread her letters and her stories, and imagine her weary gaze and her face marked by disappointment with life and with people.

Chapter 2

Jouda

Leila has gone. To Canada. She chose to go far away. Far from me, far from her father. Far even from Farida, from whom she had become inseparable. Before she left, I invited her for lunch at my place. She politely refused. "I have too much to do. I'm going a long way, you know. I mustn't forget anything, you understand?"

I understood. She was looking for excuses. A roundabout way of saying no. Gone were the days when she was close to me. When we spent every Saturday together, window-shopping and talking about everything and nothing, or watching TV on my old set. Since I had decided to remarry, Leila did all she could to avoid me and Firas, who became my husband.

I wasn't expecting such an emphatic reaction. I knew she didn't want me to remarry, but I explained my reasons to her. I told her Firas was a decent man, a man who loved me and whom I trusted. She stiffened. I'd never seen her like that. Her eyes on fire, her chin trembling, her fists clenched. She must have been about twenty and our relationship had never been better since we'd started seeing each other again. We were finishing eating. Beef stew with vegetables and potato salad. I stared stupidly at the little cubes of potato I'd spent an hour peeling, cutting, cooking, and mixing with the mayonnaise I'd patiently made, one drizzle of oil at a time. We had hardly emptied our plates when she put her spoon down on the table. She still had food in her mouth. Her anger erupted with a violence I'd never have thought her capable of. "So you want to go back to your old ways? To just drop me? To abandon me, like you always do?

The last time it was for work. And this time, it's for a man."

I couldn't believe my ears. My own daughter attacking me so viciously, as she would have a stranger.

"Why do you need a man, now, after all these years? Your work isn't enough for you? Why do I always have to pay for other people's misdeeds? My father's, then yours, and now yours again."

I didn't say a word. After that tirade that had come like a hail of bullets, complete silence.

"So you have nothing to say? Maybe you think you're the victim again? Well, I'm not going to believe your fairy tales anymore. I'm no longer the naïve, neurotic little Leila yearning for her mother's love. You can go off with your new husband. Go ahead, go to him. What are you waiting for?" She stood up and pointed to the door.

I still didn't understand how she could treat me like that. I wanted to go over to her and put my hands on her shoulders, but she refused any contact with me. She refused the mother in me.

"But Leila, I'm not doing anything wrong. I just want to start a new life and forget the years of sadness and loneliness."

"So I'm not enough for you anymore? Or do you absolutely have to have a man?"

I couldn't listen to her anymore. "Stop, that's enough! Stop it!"

The force of my command surprised her. As if she hadn't been expecting me to react, as if she had thought I wouldn't be able to answer her. As if being a mother meant forever taking abuse.

Things haven't been the same since then. We spoke again and she came to my place. But she was no longer the same Leila. She had the same smiling mouth, the same white teeth, the same long nose, but her eyes were different. Veiled in sadness and fear. Above all, there was anger in them. A different Leila, who only spoke to me superficially. Who'd make small talk, remain silent, or stand up suddenly in the middle of a film we were watching, saying she'd forgotten she had an exam to prepare for and she had to go home right away. She'd tell the same jokes as before, but avoid looking me in the eye with that look that reached deep down, that mixed our sorrows and our joys. Now everything stopped at her eyes.

After my marriage, I went to live with Firas in his apartment in Ariana. It was in an old building with poorly maintained stairways and an entrance that was missing a door and let in dust and plastic bags from

outside. But, all things considered, it was far better than the studio apartment of Si Khmaies where I had lived for almost twenty years. I was so
used to cramped quarters that it felt like a palace to me, with its two
bedrooms, sitting room, kitchen, and bathroom. I sometimes felt a bit
light-headed, not knowing what to do with all that space.

I married in secret, as if I were ashamed. Ashamed of being happy with
someone other than Leila and her father. I told Leila I was moving and
she immediately understood. She never set foot in that apartment. She
would just phone me. Voices were enough. Eyes only got in the way. When
I told her I wanted to see her, she would suggest we meet in a café and I'd
agree immediately. And from then on, we always met in the same café. I
knew every nook and cranny there, the cracked tiles, the wobbly tables, the
stained tablecloths. The waiter considered us regulars. A café crème or a
mint tea according to my mood for "madame," and a lemonade or eggnog
according to the season for "mademoiselle." Sometimes I would order a
pastry, a millefeuille or a cream puff, which we would share, but if not,
Leila asked for nothing. She would talk to me about her studies, about her
teachers, never about her father, and always about Farida.

To Leila, Farida was not just a grandmother, someone she'd visit every
Sunday, who'd give her candies on the sly, who'd tell her stories. Farida
was also a mother. A very special mother. A mother who had raised and
taken care of her after I left the house. It wasn't Farida's cakes or the
meals she cooked that Leila talked about, but rather her opinions, the
books she read, and the things she told her.

The stories Leila told me about Farida always irritated me and, frankly,
made me jealous. Jealous of that old lady who was a bit eccentric, not
always docile but always lucid, and above all, full of life, and who continued,
in spite of disease and old age, to look after her son and her granddaughter.
I would have liked to be a Farida, to have her strength and resilience, but
unfortunately, I remained, in everyone's eyes, the unworthy mother, the
woman who had abandoned her daughter for work and had now chosen to
get married instead of devoting herself to her daughter.

Even after Leila graduated, she kept telling me how grateful she was
for all the dictations Farida had given her when she was in primary school
and the books Farida had read to her every night at bedtime. And what
about me? Nothing. A temporary mother. When Leila began coming to
see me on weekends, I would read books to her. From time to time, I

would help her with her homework. She never said a word about that to me. Not one small sign of gratitude. Not one little thank you. Nothing good came out of her mouth for me. Everything was for Farida.

Maybe I deserved this, as my mother's long sighs reminded me at every opportunity. I kept my sorrow to myself. Sometimes I would say something to Firas, who would console me with a long kiss or loving words, but the pain remained rooted in my body like a weed that could never be pulled.

Chapter 3

Farida

She has gone away. My little Leila has gone to that big country, the country that gives me the chills when I just say its name. I wanted her to go, I encouraged her to leave this hole, which is what this city has become to me. This city that saw me grow up, suffer in silence, and resign myself to my fate. This city that has swallowed the past and vomited up the future. That has become a monster, a monster that has destroyed neighbourhoods, houses, and shops, and built others crowded together or scattered any which way. From the lanes of the medina, where I used to walk to school with Habib and we would be watched by a French policeman out of the corner of his eye, to these new neighbourhoods that I hardly recognize when I take a taxi and see a policeman keeping order in the urban chaos. And to think that I know my way in the labyrinth of the medina with my eyes closed, better than among the rows of houses in the new city. Gone are the days when I'd defy Kamel and leave the house alone to go talk to Tawfik's teacher. Or when I kept my father company in his room and would hear his difficult, hoarse breathing.

"Read to me in French," he would ask when he realized I was there. I wouldn't say anything. I'd open one of the books I kept on a shelf of his bookcase and start to read:

Mother died today. Or, maybe, yesterday; I can't be sure. The telegram from the Home says: YOUR MOTHER PASSED AWAY. FUNERAL TOMORROW. DEEP SYMPATHY. Which leaves the matter doubtful; it could have been yesterday.

The Home for Aged Persons is at Marengo, some fifty miles from Algiers. With the two o'clock bus I should get there well before nightfall. Then I can spend the night there, keeping the usual vigil beside the body, and be back by tomorrow evening. I have fixed up with my employer for two days' leave; obviously, under the circumstances, he couldn't refuse me. Still, I had an idea he was annoyed, and I said, without thinking: "Sorry, sir, but it's not my fault, you know."

Afterwards it struck me I needn't have said that.

My father didn't understand much of it. He didn't speak or read French. But he nodded his head to indicate a certain enjoyment despite his illness. "You have a lovely voice, my dear Farida. I don't regret sending you to school after all. Your years of school were very good for you. You could have become someone . . ."

I said nothing, Camus's *L' Étranger* still on my lap. Baba was silent for a moment, trying to find words or struggling to get air into his wretched, sickly lungs. He continued, " . . . someone important, like a schoolteacher or even a principal. But I couldn't let you grow up without seeing you married. A woman needs a man to protect her. You had to get married."

"And you married me to Kamel. An ignorant man, a good-for-nothing, an idiot, who caused you to lose your daughter and your fortune."

My father kept his eyes closed. "Keep reading to me. I like listening to your voice."

I didn't want to read to him anymore. Camus's words filled my mouth but they didn't want to come out. They remained imprisoned there as in the pages of the books on the shelves, with only the specks of dust keeping them company. Looking at my father reawakened old memories I had thought I was rid of. And yet, words, simple words, had brought them back to me, here at the door to my heart. I remained silent for a moment. The sound of his breathing filled the room. Sometimes it would stop. I'd stare at him, my eyes seeking his jugular vein. There it was, I could see it clearly, bulging, greenish, scarcely pulsing. There was still life in Baba.

Now this scene only comes back to me rarely. My father has been buried, and with him, several parts of my life. From time to time, memories re-emerge like announcements of my own imminent departure. And then I see myself newly married, struggling with the despair of being trapped with Kamel. And later, as a young divorced woman struggling with my body's desires and people's gossip, trying to raise Tawfik in a world for which I had no preparation other than the books that lived in my imagination. And today, an old lady who sees her child, the man I raised, for whom I did everything, risked everything, sees him falling deeper into a parallel world, sees him tumbling like a ball down a staircase.

My ray of hope was Leila, and I let her slip through my fingers. Yes, I was unhappy to see her leave, but glad to know she would shine elsewhere, in a new world. Yesterday I got a letter from her. The mailman handed it to me. I couldn't contain my joy, and I let loose a flood of blessings: "May God keep you, my son, and bestow his infinite mercy upon you." He was pleasantly surprised, the poor fellow, forgotten by the people and the government. Her letters travelled for six days. They crossed the ocean, then the Mediterranean by airplane or boat, then by truck, and finally by bicycle, piled in the mailman's basket, to the door of our house, where they arrived to comfort me. A few words written on a table or a desk in a library, in the morning in daylight with the timid chirping of birds in the background, or at dusk, when the horizon turned cotton-candy pink, by the light of a lamp. Words that changed my mood. From lethargy to enthusiasm. From silence to speech. That's what some letters scribbled on a scrap of paper could do to me, they could bring me back to life.

My dear Farida,

I don't know if you can close your eyes for a moment and imagine the place where I've been living for two weeks. Forget the "hole," forget the winding streets filled with traffic, garbage, and people. Forget the dilapidated buildings that stink of cat piss and drunkards' vomit. The buildings you used to show me, saying "This is La Goulette, where the family of Monsieur Giuliano, who rented my father's land, lived. Here is Rue de Paris, where my cousin Fatma lived for several years after her husband died."

Erase all those places from your memory, and open a new page. A blank page. A new file, as it's called on a computer. A file you save on the hard disc, your memory. Call that file "Leila in Ottawa." Like the stories you used to tell me when I was little. The ones you made up were the best ones. I found them the most credible and the loveliest.

Now it's my turn to tell you a story. I am the heroine of this story. In this file, you'll see wide streets, men and women rushing around, sidewalks with no street vendors, buildings with doors closed. No stray cats. Just a few squirrels, who seem to be in a hurry, crossing the street or running along the electric lines. Beggars with bushy beards and wild eyes holding signs saying they have nothing to eat.

And here I am in all this, trying to make sense of my new life, without you or my father or my mother. In any case, what would you be able to do for me? Nothing. Except maybe hold my hand, give me a hug, put your arm around my shoulders, and tell me I'll get used to it. Yes, you've guessed it, I'm homesick. I miss you, Farida. Ottawa gave me my studies, but it took away my family. I didn't know how attached I was to that "hole" until I left it. That "hole" with its misery, its little streets, its oppressive heat, its horrible men who whistle at you in the street, its sun beating down on your head, its beaches littered with watermelon rinds, with volleyballs flying at you, its women who have the nerve to tell you a few hard truths, even if they're false, its dirty, noisy, crowded markets. Can you love such things, Farida, can you be nostalgic for ugliness, dirt, and meanness?

I had no nostalgia for anything. Leila was going through a period of soul-searching. A period of contractions before a birth. If I were with her, I could help her, give her a bit of comfort, which she surely needs. A caress, a kiss, a word. But Leila needs more than that. She needs a meaning to her life. I thought I'd found mine in my son, but I was wrong. My quest was vain and my successes short-lived. Maybe Leila will have better luck in her life. I wish her that.

Chapter 4

Tawfik

Every day was the same as the next. Since my retirement, nothing changed from day to day. It was different when I was still going to the office . . . well, a bit. I'd take the bus and walk from the stop to the office, across Rue de Rome, to the Port de France, then the old medina and Souk El Attarine, to arrive finally at the Kasbah, the prestigious location of the Tunisian administration. Amor, the *chaouch*, always greeted me as if he hadn't seen me for months. And yet he was still there, sitting in the same place as the day before. He would stand up, kiss me on both cheeks, shake my hand, and say, "So, Si Tawfik, how is everything?" And I would give him a pat on the shoulder, surprised that he had been asking me the same question for years and that I was answering with the same enthusiasm. "Everything is fine, my dear Amor!" And with the same joviality, he would continue, "Shall I order you a coffee?"

"A long double, no sugar, *y'achek*."

He would walk away limping, one leg shorter than the other. This scene had been repeated daily since I'd started working in the tax audit department of the Ministry of Finance, the same day I obtained my divorce from Jouda. The end of one life and the beginning of another.

My mother thought I was a failure, a "bad egg," as our old saying goes. But she didn't tell me that. Only her eyes said it. She never criticized me. She stopped giving me advice the day I left for university. Her maternal duty had ended when I got my baccalaureate. When I was in primary school, she was the one who went and talked to my teachers. It was a way of saying I had someone to defend me. When I was in secondary school, she helped me with my compositions, changing some of my wordings. She went through my exercise books with a fine-toothed comb, leaving nothing to chance. And when I got my bac, her mission was accomplished.

I felt no resentment toward her. She had protected me from my father's violence. She had defied tradition to raise me by herself. But I made the mistake of believing that everyone was like her. I expected to give everything to the woman I married . . . love, money, and comfort. So that my wife would not have to constantly battle a tyrannical father, an overbearing boss, or relatives to feed her children. So that my wife would not have to humiliate herself in front of anyone by asking for a job. So that my wife would not endure the hell my mother had experienced. Obviously, I had misunderstood.

I didn't see it coming. I was still living with the effects of my absent father and omnipresent mother. But I wasn't the only one at fault. Jouda was intransigent. She abandoned me without hesitation. Worse, she abandoned Leila, the apple of my eye, whom I was unable to raise properly, and who then chose to leave rather than stay. Jouda made no effort to understand me, to preserve our marriage, to protect our daughter. It was work or nothing. And then after several years, she came to take Leila back, as if nothing had happened. A fruit she picked with no effort or difficulty. She left Leila when the child was one, and she came back for her when she was nine.

Farida didn't let me act like a man, she prevented me from acting as any man would in such a situation, raising his voice, shouting, threatening, imposing conditions. Farida cleared the way for Jouda to do as she wanted, without blame, without consequences. To go away to work. To come and take her daughter back. I was the useful idiot of the situation, the one everybody laughed at, even his mother.

And when Leila got the scholarship to the University of Ottawa from the Francophonie, I couldn't do anything to prevent her from going away. At first, she was not very enthusiastic about it, and I wasn't able to offer an alternative. I was part of the flotsam and jetsam from a country that had gone adrift. How could I have been useful to Leila? I don't have any influence to get her a job. I don't belong to a large clan with blood ties she could take advantage of to meet people and find a job or even a husband.

Sadly, our family exploded like a dying star, its fragments lost in the universe on trajectories that would never meet. My aunts, uncles, and cousins were taken away by illness or treated harshly by life. The new rich made their fortunes at the expense of the old bourgeoisie. Karl Marx called it class struggle; we experienced it as gradual impoverishment. Property was sold off at ridiculous prices or confiscated by the banks, fortunes dissipated. I was one of the rare members of the family to get a university degree. Without education, my cousins had nothing. They had thought the land would always produce the money they needed to live.

The houses in the medina slowly fell into ruin. It became expensive to have work done. Life itself became costly. The houses were sold and my relatives moved into apartments on Rue Lafayette or Rue de Paris, apartments that had belonged to the French colonists but since Independence were occupied by Tunisians. They were nice apartments with high ceilings, large windows, broad hallways, and airy kitchens, but nothing like the Arab houses, where the huge bedrooms could accommodate five or six children and there was still room for guests. And the houses had enormous patios where entire families would gather to celebrate weddings or circumcisions, or to mourn deaths. Compared to the old houses, these apartments were like rabbit warrens. People were crowded in them, wishing they could return to the sunny times of the past, dreaming of one day going back and drinking mint tea with pine nuts or savouring a crisp piece of baklava.

My family fell to the bottom of the social ladder. The new rich grabbed everything, the good positions, the lovely houses, and even the beautiful women. They left us nothing, not even a few crumbs. We became a handful of chickpeas left at the bottom of the pot. How could I have said no to Leila's scholarship? I had nothing better to offer her. She accepted it. I should add that her relationship with Jouda had deteriorated since Jouda's remarriage.

Never had I expected Jouda to remarry. In her forties. I didn't think she was capable of it. Just as I hadn't thought her capable of leaving me a year after our marriage. One blow after another, and I never saw them coming. That's the story of my life.

And the man she married hadn't been married before. An old bachelor who hadn't left his mother until she died. It could have been me. Actually, it was a bit like me when I married her. But that was a thing of the past. I don't want to go back there, it would open up old wounds. I too could

have made a new life, with a new wife, but I didn't want Leila to have
a stepmother, a woman who would never love her, or worse, would do
everything to humiliate and abase her and force her to do her bidding.
But what did I know? . . . perhaps it would have helped Leila to have a
stepmother—someone other than Farida, who couldn't cook or clean or
take care of the house properly. But for all her faults, at least Farida was
an intelligent woman, and I never for a second regretted that she lived
with us and was like a mother to Leila.

For the time being, I was enjoying my idleness. The garden was my
favourite place. My kingdom without a palace. The place where I didn't
have to prove to the world that I was capable, good, or intelligent. The
earth was my confidant, the trees my close friends. I talked to them,
especially when I was unhappy or when Leila was visiting her mother or
Farida was in her room reading the papers and listening to the radio. Her
way of forgetting her problems was by immersing herself in the worlds
of others. Mine was the garden. There I could forget myself and my
sorrows, my complexes, my failed life. The garden was my undisputed
territory, a battlefield where there were no winners or losers.

When Jouda left me, I thought I would die. I wanted to die. Every time
I came home from work and saw Leila growing up without a mother, my
heart sank. And then one day, I went out into the garden. A few square
metres of ground I had neglected. My pain was so intense that I couldn't
remain standing. I dropped to my knees, and the contact with the earth
was magical. I felt comforted, caressed, understood. I gave a long sigh,
a long cry that only I could hear. It freed me from all those years of suffering. I didn't believe in miracles. But that day, I saw one happen. The
miracle of a man returning to his source, returning humbly to his ori-
gins. When I touched the soil with my hands, when I dug in it or lifted
a pick and broke up the clods of clay, I had an intense feeling of joy.
Leila and Farida thought I'd lost my mind. But if I had lost my mind, as
anyone would in my situation, I found it again in my garden. The herbs
freely growing. The birds taking shelter from the heat under the leaves
of the pomegranate tree or the almond tree. The smell of rosemary in
my nostrils, a balm for my brain. The smell of sage with the sun beating down on it took me away to another world, a world of tranquility,
devoid of sorrow. My garden was all that and more. A strange place, a bit
crazy, untamed, wild, chaotic. Like me. When things weren't going well,

I would dig holes in the ground and they would gradually fill with water from the rain, and then dry out. Sometimes I would leave them like that, sometimes I would fill them with earth again, and sometimes I would buy fruit trees and plant them there. Life was beginning again.

With the years, the garden became my family, the place where I felt at home, surrounded by love and, most of all, serenity.

Chapter 5

Leila

Since my arrival in Canada, I had been hearing one word over and over: *referendum*. Of course I knew what it meant, but in this political context that was completely new to me, I wasn't able to choose "my side," as my friend Catherine kept saying I should. Quebec or Canada? The little one or the big one? French or English? And yet, from a distance, from my perspective as a Francophonie scholarship recipient and student of French literature, the choice seemed clear, even obvious. But as soon as I tried to go a little deeper, things became blurry and I'd get lost in a maze of historical events, and political ins and outs.

It was a bit like the story of my father and my mother. Sometimes I felt closer to my mother, but there were years when I was detached from her and felt almost like a stranger. It was the same with my father. For years, I felt I was the daughter for whom he sacrificed everything, to whom he gave everything. But there were days when I felt only resentment and bitterness toward him. His coldness, his stoic manner that seemed like indifference, and his inaction infuriated me. When he was silent, I just wanted to run away and never see his face again. Yet I loved him. A strange love. A capricious love that sometimes poured out and other times dried up.

When I shared that thought with Catherine Rioux, the girl who sat next to me in my nineteenth-century French literature class, who asked me if I was for the "yes" side or the "no" side, she looked at me with her mischievous eyes and said, "So which would be your mother and which would be your father, Quebec or Canada?"

I didn't know what to answer so I just smiled innocently. Catherine approached me very gently. Like an autumn breeze. Without my even realizing it. The loneliness of those first few weeks weighed so heavy on my soul that I didn't even pay attention to the other students in that French literature class. I was only interested in the professor. Monsieur Lalonde must have been in his forties, with a goatee that made him look like a rat hunting for a morsel of food. As soon as he opened his mouth and began talking about an author of the period, I felt immersed in the flood of his knowledge. Why had Flaubert used Madame Bovary to describe the new reality of his time? And could the boundless love of Father Goriot for his selfish daughters still exist today? Questions I had never thought about, but which now filled my mind. In Tunis, those novels were just stories. In Ottawa, they were helping me better understand people. I took notes. I would sink into a kind of intellectual trance that left me only when the class was over. It was during those moments of respite that I got to know Catherine. Completely by chance. She would look at me with curious eyes. Her chestnut hair reached down to her shoulders, and her eyes were almost hidden by glasses that seemed to cover her whole face and made her look like a not-very-confident teacher.

"Did you like the class? I found it a drag."

I just smiled and nodded, not really understanding what she meant.

Lowering her voice, she continued, "I mean, the prof seems very good, but there's too much information. He gives us too much in my opinion."

All the other students had left the room, and only Monsieur Lalonde was left gathering his papers.

She came a little closer and said, "I'm Catherine. Catherine Rioux. I'm from Sudbury, in northern Ontario. What about you?"

We were standing face to face. I almost kissed her on both cheeks the way we do in Tunis. But I stopped myself and held out my hand instead. I had to restrain my excessive familiarity. "I'm Leila Ben Mahmoud and I'm from the . . . from Tunis." Another near-mistake. I had almost said "the hole," as Farida called it, but I stopped myself right away.

Catherine didn't notice. She was putting her things into her backpack. Without looking at me, she said, "Is Tunis far? Sudbury is seven hours by bus. It feels endless to me."

Finally, someone who was interested in Tunis. My birthplace, which I'd barely left, was taking revenge on me, like an abandoned lover, leaning with all its weight on my memories.

"Tunis is almost ten hours' flight all together. And first you have to go to Montreal by bus. Then you go by plane, with a stopover in Paris. That's the route I took to come here, in the opposite direction."

"When did you get to Ottawa?"

"August 15." Saying the date made me queasy. My leaving home was the source of endless pain.

"Almost a month ago!"

I was trying to contain myself. "Yes, and I'm homesick for my country." I nearly burst into tears. Finally I was talking with someone face to face rather than on the telephone, someone other than an officer responsible for the Francophonie scholarship, other than the administrative assistants, other than my professors. A flesh-and-blood person talking to me. She was talking to Leila Ben Mahmoud.

"I understand."

We both had tears in our eyes. We were both emotional, each in her own way. It was our loneliness that brought us together. I wasn't only feeling sorry for myself, I also empathized with Catherine. But when Catherine talked about politics, her eyes weren't sad anymore, they sparkled.

"Why didn't you go into political science, or law?" I asked her one day when we were sitting in the university cafeteria.

She was eating a salad and I was eating a tuna sandwich. She took a mouthful of her salad, chewed it slowly, and said, as if she were revealing a secret, "I don't know if I could ever go into politics. Most politicians are men, aside from Kim Campbell, that is, who was the first female Prime Minister of Canada—but only for a few months. Becoming a college teacher seems more realistic."

"But you have nothing to lose. You can try. After all, there *are* women in politics, aren't there?"

"A few, very few. Anyway, not many in my region in northern Ontario. Plus my family is rather poor and not very well educated. I'm the only one who's gone to university. Nobody in my family likes politics, and even less, women in politics."

"All the more reason for you to take your chances."

She continued eating her salad. Her eyes had lost their sparkle. She was expressionless. Her mind seemed to be elsewhere. Wiping the dressing from her mouth, she explained the Canadian political system, which I knew very little about.

"A dictatorship is a lot easier to understand. There's just one person whose name you need to remember, and that's it. For us in Tunisia, it's Ben Ali."

She smiled at my sarcasm, but she wasn't convinced. "And did you like living under a dictatorship?"

"Not really, but did I have a choice? Did I choose my parents? Did I choose where I was born? No, not really, you understand? In fact, dictatorship becomes so subtle that you don't feel it anymore. Except for a few activists and a handful of political opponents, who are seen as the enemy, there's nothing. The people learn to live with their misery. And with time, they can cope with everything—poverty, injustice, and even dictatorship."

She couldn't relate to what I was saying. "What do you mean, cope with oppression and injustice?"

"Yes, you learn it in school, in the street, on the bus, even at home. You can't talk back to your teacher, even if he treats you unfairly, you can't confront the policeman who stops you for a supposedly random identity check, even if you've done nothing. You can't lodge a complaint about the bus driver who calls you all kinds of names if you ask him why he didn't stop at the usual place. You learn to live with injustice. You cope with it. You justify it. Until the day you wake up and you yourself have become a little oppressor." I didn't know how those words had come out of my mouth. It was as if I had harboured them in me for years, and now they were coming out in that university cafeteria in Ottawa, where everyone only wanted to satisfy their hunger.

"And did that happen to you?"

I shook my head.

"I left before that. In fact, Farida pushed me to leave."

Catherine didn't know who I was talking about. Her eyes were wide. Confusion had replaced her initial surprise.

"Farida is my grandmother, she raised me and I lived with her, until I left for Canada."

Family relationships had somehow entered the conversation. Everything was getting mixed up.

"And why did she encourage you to leave? In my case, my parents always wanted me to stay in Sudbury. At most, to become a teacher. They would have been proud to see their daughter stay in her home town. They would have been able to say to their neighbours and friends:

'Here's Catherine, our daughter. She's a teacher at the high school.'"

"My father would have liked me to stay in Tunis. My mother too. She would have wanted me to continue seeing her in the same café and maybe sometimes go to her place. In fact, Farida is the only one who openly encouraged me to leave. For me, it was different. Staying would have meant dying a little. Losing my capacity to feel, losing that innate sense of justice we all have . . . basically, forgetting my humanity. That's why I followed Farida's advice. Beyond all the conflicts between my father and my mother, I was afraid of losing my humanity. I was afraid of losing my life."

She put her hand on mine, as if she wanted to tell me that words were no longer needed and that her heart had understood everything. "Maybe you also came so that we could meet!"

We burst out laughing simultaneously. It was the first time I'd laughed since my arrival in Canada.

I was gradually starting to get used to my new life. First of all, because my classes didn't leave me time to lament my fate or feel lonely. But also, after meeting Catherine, I was able to talk with a real person. To talk about my life in Tunisia, to forget my homesickness, to put aside my sometimes glum feelings, and especially, to get to know myself a little better.

Back there, in the "hole," I lived always surrounded by others—Farida, my father, my mother, my friends, the whole "system." I existed through them. I was in turn a child, a little girl, a student, and even, for the police, a number on an identity card. But never a person who loved, who hated, who simply existed. Here, far from my family and my reference points, solitude let me discover my true self.

Who was I really? The fruit of a failed marriage? The product of two ruined generations? Or Farida's granddaughter, who still thought and lived through her grandmother? I would think about these questions on the bus that took me from the supermarket to my apartment, two plastic bags containing my purchases pressed between my legs, or when I was cooking and the pasta I was boiling overflowed and splashed water on the stove and the pot, which I had a lot of trouble cleaning. And I would think about them when I forgot that the radio was on and went into the bathroom, and the muffled sound made me think for an instant that someone had come into my apartment, giving me a fright. Those thoughts pursued me like sticky, persistent flies on a summer day that would stop for a moment only to start again, more annoying than before.

Chapter 6

Catherine

If it weren't for political activity, I'd be dead, deceased, vaporized like a snowflake in the sun. If it weren't for politics, I'd still be suffering under my father's control and my mother's apathy. If it weren't for politics, I would never have been able to stick it out and live with the wounds of my adolescence.

Every night before going to bed, I would recall the "incident." That's what my mother called it. I told her so many times that it wasn't just an incident. She would roll her eyes and go into the sitting room, which stank of damp and cigarettes. My father refused even to talk about it. In any case, he was never good with words. He would just stare at me as if I were one of those visions his mother had apparently experienced in his childhood, which he would often recount to us in every blessed detail. He would peer at me with his weak eyes and fall silent.

I had told them all about the "incident," all the details, from beginning to end. I was coming home from my classmate Natalie's house after spending two hours with her. We had a biology project to hand in the next day. It was dark. I was never afraid walking in the streets of Sudbury. There were sometimes drunks, homeless people, some arguing loudly, some who asked for small change. Occasionally, I would give them a few coins. Or I'd continue on my way with just a "good evening."

That evening, I was walking along Mackenzie Street, which runs past the public library. My mother used to take my brother and me there every Saturday afternoon and leave us for two or three hours. I have no idea what first led her to take us to a place where she didn't feel at home. Maybe her feeling of inferiority because she hadn't gone to school, or the fact that she didn't have much to offer us for fun. Everyone in the library knew us, the clerks, the librarians, and even the regulars. They recognized us with our hair always cut short and the second-hand clothes my mother got at the Saint-Vincent de Paul store, which I was ashamed of because they were always out of style compared to those of the other kids at school.

I'd barely gotten to Baker Street, just two blocks from our house, when I heard Paul calling to me. Paul was our neighbour. We had played together when we were little. It was really my brother who played with him. I never liked him. I could hardly stand him. He always bothered me, called me a tomboy and tried to get me to play hockey with him when I didn't want to. I didn't like his fake innocent look, I sensed it was a cover for nastiness. My mother had often suggested that I might one day marry him, and my father had hired him at the mine when he got expelled from high school. That evening, Paul's voice was different. It was hoarse, not his usual calm, low voice. There was only one streetlight on our street, which was out that evening. It was totally dark. Paul was tall and all the girls in our school found him handsome. Except me.

"Why are you coming home so late, baby?"

I didn't understand why he was calling me "baby." I wasn't his girl-friend, and I didn't want to be. Something didn't feel right. But I wasn't afraid of Paul. And in spite of everything, I thought of him as a friend, our neighbour.

"I was working on a project with Natalie. And you, what are you doing out here?"

He didn't answer. I was starting to feel uneasy. I wanted to get home as fast as possible, and his sudden appearance and the strange way he was looking at me were making me more and more nervous.

He came close to me and I felt his two heavy hands on me, one on my arm and the other on my back. "Come over to my house, Catherine. I have something important to show you."

What was he talking about? I tried to free myself from his grip, but he held on.

"Let me go, Paul, I want to go home, you can show me what you think is so important some other time."

He acted as if he hadn't heard me. He was holding on to me and pushing me farther and farther away from our house in the darkness. I was afraid. I wanted to cry out. "What are you doing, Paul? Are you serious? If this is some kind of joke, it isn't funny."

"Shut up, you'll do what I tell you or you'll be sorry."

My heart was pounding like crazy. I opened my mouth to scream, but before I could, his hand that had been on my back was over my mouth. He kept pushing me. Our house was gradually disappearing from my field of vision.

I found myself in the backyard of Paul's house. He pinned me against the crumbling brick wall and kissed me on the mouth. He stank of alcohol. His whole body was pressing against mine, crushing me. His hands grabbed my breasts, dug into my belly, clutched my hips. He bit my neck. I tried to dig my fingernails into those grabbing hands. I kept struggling, and I was finally able to free myself from his grip. I ran like crazy, away from that dark silhouette. He ran after me but I yelled, "Take another step, Paul, and I'll scream as loud as I can," and he stopped. I was shaking and about to collapse.

He pointed his finger at me and threatened, "Don't say anything to your parents. Nobody would believe you anyhow."

I don't know how I found the strength to turn around and go home. Paul walked away as if nothing had happened. He climbed the steps to the porch of their house and went in. I stumbled home, shaking with sobs. I didn't know what to do.

Paul was right. No one believed me, starting with my parents.

"Are you sure it was Paul? Our Paul? Paul Gagnon?" my mother finally said after I told her the whole thing. She had the same look as when she watched the news on TV. A look that was puzzled and incredulous.

I was crying. I had my hand over my mouth. I was trying to get rid of Paul's smell.

My father was obviously upset, but he was looking for excuses for Paul. "Paul's a nice guy, how could he do something like that? Maybe he was drunk and didn't know what he was doing."

I got up from the chair I'd thrown myself into and headed to the bathroom. Everything felt slimy, the soap, the sink, my hands—and my parents' words that echoed in my ears. I scrubbed my mouth, my fingers, my fingernails, and my arms up to the elbows. The hot water made

my hands more and more red and swollen, and my mouth looked like
the mouth of a clown. I stood there without moving. I didn't want to
walk out and see my parents and hear their words. I looked around me
at the little white and black tiles, the bathtub, the shower curtain with
its happy-looking multicoloured fish, the sink, the faucet, the water running. Everything was the same, except me. A new me. A girl who had
been assaulted. A girl defiled.

When I left the bathroom, my face still covered in tears, my fingers
swollen like sausages, my parents were in their usual places in the sitting
room. "Don't say anything to anyone. I'll talk to Paul tomorrow." "And
above all, not a word at school. It has to stay between us." That was all
my parents had to say to me.

"But Maman! Paul attacked me. Don't you get it? He has to pay for
what he did. We have to report him to the police!"

"What are you talking about? It was just an incident. These things
happen in life. After all, Paul's our neighbour."

"An incident? What do you mean, an incident? Our neighbour, our
childhood friend, stops me in the street, asks how I'm doing, and then
assaults me . . . you call that an incident? Are you defending him, or what?
I'm your daughter. Why are you defending *him*?"

"Go to bed now. We'll talk about it tomorrow."

My parents never discussed it again. Paul never acknowledged what
he'd done. He told my father that I had made it all up and that he would
never do anything like that. My mother still looked at me with doubt
rather than trust in her eyes. And my father told me not to talk about
that "story," it was in the past and after all, everything had gone back to
normal. A few weeks after the "incident," Paul left for Alberta, for Fort
McMurray, to work in a mine. I never saw him again.

For months on end, I cried every night. Just when I was about to fall
asleep, I would see Paul's face again, his hard eyes, I'd smell his acrid
smell, and I'd feel his mouth on mine, his sweaty body against mine.
Those images would come back once, twice, three times, hundreds of
times, and I would force myself to shut them out as if they were shame-
ful. Only tears relieved my despair.

That "incident" practically took over my life. I lost my desire to live.
I no longer wanted to talk to people. I would go to school and then go
straight home and shut myself in my room. I didn't want to talk to my

parents anymore. And then one day, I met Guillaume, in the social sciences club at my school. It was just by chance. But it gave me a chance to come back to life. Another irony. Paul had pushed me into the void and Guillaume had thrown me a lifeline. Our budding friendship led me to throw myself heart and soul into politics.

During the election campaign, Guillaume and I did everything together. We went door to door, made phone calls, went to rallies, and discussed which neighbourhoods to target and what messages to use. I'm not sure which helped me most to get my head above water, politics or Guillaume. It doesn't matter. The important thing is that, little by little, I forgot the "incident." Or rather, I learned to live with it.

Chapter 7

Leila

For a few days, Catherine and I had been making plans to go to Montreal for the big "love-in." We came up with the idea after one of our long discussions about politics. We were an odd couple. Catherine was Canadian, had been following the political scene for years, and had strong, opinions, while I had only been in Canada for a few weeks, and barely knew anything about life here. Yet we were both fascinated by the historic moment the country was going through. For me, seeing a country choose its destiny was marvellous, unprecedented, an opportunity that I would have wanted to experience in my country. And for Catherine, who loved politics and who was born here, the referendum was like a once-in-a-lifetime experiment, but one that would have real consequences. She thought the sovereigntists would win the referendum and Quebec would become independent. That was her greatest fear, her constant preoccupation, her obsession. The danger of losing part of her country and the mother tongue she loved. She sincerely thought that the "yes" camp would prevail in the end.

"This time they'll win, you'll see. The Québécois are fed up with being told what to do by the rest of Canada. Never again. This time, they're going to have their country." She spoke with absolute certainty.

"What makes you think it will work this time?"

"The polls . . . all the polls say the yes side will win. Those in favour of Quebec's independence will win, you'll see."

I took pleasure in playing devil's advocate. "Okay, but aside from the polls, are there other indications? Maybe when they're marking their ballots, people will change their minds at the last minute. It could still be possible . . . "

Catherine smiled feebly. She didn't seem convinced. It was as if she was letting me talk just to humour me. "Yes, maybe. But this time, it seems to me, the Parti Québécois has learned from its past mistakes. They're all fired up. The time seems right to me." She was speaking absent-mindedly, as if she was tired.

"Do you really believe that?"

"Yes, I do. But honestly, I don't want it to happen. I don't want Quebec to separate, I want all the francophones to stay in Canada, strong and united."

"Maybe you're wrong and in the end Quebec will stay . . . "

Our discussion remained unresolved. Her rigid ideas did not fit with mine, which were fluid and not quite defined. Catherine was not convinced by my doubts. And for my part, I was clinging to doubt, which continued to mark my life, even in Canada.

I'd been in Ottawa a month already. Farida, my father, my mother, I missed them all. But Catherine and my classes kept me busy. I was spending a lot of time in the university library. It was a way of dealing with both the huge number of assignments I had to hand in and the loneliness that took hold of me when I returned to my apartment. In the library, there was silence and work. There were books, and people walking around, and those I would watch out the window when I raised my head and looked beyond the study carrel where I spent hours. It was only mealtimes with Catherine that freed me from that near-prison.

In the evening, when my reading was done and my brain exhausted, I would take Louis-Pasteur Street, cross Mackenzie King Street, and head to my apartment in Sandy Hill. At the corner, some students would be smoking and talking loudly in English. I didn't understand much of those strange sounds. I'd hear the echoes of their laughter and I'd wonder what would become of me if Catherine's prediction came true, with the English living on one side and the French on the other. What would happen in Ottawa, the capital, where I had been living for several weeks and which already seemed more anglophone than francophone? Would I still have a reason to stay here? And having come here thanks to a scholarship from the Francophonie, why wouldn't I be tempted by the idea of an independent francophone country? In fact, I still didn't know which side I was in favour of. The "left" side, with the *indépendantistes*, or the "right" side, with my friend Catherine and those who wanted to keep Canada united, even if it meant shattering the hopes of a people. And why would I take the side of the strong, the dominant, the oppressor? Wouldn't it be more appropriate, more natural, for a foreign student who has lived under oppression to join the ranks of those fighting for their freedom and independence?

When I got to my building I was freed from these thorny questions that plagued me. A letter from Farida was waiting for me. I climbed the stairs to my door. Everything was quiet except for the purring of my fridge. My little bedroom was overheated and I opened the window to let in some fresh air. The light breeze that came through the window, which was held up by a stick of wood like a crutch, felt good. I sat down on the edge of my bed, repressing the gurgling of my belly and promising myself a visit to the fridge once I'd read the letter.

Seeing Farida's handwriting transported me thousands of kilometres away, far from my solitude. I felt close to her, I could almost see her lying on her bed, her radio beside her. On her dresser, a piece of bread or a biscuit in case she felt peckish, her glasses, held together in the middle with a band-aid, the little bottle of rosewater her cousin Fatma had given her and she had never opened, and a picture of Tawfik, my father, the day he graduated, a cherished memento that was a constant reminder that she had raised a boy on her own in a man's world.

Dear Leila,

It has been so hot these days. Especially in the afternoons. Siesta time. The siestas that "ripen the quinces and the pomegranates," as they're described. I stay in my room and keep the French door ajar, the one that looks out on the garden, to let in a little coolness. The radio isn't much use anymore, they keep repeating the same old news day and night. Like a piece of gum you chew over and over again, then spit out. Weary, I turn it off. I close my eyes and take a little nap. I see you in my dreams. I can't make out the shapes or the other faces, only yours. I recognize you. You're walking alone and you smile at me. You wave to me. Then I wake up, my hand raised as if I wanted to touch you.

Your father is going to the mosque now. Since your departure, he's been going regularly. I have never seen him so constant and so devout. Your departure revealed our weaknesses to us. We face them, each in our own way. Your mother called me the other day. She wanted news of me and of you. She seems happy with her new husband. I know you detest him and that you haven't forgiven her for that "betrayal," but why stop her from being happy? She never was with Tawfik. Twenty years later, she's fully in control of her destiny and she has chosen the man she wants to share her life with. I never had the good fortune to do that. Can I call it that? I don't know! I always submitted to the choices of others. First those of my father, then those of my husband. And when I could finally choose, I chose to raise my son, on my own. In those days, I never would have been able to remarry. First of all, I didn't want another man to force me to choose between him and my son, but even when I felt I'd found a man who loved me, my father wouldn't hear of it. So, once again, I submitted. Your mother did not submit, and I respect her for that. Would I have been able to do the same if I had been born in her time?

I didn't want to go on. I gently put the letter down on the bedside table. The curtains fluttered in the breeze from the window. The northerly wind was doing its job. In a few minutes, the temperature in the room had fallen and I was starting to feel the cold on my skin. I lay down on my bed and saw my mother and Farida again. Two mothers. The one who birthed me and the one who raised me. Two lives. Farida tacitly accepted my mother's leaving in order to fulfill her own dream. A dream she lived vicariously. Happiness deferred for a generation.

I didn't know whether to laugh or to cry. To cry for the years when my mother chose her work over me or to laugh at Farida's audacity. I didn't know whether I should love my mother or hate her, or if I should treasure what my grandmother had done for me or curse it. I got up like an automaton and went over to the window, shivering in the breeze. Outside, snowflakes were fluttering down. Was it the beginning of a storm or just a warning that wouldn't amount to much?

Farida and Jouda were thousands of kilometres away. And yet, they had followed me into every nook and cranny of my life. In the morning when I looked at myself in the mirror and saw my eyebrows that met in the middle like two palm fronds, I remembered Jouda. In class when I answered the profs' questions, I sensed that I had the same expression as Farida did when she talked about her favourite books. Everything was like her, my bearing, the timbre of my voice, my way of hesitating for a moment in search of a word and then continuing without stopping. Farida and Jouda were both part of me. How to detach myself from them? How to cut those cords that were so long, so deep, so tenacious, and live my life without them coming back in a look or a word, making visible the twisting paths of my past?

I removed the stick of wood and the window slammed shut, blocking the cold air that had turned the room frigid. The snow had stopped falling and the wind had swept it away. Maybe my distance from home would help me find the path to forgetting, the path to peace? To find peace between my two sources of life, those two women who had formed me and who haunted me although I no longer lived with them.

This new country fascinated me. One side was natural and almost wild, despite the city's modernity that made it seem disciplined and ordered. I had a feeling I was hearing its muted growl in each gust of wind or rustle of tree branches. Hidden behind the calm side that seemed to have been tamed by men, there was a limpid, rebellious nature waiting to spring out. Wasn't that what I, too, needed? To rediscover what is deepest in me, not the refinement of my mother nor the archaic quality of my grandmother, but something that belongs to me, an innate part of me that one day will emerge to guide me through the labyrinth of life.

Chapter 8

Tawfik

I never thought I was capable of faith. Not to this extent, anyway. Never had I imagined myself, Tawfik, praying, kneeling, prostrating myself and standing up with my palms held up to the heavens to thank God. Never had I seen myself this way. And yet, it happened. A miracle, a second miracle, after that of the garden. I can't explain it, but it is surely God's light that touched me. Since my retirement, I have divided my time between the garden and the sitting room, a little more in the garden than the sitting room. I would go out occasionally to do errands. I was the one who did the cooking. My mother never felt at home in the kitchen. When she grew old, I prepared our food.

Solitude was suffocating to Farida. Only visits by a few women neighbours provided some air. She missed Leila, and the letters they exchanged regularly helped her overcome the sorrow and emptiness Leila had left behind her. When a meal was ready and I called her to come eat, Farida would put on her slippers and quietly shuffle into the kitchen. Everything about her had changed. Her face was furrowed, her hair, for a long time completely white, was now yellowed, especially at the nape of her neck. But her gaze was still lucid and alert. Her whole body seemed frail, weary of life, tired from having experienced too much, endured too much.

She would sit down and talk to me about the neighbours. Weddings, births, sudden deaths and expected deaths, the stuff of everyday life, she'd recount it all in a rather detached way while eating her soup. Sometimes I'd listen, and sometimes I'd pretend to listen, my mind elsewhere. She didn't tell me the news from the radio anymore. It was strange, the relationship she'd always had with the radio was disappearing. And she had given up cigarettes. From one day to the next. Now all she had was her books.

I remembered her in her youth, in my grandfather's sitting room listening attentively to the tales beautifully told by Abdelaziz El Aroui, a famous storyteller of the time. Tales of secret love and burning jealousy, of incredible adventures, whose heroes visited exotic lands and came back home years later with gold coins and stories of amazing people and places.

In those days, the radio my grandfather had bought was treated with all the care and reverence accorded to a high dignitary. It stood between two ancient armchairs, covered with a piece of lace and regularly dusted. Later, when we lived in the house my mother inherited from her father, a black radio had replaced that big brown one with its golden knobs. My mother's radio looked like a shoebox, with a large dial on the side that was always tuned to the same frequency, the national radio station. When the big cylindrical batteries were running low, she would take them out of their little compartment at the bottom, clean them with a cloth, and rub them vigorously in her hands before putting them back. "I'm giving them a bit of life," she would say with a little smile, seeing my look of surprise and curiosity. I didn't question what she said. Farida was my living dictionary, where I found all definitions and facts, and I innocently swallowed even the trivialities and the myths she occasionally threw in. But now she no longer listened to her radio all the time. She would leave it on her dresser or her bed, preferring the newspaper I bought every day or the neighbours' stories.

When she finished her soup, Farida would dab her lips, which had become almost invisible, now that her teeth were gone. "The soup is rather bland, Tawfik, you should have put in some leeks, that would have substantially improved it." Typically Farida! Always keeping up appearances, covering her faults and weaknesses with her words, her knowledge, her good manners.

The only times I saw her regain her old energy were when she was writing to Leila. Her back would straighten, her fingers would move with their former vigour, and her eyes would fill with a tenderness I had thought gone years ago. An expression that brought back the tender kisses she would shower me with when I was a child, especially when my father scolded me and I took refuge in her arms.

The first time she saw me go out to pray at the mosque, she asked, "Where are you going at this hour? It's almost night."

"To the mosque," I answered, without adding anything.

She remained silent. The next day, she asked if I had started praying regularly, and I said yes. She didn't say anything. Religion had never been very present in our lives. Sometimes nonexistent; at most, very subtle. As a child, I sometimes went to the mosque with my father for the Friday prayer. My father was not especially observant. My mother had told me he drank, and that he had stopped drinking just after my birth. Later, I knew he never stopped seeing his mistress. But every Friday, he would put on his best *jebba* and go to the mosque. Was it to do as others did? To see his friends? To show that he was a still a believer in spite of his sins? I never understood.

For my mother, religion had a different flavour. No special prayers or fancy clothes, but certain gestures that she reserved for religious ceremonies. The Eid was the only time I saw her put kohl on her eyes. And on the eve of Mawlid, she would make *assida zgougou*. That pine-nut cream was often not a culinary success, it was sticky and greyish, but she seemed happy while making it and garnishing it with almonds, hazelnuts, walnuts, and pistachio nuts, whose delicious taste made me forget its unfortunate texture.

She would also take me with her to religious ceremonies at the cemetery, where she would stand silent and meditative in front of her mother's grave. Together we'd climb the stairs leading to the Sidi Belhassen Mausoleum, on the hill overlooking Tunis. She would buy me nougat or *halkoum* from one of the itinerant vendors, who displayed it on wood with a cotton cover to keep the flies off. Visitors would come to the prayer circles there every Thursday evening in a little room with one section for men and another for women, where poetry was recited or chanted to celebrate the life of the Prophet. I often attended these rituals in silence, dazed by the rapid rhythm of the words filling the sombre, mystical space. Sometimes a woman would stand up and start swaying her head from side to side, loosening her hair, so that she looked like a tree buffeted by the wind. I would stay close to my mother, not knowing what was going to happen. The faster the movement of the woman's head, the closer I would move to my mother. Sometimes my mother would suddenly decide to leave, and sometimes we would stay until the woman fell to the floor with dizziness and the other women helped her up and held cologne under her nose. One day my mother stopped going to visit her mother's grave, and I gradually forgot those rare times I saw her fascinated by something other than books or the news.

Prayer came to me almost crawling, one day after I had spent several hours in the garden breaking up clods of clay and watering. It was well into fall. The almond and apricot trees had lost their leaves and soon the pomegranate trees would lose theirs. The sun was setting earlier and earlier. Suddenly I heard the Adhan. As if for the first time. And yet, how many times had I heard that call to prayer without being moved? Without really paying attention to it. It was not so much the voice that I responded to that day, it was nothing new, nothing unusual. But something in me moved, and I felt it. *"Hayya ala salat, Hayya ala falah, Allah hu Akbar Allah hu Akbar, La ila ha il lal lah."* I was paralyzed by the impact of those words, so many times heard and so many times ignored. What was different that day? Faith, I would say. Mere coincidence, others would say. "You're getting old," my mother said, a few days later when she saw that I was now going to the mosque regularly and praying five times a day. She was right. Farida was always right.

After my discovery of the joy of working the earth, never had I felt as happy and serene as when I was praying. After twenty years of separation, of conflict, solitude, jealousy, and doubts, I had finally found my remedy. "Belief in God, belief in the Absolute." Before, I was living surrounded by doubts from morning to night. Doubt of my intellectual abilities, doubt of the value of my long career as a dedicated public servant, doubt of my mother's love, doubt of my role as a father. All that was in the past. My new faith erased my doubts, my hesitations, my fears, and the ups and downs of my life in one stroke. I replaced them with a single certainty: God.

Chapter 9

Farida

I could feel the end approaching, tiptoeing quietly toward me. Especially at night when sleep dissipated, when my heart rhythm became as chaotic as my life, when memories became more vivid than the light of day and I felt alone even though my son was asleep in the next room a few metres away! Death was solitude, and it was prowling around me. I'm not afraid to go, but I would have wanted Leila to be with me. To be sitting on the edge of my bed or in the tattered armchair in the corner looking at me with eyes filled with stories and words! She'll be far away when my soul leaves my body and I turn cold as ice. She'll be very far away, in Canada, with her books, her new friends, her new life. And when she receives the news, it will be too late for her to get here to see me one last time before I'm washed, wrapped in a white shroud, and buried, and my cold body in the ground is being covered with shovelfuls of earth. She'll have to take a bus, two planes, and a taxi to come say a last goodbye to me, and I will already be a lifeless body in the ground.

So many experiences and stories vanished! Today I still have a faint, barely recognizable taste of them. Is it bitterness or regret or just age? Forgetting, melancholy, nostalgia, or confusion? Death seemed to me the greatest certainty. I'd see it pass in front of me again and again without being able to hide from it or ignore it.

Tawfik, since the beginning of his new life, would talk to me of religion and prayers.

"It's time for *al Asr*, the afternoon prayer," he would say. Coming in

from the garden, he would immediately go into the bathroom and perform his ablutions, washing his face, hands, and feet, and then leave to
go to the mosque. I had no explanation for this new love of prayer he
had shown in the past few weeks. On one hand, I was glad for him. He
was no longer alone, he no longer spoke only to the trees; now he spoke
to God. When I'm gone, he'll cry for me, but he won't be inconsolable.
He'll be sad, but he won't despair. He'll have a branch to cling to. That
will be better for him. But I fear that this sudden love of religion could
take him far away, far from me and far from Leila, even farther away than
he already is. That he'll become a sort of half-saint, half-madman and the
neighbourhood kids will throw stones and laugh at him when they see
him walking with his head down and his hands behind his back.

Who would have thought that my son would become an eccentric that
people laugh at? And yet anything is possible, today more than ever. Will
I finally have failed as a mother? Will my womb have produced a boy who
ends his days as a dervish? Will I have given up my whole life for nothing?
To reach the end of my journey only to see all my dreams destroyed,
demolished one after the other without my being able to change anything?. That is what I fear most of all.

A few days ago, my cousin Fatma came to visit me, and the way she
looked at me made me realize I would soon be going. Her gaze was different. I've always known her to be a bit bold, with a direct gaze that
bothered people, especially men. Fatma, my favourite cousin, my childhood friend, my partner in crime. She had suffered in silence, but her
spirit had not been bowed despite the damaging violence done to her
body. She struggled alone and held her head high in spite of the malice
around her. She survived her destiny and never gave in to the loud whispers, the veiled insinuations, the nasty looks. I loved Fatma and I will
always love her. That day she seemed full of pity for me. Perhaps for my
loneliness, which had become obvious after Leila's departure. Perhaps
also because I have never experienced love, and even when it came knocking at my door, it was impossible for me to let it in. It was not welcomed.
Perhaps Fatma knew how hard it was to live without love. For a few years
she'd had a kind, generous husband who had given her children and had
believed her when nobody else would. He had been taken from her by
sickness, but at least, she had tasted love, joy, and happiness. Words that
never existed for me. Words that had been erased from my life.

Fatma will always be my mirror, the person on whose face I can read my own life. The one who reflects my feelings without distortion or exaggeration. And now I saw it in her eyes. She was afraid that I would go. I immediately understood. We looked at each other in silence. Her straight grey hair was now cut short. Her fingers were deformed by the hours she had spent working at her sewing machine. Her fingers had made my first dress. Her fingers had freed her from poverty and misery and enabled her to raise her children after her husband's death.

During that visit, I would have liked to hold her in my arms and kiss her for perhaps the last time, a goodbye before the final parting. But I didn't have the courage. Instead, we sat face to face looking searchingly at each other, reading the invisible stories written on our foreheads.

"Remember the days when we would catch a *bibi* and go to the *Saf-Saf* in La Marsa without anyone knowing, and eat fried potatoes and sip *gazozas* and spend the afternoon together, and then sneak back home unnoticed?. Without a word to anyone."

Her eyes filled with tears. "That's what I want to remember of our lives . . . our lives were adventures . . . weren't they, Farida?" She looked at me again with her beautiful dark eyes. Tears were flowing down her cheeks.

Outside, I heard the garden gate creak. Tawfik was going out for the sunset prayer.

Chapter 10

Jouda

Leila wrote to me. Her first letter since she left for Canada. She had phoned me a few days after her arrival in Ottawa to tell me everything was fine—and then, silence. That silence filled me with doubts and apprehensions. Had she forgotten me? Did she still resent me for my marriage to Firas? Did she see it as still more evidence that I didn't love her and would never be a mother to her like other mothers?

I've understood for a long time that my relationship with my daughter would not be a normal one, with kisses and hugs and, from time to time, a few tears and some innocent sulking. Our relationship was complex. Layers upon layers, each one thicker than the next. And yet, it had begun so well. The outings, the meetings, the hours spent together without tiring of each other. But it seems to me that my marriage brought out all the feelings we had hidden from one another. The bitterness, the darkness, and especially, the fear. Yes, her fear of being abandoned by me and my fear of being forgotten.

But I finally had her letter in my hands. I had the proof that she hasn't forgotten me and that I'll always be her mother. Despite our complicated relationship, despite her hurried departure, despite my new marriage.

It was raining. An autumn rain that brought out the smell of the earth that was dry from the summer heatwave. The big drops were falling noisily on the windows, on the walls of the balcony, on the few cars in the parking lot. The dust they raised looked like the smoke from a fire that was slowly dying out. Firas was at work and I wasn't teaching. I had a few students coming to the house for tutoring, but they wouldn't be here for an hour. I opened Leila's letter. The stamp on the corner of the envelope caught my attention. A red maple leaf, the emblem of that country. I imagined Leila surrounded by trees with those bright red leaves and I shuddered. The colour of blood, the colour of martyrs, the colour of the Tunisian flag. My heart had experienced our separation like a bloody wound and that colour of fire and blood rekindled my fears. I turned the envelope over and saw Leila's address written in her hand, cramped as if she was afraid of not having enough space.

I closed my eyes and imagined that foreign place. A brick building, like those we sometimes saw in the news on TV when they showed images from abroad of buildings in flames or cats stuck in trees being rescued by firefighters. Gloomy buildings, grey or brown, with peaked or flat roofs and almost invisible windows framed in steel. Streets with bare trees. No dust, only snow. Was it possible that my daughter had gone to live in such a place? I still felt guilty for letting her leave and not trying to stop her.

My hands were trembling as I began to read:

Dear Maman,

This is my first letter from Canada, the country I chose in spite of myself, or that chose me. Actually, I'm doing all right. Many times I've thought of packing my bags and returning to Tunis. Forgetting this country, this city, this winter that engulfs us a little more every day. But I thought of the scholarship I would lose, the classes I would miss, and the pain I would cause you. And so I told myself it would be better to stay, despite the loneliness, despite the anxiety, despite the cold. And I stayed. I stayed to save you worry. But also because I realized that with every day that went by, I was forgetting Tunis a little more and getting to know Ottawa a little better. In a way, every day was making me a little less Tunisian and a little more Canadian. Yes, that seems a bit strange, but it's true. It's the distance that does it. I miss you, I think of you, but I'm also beginning to look around me, and I see another country, another city, and other people. I have a new friend. Her name is Catherine. She's francophone and comes from northern Ontario. I don't know if she's keeping me company or if I'm keeping her company, but we get along very well. She talks to me about politics and I listen to her. Just as, when I was a child, I used to listen to Farida tell me the fantastic stories she made up from I don't know where. But Catherine's stories aren't extravagant or invented. They're true stories. I listen to them, thirsty for words, for emotions, for human warmth. I'm understanding this country through Catherine. Through her explanations of the politics. A story of different peoples, different languages, and especially, of power. Who has the most power? Isn't that fantastic? In Tunisia, they had us believe that political power belongs to the "Father" of the nation. Our father, the "combattant suprême," President Bourguiba, who fought for us, to liberate us from the French. Then one day, that power was given to or seized by—depending on the version—his successor, Ben Ali. Never have I thought that power belonged to the people or to those who represented them. Catherine is very enthusiastic, she always seems happy when she's talking about politics. When she isn't talking about politics, she's silent. Something veils her eyes, I don't know what. A profound sadness you can see only with the eyes of the heart. Maybe she talks so much to cover up the silence deep inside her, the silence that's really frightening and that we try to stifle at all costs, to push down deep inside so as to no longer hear its echo. Perhaps, I'll understand better one day.

But for now, I consider Catherine my friend. I'll be going with her by bus to Montreal, another Canadian city, which I saw only briefly when I arrived in this country. I'll tell you about it when I go there. I've heard that it's a big city, bigger than Ottawa, which I already find huge. My classes at the university make me forget the strangeness all around me.

When I'm not at the university or with Catherine, I'm submerged in loneliness. No one looks at me, no one even pays attention to me on the bus or in the street. They all walk with their heads down, lost in their thoughts or focused on a newspaper. To escape that loneliness, I throw myself heart and soul into my studies. And when that becomes too much, Catherine rescues me with her long speeches about politics. But don't worry, I'll get through this.

And now I get to you. How are you doing? Your work at the school and the tutoring? Do you still go to the Café Les Palmiers, our secret place, where we got together just before I left? Lemonade in the summer and eggnog in the winter. Do you remember? And the millefeuilles that you always insisted on sharing with me. I still remember their sweetness on my tongue, the pastry cream that melted in my mouth, and the crumbs that would fall on our clothes. I recall all that because it's precisely those memories, those insignificant details like the red and white checkered tablecloth that remind me of my more personal memories, like the colour of your eyes. That's what enables me to keep going to my classes, writing my papers, and taking my exams. That's what's keeping me alive and I'm grateful to you for it.

I love you.
Leila

Chapter 11

Catherine

I was going to Montreal. And Leila would come with me. We were going to the big rally on October 27, three days before the referendum. It was a week from D-Day, and I could already see myself sitting on the bus that would take us from Ottawa to Montreal. It was my member of Parliament herself who told me about it on the phone. Guillaume, her assistant, had already mentioned it. I've known Guillaume since high school. We met by chance in the social sciences club of our school. In my last year, he was the director of the club. I had gone to it because I was bored at lunchtime. But little by little, I got to like the discussions. Guillaume drew me out of the solitude I had sunk into and introduced me to politics. To real-life politics, grassroots politics. We were both volunteers even before the 1993 federal election. Then, when he finished college, he became an aide in the member of Parliament's office.

I was immersed in politics. Riding meetings, distributing pamphlets in mailboxes, community fundraising suppers. It was my new family. And then there was Guillaume. Our friendship was solid and indestructible. He knew everything about me, I had told him all of it. He always supported me without hesitation. He listened and understood. Understood the baseness of our world, the vileness of some people, and the pain I had lived with since the "incident." What I liked most about Guillaume was that he never tried to take advantage of my weakness or my wound to present himself as the model man or the perfect man. He never tried to exploit my situation by trying to appear friendlier, kinder, or gentler.

That, in a way, was the therapy I needed. To find honest people. People I could trust. People who didn't want something from me or dislike something in me. After the "incident," I no longer had faith in men, especially the ones around me. When I met Guillaume in the social sciences club, I thought he was like the others. Just another young guy from Sudbury who was crazy about hockey or who dreamed of getting out of there and making his life somewhere else. But Guillaume was different. A young man who was interested in politics and books. Sort of my male alter ego. When I decided to leave Sudbury to come study in Ottawa, he was the first one to encourage me. "Don't even think twice, go for it, it's a chance to see the world." I still smile at those words. Ottawa wasn't the world, just a little bigger than Sudbury.

With politics on the one hand and literature on the other, here I was, finding my way in life. My own way, mine alone. My parents had wanted me to stay in Sudbury. They had already put the "incident" behind them. I never would. It was part of me, like a second skin. A burdensome shell I constantly tried to shed, in vain. The scene of Paul pinning me against the wall with his mouth pressing heavily against mine kept replaying in my head. Leaving Sudbury was an opportunity to expel that image from my memory, to clear it from my vision and see something else.

When I met Leila in Ottawa, I immediately felt we could become friends. She knew nothing about me. Nothing of my pain, nothing of my parents' indifference. I felt safe, precisely because she didn't know that dark side of my life. I didn't yet feel able to tell her what had happened. Our discussions of politics were enough. They drew us together. Leila liked school more than I did. She wanted to become a literature teacher, a really good one. I had no doubt she would do it. I had the impression that her whole family was behind her. Including Farida. Yes, I called her that too. Leila had shown me a yellowed photo of her and her grandmother. A small woman, frail, but standing very straight despite her age, with one hand on Leila's shoulder, and Leila with a hesitant smile on her face. Leila often talked about Farida. I imagined that I had already met her or had known her in another life. How I would have wanted a grandmother like that! She would have understood me and consoled me. Certainly better than my parents. She would have taken me in her arms and let me cry until the pain went away and became just a scar.

Guillaume had told me to go to Algonquin College. It was the students' association of the college that was taking care of the transportation from Ottawa to Montreal. As we got closer to the date, my anxiety went up a notch, then another, and then took over my whole mood. Fortunately we had no classes on Friday.

On the day before the trip, I couldn't follow the literature class. I could see Leila fidgeting in her seat, and she occasionally turned around and gave me a quizzical look as if to say, "Why are we still here?" She, who was usually so studious and conscientious, hardly seemed to be paying attention. And neither was I. Monsieur Lalonde's words were going in one ear and out the other. I was too tired and too anxious about the referendum and what would happen in the days after it. Would we be two countries or one? Would Quebec become a new country in the world? Or would everything go back to normal? Those questions were constantly in my mind, and Monsieur Lalonde's talk only added to the confused muddle in my head. When he finally got up from his chair, indicating that the class was over, I was barely able to restrain myself from rushing over to Leila and running from the classroom. Monsieur Lalonde noticed, and took advantage of the opportunity to say pointedly, "I have the impression that things are not as usual today. Heads are turning, eyes and minds are wandering . . . and bodies too."

I pretended I hadn't heard. I looked around for Leila, but she was already beside me. I didn't know if I should respond to Monsieur Lalonde's remark, which was aimed at me.

Leila's presence gave me courage and I decided to keep quiet for the time being. I would just let Monsieur Lalonde get on his high horse and play his word games, as he was in the habit of doing. Leila and I were already far from his little show. In a few hours, we would be on the bus heading to Montreal. Our heads lowered, we left the classroom like little girls caught red-handed, with Monsieur Lalonde's words ringing in our ears and his eyes following us.

"Are you ready for tomorrow?" I wanted to double-check that Leila hadn't forgotten anything. I was acting like an overprotective mother.

"Yes, yes, I told you twice this morning before class!"

"I'm sorry, Leila, but Monsieur Lalonde got me flustered. He was annoying me with his blather. And did you notice how his last remark in the class was aimed at me?"

"Forget Monsieur Lalonde. What time are we meeting tomorrow?"

"Seven o'clock sharp, we take the bus to Algonquin College, where our bus to Montreal leaves from. Guillaume said a guy named Yves, one of the organizers, put our names on the list. The students will meet in the cafeteria."

"Okay!"

Leila left me, practically running, to go to the library. She wanted to spend a few more hours there so that she wouldn't fall behind in her reading. The weather was sunny and cold. Montreal awaited us! The countdown was about to begin.

Chapter 12

Leila

I knew Montreal. Well, just a bit, from very far away. More precisely, from the airplane window, the day I first arrived in Canada, when the plane touched down. That first day, I caught a glimpse of the expanse of the city, the blocks of buildings that seemed to go on forever, the St Lawrence River that encircled the city like a silvery belt, and especially, all the green. Trees everywhere. In concentric circles or straight lines or scattered. I compared those living landscapes with the dry, yellowed images of Tunis on the day of my departure. And yet there was a time when it was known as "Tunis the green." Where had the trees of my childhood gone? And the moist green grass where I would frolic and do somersaults until my feet and my head hurt? The cypress trees, tall and straight, standing like a fortress against the winds from the west? Where had those vestiges of my childhood gone? Was it a myth they taught us in school like so many others, or a reality that gradually disappeared, swallowed up by the creeping advance of the desert and the destructive march of urbanization?

When we arrived at the meeting place at Algonquin College, the organizer, Yves, checked our names against the list he was holding, nodded, and asked us to wait in the cafeteria. Catherine told him that it was Guillaume, her friend from Sudbury, who had sent in our names. He smiled then, displaying crooked teeth, and asked if we wanted something to drink. We sat in a corner of the cafeteria watching the students arrive, some greeting each other and others keeping to themselves like us. I was neither hungry nor thirsty. Catherine was beside me. At times I wondered what I was doing there. Why was I here with these people who, weeks before, were unknown to me, strangers? Catherine, Guillaume, Yves, all the others. A few months ago, the people I knew had other names and other faces: Farida, Jouda, Tawfik.

What was I going to do in Montreal? Witness in person the break-up of a country, or maybe participate in a collective jolt that would keep it together? And why would I want to get involved in this puzzle in which I felt more and more lost?

Catherine roused me from my reverie and we got on the bus, which was already filled with young people talking loudly and laughing. During the ride, I was seduced by the excitement around me. The songs, the slogans, and the little flags gave the bus a festive atmosphere. Catherine swung between two moods. At times, she would get excited and carry on as if she was a modern-day Joan of Arc trying to conquer fate and keep the country united. At other times, she would withdraw into silence and just stare at the road, discouraged by the recent polls she'd heard about on the morning news.

We arrived at a big parking lot. Our yellow bus was one of hundreds waiting in a long line for places to park.

"We're not far from Place du Canada. That's where the centre of the demonstration will be. We'll head there together. You and I will have to stick together like magnets. I'm the north and you're the south." As she said those words, Catherine burst out laughing. A nervous, contagious laugh that I caught too. Hand in hand, we fell silent, ready to melt into the crowd, ready to write history.

A human tide doesn't begin to describe the mass of people in front of us. It went on forever. Everyone was wearing red and white. Draped in red and white flags, maple leaves painted on their faces in lipstick or children's paint. Catherine was transported, her body beside me but her mind in communion with the crowd. We were surrounded by buildings, skyscrapers that made me dizzy. The trees had lost most of their leaves, which now formed a carpet under our feet, brown and yellow with patches of orange and red, and blew around with every gust of wind. The singing and chanting never stopped. About anything and every-thing . . . love of country, love of another people.

Immersed in the crowd, jostled from side to side like a boat on a stormy sea, I kept thinking about Farida. Here I was with all these people she had never met, and would never meet. Here I was, no longer in the "hole" where she had grown up and where I grew up. To find myself here in the street surrounded by political slogans and passions for a country that was not mine.

So much to tell her, so many stories! The story of a woman dressed all in red, eyes shining, one hand on a flag and the other on her heart as if to say that the two were one. That of a man dressed half in blue and half in red, as if to show that the two colours lived together in him without fear. Stories of streets packed with cars honking and people marching, conquering the public space and making it theirs.

And then, of course, the politicians. One after the other, their voices of different timbres, melodious intonations to stir the crowd, words that played with hearts as if they were yoyos. And the shouting of the crowd, the songs on the loudspeakers. I would tell Farida all about it. Write to her about everything, word after word, sentence after sentence. She would be witness to what I was discovering. As if she were beside me, as if she were our friend, mine and Catherine's.

Catherine, looking a little lost, caught up in the excitement of the crowd, the noise, the words, was walking, her body close to mine. I put my arm around her. She was surprised by my spontaneous gesture and did the same. The physical warmth brought us closer together. Something in the buildings around us also comforted me. The solid old stone looked benevolent. The magnificent old architecture observed us in silence. How many people had these stones seen passing since they were piled one on top of another by the hands of anonymous workers? Today I felt that I was part of this country that was still being created despite its birth pains, despite its differences of opinion.

Chapter 13

Farida

Last night I didn't sleep a wink. Was it the presence of death that was keeping me awake? The beginning of eternity. Neither day nor night. Constant awareness. Or dreaming without end. Sounds barely noticeable during the day became overpowering at night. A cat meowing became a lion roaring, the branches of a tree tapping on the window became the claws of a monster dismembering its prey, and the grating of the hinges of a gate became the fearsome rumble of distant thunder. That's the state I was in. A frail body and a raving brain that wouldn't calm down. Only death would deliver me from this ordeal. Neither the pills Tawfik brought and insisted I take at the same time every day nor the prayer he murmured with his hand on my forehead nor the daily visits of the women neighbours brought me relief. They helped me forget myself for a few moments. Then the thoughts would start again and would not let up. The pills made me so lethargic that I would pretend to take them and then flush them down the toilet. I didn't want Tawfik to know. It upset him. The prayers he read while touching my forehead or the palm of my hand calmed me briefly. It was really his presence that reassured me. I could barely make out the words, but the warmth of his hand in mine comforted me and made me feel I was still the young mother who sacrificed everything for her son's happiness.

It was the feel of our skin touching once again that soothed me. The return to a time when we were both immersed in the liquid warmth of my body. Words came faintly to my ears, they didn't matter anymore.

And there were the neighbours' visits. Vegetable soup, hazelnut cream, mint tea, their sweetness calmed my emotions and made the blood run in my veins. These women brought me the gift of a different flavour every day. Flavours that had disappeared with the death of my mother, and that, all my life, I was never able to recreate when I prepared food myself. I never had the ease in the kitchen that Fatma and many other women in my family had. My passion lay elsewhere, in words and books. In contemplation and silence, in poetry and sensibility. Meanwhile, I let my life go to ruin. Unhappiness took hold of me, and happiness, whose outlines I knew only through my books, gradually vanished. Even the one time I dared to love a man was a mirage. A stolen kiss and a fleeting caress, a minute long, the effects lasting an eternity. A wall separated us for life. Kaddour could never become my husband. Nobody wanted that, starting with my father. The man who had chosen for me the husband I did not love refused the man I did love.

"Kaddour is just a clerk, he doesn't even have a father. His name is Kaddour Ben Mbaraka. *Mbaraka* is a woman's name. This Kaddour bears the name of his mother. Don't you see, he's a bastard? How can a woman from a prominent Tunis family accept a man from the country, and worse, one with no father? I will never approve such a marriage!"

And he backed up his words with actions, willing me his house on condition that I not marry Kaddour. I found myself having to choose between the man I had dared to love and my son's future. Between living with my son with a roof over our heads and living in the street with a man. I defended Kaddour as I had never defended anyone in my life. I defended his family name as if it were my own. "And why shouldn't a bastard have the right to marry and live like anyone else?" I repeated this question dozens of times to my shocked father, my indifferent Uncle Salah, and my sympathetic cousin Fatma.

"He has the right to marry, but not to a woman from a good family, maybe to a bastard like himself, a *goora*, from his own class," my father answered. "You wanted a divorce and you got your divorce. Very well! Now don't try to convince me to become associated with a poor fellow like Kaddour, who works as a *chaouch*, sitting from morning to night in front of the courtroom. A disgrace, I would be a disgrace to all the families."

"At least he finished primary school. Kamel had no schooling and he made us a laughingstock. He's the disgrace to us."

Yes, I had become that impudent, insolent woman capable of talking back to her father. But nothing worked, not even insolence. My father had the upper hand, and above all, he still had money. I had nothing, only a few words that couldn't change anything.

My father made me choose between two men. To choose between the man I loved for himself and for the happiness he would bring me, and the future of my son, whom I was raising with my father's money. Which of the two would prevail?

It was my love for my son that prevailed. Fatma said I should choose Kaddour, because he seemed like a decent man, and even if I were poor, I would at least be happy. But I didn't listen to her. Not that what she was saying was untrue, but because I couldn't convince myself to do it. I've never had the courage to leap into the void. With Kaddour, it was the void. And I hesitated. Motherly love left me no real choice. Motherly love is the most oppressive force I have ever known. I couldn't free myself from it, and this is the result, here in this bed, alone, a few steps from death, listening to Tawfik's heavy breathing in the next room, which was actually comforting. It told me I was alive . . . still.

Chapter 14

Tawfik

I found her this morning. Stiff. White. One hand on her heart, her other arm extended along her side. Her eyes open, looking at the ceiling, as if something had drawn her gaze upward. She seemed to be smiling. I recognized that almost imperceptible hint of a smile. I had grown up with it. She went during the night, without calling me, without warning me, without a sigh. She went in silence. She who had brought me into the world, who had never abandoned me, who had sacrificed her life for me, who had raised my daughter. She went in the night while I lay snoring, my eyes closed, my mind far away.

She was gone, that fighter who had defended me through thick and thin. She went without me holding her hand, without me sitting at her side, without me rubbing her hands and feet one last time to warm them. She went without saying goodbye to me. My mother was everything to me, from the time when I played in the courtyard of my grandfather's house to the day she came to live with me and take care of Leila, after Jouda left. What didn't she do for me? And even when people, starting with my grandfather, said she was raising me like a girl and I would grow up incapable of anything, she never stopped loving me. All her life, she pretended not to hear the criticism, the slights, the insinuations, the sarcasm, and even the insults couched in unsolicited advice that were lavished on her. She overcame my grandfather's oppression disguised as fatherly love and she survived my father's failures and his violence. She got through it all alone. Always standing strong. Sometimes weakened, but never bowed, never defeated. Even when everyone wanted a piece of her. Starting with my grandfather, who married her off to his nephew in order to preserve his fortune, which ended up being squandered anyway. And who insisted on keeping her at home with him when he was facing his own lonely and troubled old age. Then my father, who always saw my mother as more intelligent than he was, a threat and a constant reminder of his own weakness. My father hid behind the excuse that my mother couldn't cook or keep house properly and used it to diminish, humiliate, and mistreat her. And as if that weren't enough, he tried to break her, to abase her, to make her malleable. But he underestimated Farida. She resisted and resisted, until he went away. My father finally lost the battle. Lost his fortune, his wife, and his son.

She's gone, the one who taught me to read, who sent me to school and did everything so that I had a good education and got a degree. She's gone, the one who was never able to fulfill her own dream of becoming a schoolteacher. In spite of everything, she succeeded in becoming the mother of an educated man, and especially, the grandmother of a young woman studying literature in that faraway country, Canada.

Faced with this fragile, immobile, shrunken body, I was at a loss, I didn't know what to do or how to behave. Whether to call a doctor to attest to her death, go to city hall and get a death certificate, or make arrangements for her burial. Where to start? In front of her inert, lifeless body, I felt like the little boy I once was, seeking refuge in his mother's warm arms. When my father flew into one of his frequent rages, she would protect me. After he abandoned us and we were practically hostages to my grandfather, she persuaded that greedy man who lovingly counted his every penny to buy school books for me. And when all the men in the family laughed at me and insinuated that I was effeminate, pampered and spoiled by my mother, and that I had no future and would be a good-for-nothing, she fiercely opposed their malicious gossip and threw their hypocrisy in their faces. "If you're so well-meaning, if you're concerned about my son's future, why haven't you found his father and forced him to take care of his boy? You know very well where to find him, don't you? At his mistress's house."

She never shied away from telling the truth to anyone who seemed to doubt my virility and my future. But she had few allies. My Uncle Habib, who could have been her saviour, always remained silent. He had become a brilliant professor and a recognized poet, but he let his sister struggle under the yoke of both her husband and her father without lifting a finger or making a peep. Nothing. Only my Aunt Fatma, my mother's cousin, who remained faithful to their childhood closeness, their shared unhappiness. Aunt Fatma could hardly read, much less write, but she could read people's eyes and hearts. She always treated me like her own son. She prepared dishes I adored and that my mother couldn't make. All the *briks* with egg I ate at her house, and the plates of *madfouna*[1] with tripe and meatballs and a sprinkle of lemon juice that she insisted I eat down to the last morsel. She was always well-groomed, and always generous with her cooking and her affection.

I was letting my thoughts run away with me, forgetting my mother's body on the bed. *"Inna Lillahi wa inna ilaihi raji'un."*[2] I gently closed her eyes. I pulled her blanket back up over her. It was the one with the little gazelles on it that I used to count to show her I knew my arithmetic. We had used it to try to keep warm on winter evenings, sitting in front of the kerosene stove shivering, with the damp oozing from the walls. Now that blanket, worn and tattered, was covering my mother's cold body.

I was filled with sadness. I would not see Farida ever again. What would I say to Leila?

---

1   A traditional dish made of spinach, white beans, meatballs, and sometimes offal.
2   We belong to Allah and to Him we will return.

Chapter 15

Jouda

He called me at home in the morning. I hadn't heard his voice in years. But I recognized it right away. A little older, a bit tired, very weak, a murmur of distress. "Only God is eternal."

I understood that there had been a death. "Farida?" I asked, my voice already choked with emotion.

"Yes, she's gone." He started to sob. Like a little boy. First a succession of hiccups, then big sobs. Never had I heard him so upset and confused. It pained me just imagining him like that.

"Jouda, my mother is gone. She's no longer of this world."

The man I had left years ago was calling me in tears to tell me he had lost his mother. Who would have imagined it? I never thought about Tawfik anymore, I had removed him from my life. He had become just a vague memory of a relationship I'd never been committed to. In spite of everything, Leila was still the link between us. Farida had been a bulwark protecting and sustaining that link. Now Farida would no longer be with us to keep us so closely connected. I didn't know what to say.

"How did she die?"

He was still crying, the sobs replaced by whimpers punctuated with pauses. "In her sleep. I found her this morning in her bed. The doctor told me her heart had stopped beating."

Such a complex life had ended in such a simple death! Perhaps it was a gift from heaven for a woman who had done nothing but fight for those she loved. Her heart had given out. The time of eternal rest had come.

Leila suddenly appeared before my eyes. "And what about Leila?"

He gave another moan, like an endless sigh. "I don't know how to tell her, she'll be devastated."

"I'll call her, I'll take care of it. You can talk to her after . . . after I phone her."

He seemed relieved by my words. "Jouda, could you come today? We're going to try to bury her this afternoon."

See Tawfik? See the man I'd never wanted to see again? And without even Farida's presence, or Leila's. I couldn't talk anymore. All I could say was a few abrupt words. "All right, I'll be there. I'll have to take the day off. I'll call work first."

He said nothing. He just hung up. Or maybe I heard a thank you, I wasn't sure. Perhaps I imagined it. He had never wanted me to have a job or be independent. He had wanted to give me everything, and he had lost me. But all that was in the past. I had to deal with the present, and quickly. I would go to his house out of respect for Farida's soul, and especially, because Leila would not be with us.

Thoughts were swirling around in my head. Should I call Leila now or should I wait? Wait for the body to be buried, wait until things were calmer? But exactly what would I say to her? "Hello, Leila, how are you? I wanted to tell you Farida has passed away"? And how would she react? All alone, without family, without anyone. Maybe she would want to come here, maybe she would be inconsolable. And besides, I had only called her once. We wrote to each other from time to time. If I told her nothing and hid Farida's death from her for a few days, she would never forgive me. She wouldn't speak to me again for the rest of my days. It was ten o'clock in the morning here, therefore four o'clock in the morning in Ottawa. Too early to wake her. I decided to call a little later in the day, in the late afternoon or evening, when she would be finished with her classes and would be back home.

When I arrived at Tawfik's house, I felt a pang of anxiety. I would have liked to turn around and never see him again, neither him nor the house nor all those people. I didn't want to relive the past and remember the pain of those years. But the sight of the chairs lined up along the fence around the garden and the few men who had come to offer their condolences sitting there in glum silence made me change my mind. I couldn't turn back. It would be like betraying the memory of the woman who had without hesitation allowed me to leave. Farida had opened the door to freedom for me. Farida had saved my life. I could never let her leave without kissing her and whispering a final thank you.

I found Tawfik sitting inside surrounded by some men I didn't know. I remained standing in the foyer, a little disoriented at seeing Leila's house again. Not much had changed. The same furniture, old and dreary, like that we had in our first apartment. A few new photos had appeared on the walls, Leila's work, no doubt. Otherwise, the same carpets, a little more threadbare with time and footsteps, and above all, the same atmosphere. Tawfik came over to me. I barely recognized him with his grey beard and receding hairline. Only his eyes were the same, keen and a little cold. Everything else had changed, age had done its work. We stared at each other without a word. Death had swept everything away, had left us naked and vulnerable, facing one another. Then, as if he were waking from a dream, he motioned me to a room with the door ajar. "The women are here. My mother too."

Fatma, Farida's cousin, recognized me and led me to the body of the deceased. Farida was very slender, and she looked even more tiny than she actually was. Covered in a white shroud with only her face visible, she seemed younger than her age, her wrinkles almost vanished. Her eyes were closed, and she looked as if she was already in another world.

Fatma, her eyes red, her straight hair completely grey, said in a low voice, "You can kiss her and say goodbye."

I placed a quick kiss on Farida's hollow cheek. It was as if death had devoured all her flesh, leaving only a thin skin and protruding bones. I quietly found a place among the women—neighbours, friends, and members of the family. I silently thanked my former mother-in-law, the woman who had once saved my life. Saved me from the life that Tawfik, her own son, had created for me, in which I played the part of a doll, smiling and proper. Farida enabled me to erase that picture and draw a different one. My own. A clumsy one, in which I appeared with my flaws and my weaknesses and, above all, my dreams. A complicated picture, with clouds, a sun, an airplane, a desert, and snow. A picture with Leila in the middle. Her face was still very much with me. How was I going to tell her that Farida had died?

Chapter 16

Leila

I've almost forgotten the whole debate about the independence of Quebec. My trip to Montreal with Catherine ended when our bus dropped us off where we had left from in the morning. Our excitement had turned into fatigue. Our lively discussions had gone silent. My assignments were piling up and I had to get to work. I promised Catherine that on Monday evening, I would go to her place to watch the referendum results on TV.

I didn't have any classes Monday mornings and I usually went to study in the library. But not that day. I just knocked around the apartment. I looked out the window. The garden behind my building was strewn with dead leaves. A brown blanket on which the squirrels were happily frolicking, sometimes stopping to scratch the ground frantically in search of an acorn or a berry they had saved. The winds of the last few days had stripped the trees of their leaves, except for a few that were barely hanging on. I had an assignment to hand in for my literature class. I wanted to write about Victor Hugo. Farida was the one who introduced me to reading and then to literature. The first words I read, the first sentences I wrote, the first books I devoured.

Of course there were the good little girls in the novels of the Comtesse de Ségur and the adventures of Martine, those little heroines that lived in my childhood imagination, but later she talked to me about Victor Hugo. Farida was obsessed with him. His genius as a man of letters, and the successive family tragedies he experienced, always fascinated her and in a way inspired her in her own life.

I remembered that, one day, when I got bored sitting in my room, I went to Farida's room to kill time, as I often did on days when I didn't have school. I found her as usual, on her bed, her legs crossed and her radio on the dresser. I sat down in my favourite chair. I wasn't sure if she'd noticed me coming in. She was immersed in her reading. I gazed out the window overlooking the terrace. I must have been twelve or thirteen years old. The garden was in full bloom. It was the time when I was seeing my mother more and more, and Farida mattered less and less in my life. Farida sensed that detachment, and with time I realized that it hurt her.

I stayed in her room for a moment without saying a word. I waited. Then, finally, she put her book down on the dresser beside the radio. Our eyes met. She looked upset. Something strange had taken hold of her that day. She told me things a little girl like me didn't usually hear.

"I've just reread Victor Hugo. The poem on the loss of his daughter. It's overwhelming, it's sublime."

"Did his daughter die?"

"Yes, she drowned in a boating accident."

I was shocked. "Can you die young? Even before your parents!"

"Death lives among us," she answered without looking at me.

"Why do you read sad things? Why not cheerful, funny stories, things that make you happy?"

"I've never been happy and I don't want to be anymore. At one time, I wanted to be happy, but sadness got hold of me."

"When was that?"

"When I thought I'd found a man I loved."

I blushed. I'd never talked with Farida about love and boys.

"Don't be embarrassed, these are normal things that happen. Didn't your mother tell you about them?"

"No."

"She should. One day, she will, I'm sure."

"And what happened then?"

"Nothing. My father didn't let me marry him because he wasn't a rich man. He was poor and didn't come from an important family. That was his crime. Your grandfather, my ex-husband, was supposedly a rich man, but he died penniless, living in an *oukala*, like poor people. He wasn't very intelligent. He could barely write his name. And worse, he hated anything or anyone that reminded him of his ignorance, me in particular."

"And why do you like Victor Hugo's stories?"

She didn't answer. Instead, she started to read:

Tomorrow, at dawn, the time when the country goes white,
I will leave. You see, I know you wait for me.
I will go by the forest, I will go by the mountain.
No longer can I live far from you.
I will walk with my eyes on my thoughts,
Seeing nothing outside, hearing no sounds at all,
Alone, unknown, back stooped, hands crossed,
Sad, and the day for me will be like night.[3]

Her voice was trembling. She hesitated for a moment, then, looking me straight in the eye, said, "You know, Leila, if I had to choose a man, I would prefer a man like Victor Hugo. Intelligent, cultivated, and above all sensitive. A man who could make me cry with words. My brother, Habib, became a great man of letters, but he didn't help me. Fatma was right, he was afraid. Victor Hugo is far from me, and yet he has comforted me so much in my moments of pain."

Back then, I didn't really understand what she was trying to tell me. But now, I felt better able to appreciate the subtleties of her actions and her words. They were like a needle that pricked the bubble I had shut myself up in with the reappearance of my mother in my life. Farida was a little jealous of my mother, who had been late to take on her role as mother and had found the work already largely done. Time heals all wounds. It made me more sensitive.

I was making a chicken and vegetable stew. I'd found the recipe by chance in a magazine that was lying around in our department office and I'd decided to try it. While the pot was simmering on the stove, I was finally able to collect my thoughts, which were flying off in many directions, and sit down to write. Farida, my mother, my father, the referendum, everything could wait. I wanted to write about Victor Hugo, and how he had found in the heartbreaking death of his daughter the strength to write his most famous novel, *Les Misérables*.

I had barely begun to write when the phone rang. Usually it was Catherine calling to talk about school or complain about all the reading

---

3   From "Dès demain l'aube," poem by Victor Hugo, translation.

they made us do. We spent more time joking and laughing than anything else. Sometimes it was my father asking for news. We didn't talk for long, it was expensive. He would say what he had to say and that was the end of it. He would talk about the weather and his garden, nothing else. And I would talk about the weather here, about my classes, but never about how lonely I was. In between his calls, the letters from Farida filled my solitude.

Picking up the phone and hearing a distinct little click, I quickly realized that it was Tunis.

"How are you, my dear Leila?" My mother's voice was trembling a little.

"Fine, I was about to write an essay."

"Ah! That's good. I didn't want to disturb you."

"No, not at all, how is everyone there?"

She didn't answer. A brief silence that I couldn't interpret. It was a bit strange, because my mother was never at a loss for words.

"Leila, I have some bad news . . . "

My hands became clammy. The receiver almost slipped from my grasp. An illness, a car accident, a death? And suddenly, I thought of Farida. I wanted to see her again. I didn't want her to go.

"You know, Leila, we all have to go one day, it's God's will."

My heartbeats came one after the other like the few leaves that were still falling. Farida was gone. I didn't want to hear those words. I wanted to hang up the phone.

"Farida, your grandmother . . . "

A sound came out of my mouth. Not a scream, not a howl, but a long moan I'd never have thought myself capable of. Even the announcement of her death made me discover something new.

I heard my mother's voice saying the standard phrases that are automatically repeated with every death: "she went peacefully" . . . "she didn't suffer" . . . "it was very quick" . . . "she's in a better place." But those words were so weak compared to the sounds that wanted to pour out of my mouth.

"Leila, your father didn't have the strength to tell you. I'm doing it in his place."

Who the messenger was didn't matter. The message was horrible. No one could soften it. Neither my father nor my mother. Farida was gone, despite my believing all this time that she would never go. Everything was happening in slow motion. My mother's words, the thoughts in my head.

"Leila, you're a big girl . . . Farida is gone, *rabbi yarhamha*.[4] You have to stay strong, you know, *ya aziziti*, my dear."

"I want to come back to Tunis." I didn't know what had gotten into me, but it was the first thought that came into my head.

"Don't be silly, Leila, you can't drop out of school. You've only just started."

"Now that Farida is gone, my studies don't matter . . . I want to see her one last time."

"No, no, Leila, you can't do that. Farida, may God bless her soul, was buried this afternoon. Even if we'd waited until tomorrow morning, you would never have been able to get here in time. Listen, my dear, try to remain calm. There's nothing to be done. It's the will of God."

I want to sit beside her grave, I want to say goodbye to her even if she's already buried.

"Yes, and you will, *Insha'Allah*, but not right away. When you're in Tunis, during the holidays."

The kitchen was filling with smoke. The stew was burning. I put down the phone, turned off the stove, and opened the window. The fresh air felt good. Farida was really gone, and I was in Ottawa, six thousand kilometres away.

I picked up the phone again and my mother was still talking.

"Leila, Leila, where are you? Are you all right, sweetie? Listen to me . . . "

"I'm here," I answered feebly.

"*Alhamdulillah*, don't leave me torn between here and there. Calm yourself. Farida has been buried. She is beside her brother, Habib."

I knew the spot. I had visited Uncle Habib's grave with my father after his death. We had walked a long time before finding it. The face of death was always the same . . . a grave, grass, sometimes a few shrubs. Or nothing. Everything looked the same. You could easily get lost in the labyrinth of death. Farida would be one more grave, hard to distinguish from the rest. Yet she had always been unique.

"Leila, promise me, my dear daughter, that you'll take care of yourself. *Rabbi yarhamha*, Farida. We'll miss her."

---

4   May God bless her soul. Expression used when a person has died.

I didn't want to talk anymore. All I could say was yes. Reassured by my near-silence, my mother said goodbye, promising to called again the next day.

Alone with myself again, I became aware of the scorched smell that filled the kitchen. Farida was dead and I had spoiled my dish. How ironic! I went to my bedroom and lay down on my bed. I let out a great sob. My whole body was shaken by spasms of sorrow.

Chapter 17

Catherine

I could hardly believe the day had come. Referendum day. And the world was still turning. I had almost convinced myself that it would never come, that the referendum would be cancelled for some reason and life would go back to normal. It may seem a little crazy, but I had found a kind of comfort in that fantasy. And what if Quebec were to separate from the rest of Canada? Would we have two countries, Canada and Quebec? Would Franco-Ontarians then have to make a choice between staying in Canada and immigrating to Quebec out of solidarity with our fellow French speakers? I didn't have any answers to those questions, and I got caught up in dark thoughts that only nostalgia for the time before the referendum campaign could dispel.

But luckily I had Leila to share my fears with. I had never thought I could become friends with someone so quickly. Guillaume was the first friend I'd made after the "incident" and now Leila had become a friend too. We'd become so close in the past little while that I couldn't see myself managing without her. We had developed a closeness that it takes other people years to forge. For us, it grew out of our shared loneliness. Leila had just arrived in Canada—a new country, new studies, another culture. And the referendum question that I would go on about endlessly. My loneliness had a different quality because of the bitterness of my experience when my parents refused to take action against Paul, to report him to the police or tell his family what he had done. They claimed they were trying to protect me. "What good would it do you to talk to the police?" asked my mother, puffing on her cigarette as if it held the answer.

"He'd be punished, he'd pay for his obscene act. I don't know exactly what they'd do to him, but at least he wouldn't do to other girls what he did to me." The words came out of my mouth automatically. I wanted my parents to show that my suffering really mattered to them.

Maman gazed at the smoke coming out of her nostrils, still focused on the cigarette she was holding between her thumb and index finger. "But you, Catherine Rioux, it wouldn't do you any good. Your teachers would know about it, and so would your friends and the neighbours, and they'd imagine all kinds of things, and your future would be compromised."

It was no use. My mother was thinking of the future and I was thinking about the present, about the suffering Paul had subjected me to, which she and my father refused to acknowledge.

I had invited Leila to my place to watch the referendum results on TV. When I phoned her, I got her answering machine. "Sorry, I can't answer the phone now. But if you leave a brief message, I'll call you back as soon as possible." We had made that recording together. We never stopped laughing that day. Every time she made a mistake or stumbled, we would burst out laughing, and she would repeat the message and I would patiently press the button to record it. Again and again.

I wasn't worried. Maybe she was out doing errands or hadn't yet come back from the library. I remembered that she'd said she wanted to write a paper on Victor Hugo, but wasn't sure how to approach it. I decided to wait and try to reach her a little later. Or else I'd go over to her place and get her, and then we could go back to my apartment.

When I knocked on her door, no one answered. Usually she opened the door after the first knock, as if she were standing behind it, ready to open it. I was carrying two bags of chips. One plain, which Leila loved, and the other with ketchup, my favourite, which she hated. I knocked again, lightly at first, but then more loudly and emphatically. I was starting to get worried. When I heard the sound of heavy footsteps, I stopped. It was Leila. She opened the door a crack and I could see her. Her face was livid, her eyes wild, and her hair messy.

"What's happened?"

She didn't answer, but she opened the door a little more so that I could slip inside. I sat down on a chair in her little sitting room.

She stood motionless in front of me. "Farida is dead," she said. Her words hit me like a cold shower. "I feel like I'm going to die too." She started sobbing.

I'd never seen her in such a state. I wasn't sure how to console her. I let her cry. When she regained her composure somewhat, I went over to her and said very softly, "I'm sorry, Leila. I'm really sorry for your loss of your grandmother."

Her tears started flowing again, and I saw the suffering in her eyes. The suffering of losing someone dear, the suffering of losing oneself too. "Thank you, thank you, Catherine, for being with me. I want so much to go see her again . . . one last look, a goodbye . . . but I can't. I'm here, and she's there."

"It's true. You can't go. We have classes and assignments to hand in and exams soon."

She nodded.

"How did she die?"

"A natural death. My mother said my father found her in her bed. She must have died in her sleep. I don't really know."

I was afraid to say something stupid and cause her even more pain. "Maybe it's better like that? She didn't suffer. No stay in the hospital, no intravenous needle in her arm or tubes in her nose, none of that end-of-life suffering."

She gave me a look as if to say she'd never thought of that, and then nodded. "Yes, maybe you're right."

I didn't reply, I just looked at the two bags of chips that were lying on the little white table in the middle of the room. The light of the setting sun gave the apartment a warm feeling. A police siren shattered the silence. We glanced at each other, then lowered our eyes, both staring at an invisible point on the floor. I don't know how long we stayed that way. An eternity. A few minutes. I forgot about the referendum. I didn't care who won and who lost. Leila had lost her grandmother, who had raised her, who had been everything to her. I couldn't forsake her for the referendum results. I knew Farida only through what Leila had told me about her. That woman was unique. She had surely chosen the time of her death.

Chapter 18

Leila

I went to pay my respects at Farida's grave eight months after her death. For eight months I was a zombie, a hostage to life and pain. Fortunately, there was Catherine. She saved my life. In fact, we saved each other's lives. I didn't want to live anymore because I'd lost the person who mattered most to me in life. She didn't want to live anymore because she'd been molested by a boy. That was the secret she'd been hiding from me since the beginning. It was the veil over her eyes that I had never been able to lift. It took a catalyst to make it happen. And that was Farida's death. It all poured out without warning, the way someone suddenly vomits an indigestible meal. She told me everything down to the smallest detail . . . the violence of the hands that restrained her body, the mouth that prevented hers from making a sound. Everything. And I listened to her story, at first shocked, then overcome by sadness. How had she managed to survive all that pain and bury it in the deepest recesses of her being? She felt she had found a refuge in politics, where she could unleash all her passion and find a release for her anxiety, but with the slightest upset, her shell fell away, leaving her completely exposed, more vulnerable than ever. Catherine had fallen apart in front of me, a few days after Farida's death. I didn't know if it was seeing me suffer that made her want to share her own suffering, as a way to comfort me and alleviate my pain. Or maybe it was the emptiness caused by the referendum result.

The "no" camp had won, but just barely, and Catherine's fears had dissipated, leaving her rudderless, adrift from the cause that had given her life meaning. Once the night of October 30 faded into the past, the emptiness crept in to fill the space. Tentatively at first, but a little more vigorously each day, to become an undesired part of her being. I'll never know what happened in Catherine's head, but I witnessed the result—a descent into hell. Fortunately she never hit rock bottom and she was able to come out of it.

How could a friendship that began so simply, so spontaneously, become a lifeboat that would save us both? In the months following those two events, our lives were turned upside down. There was no going back. We were bound together by sorrow. I almost dropped out of school. I didn't want to go to my classes anymore. My words dried up and so did my compositions. It was as if Farida had been my muse, my source of inspiration, my reason for living. With her gone, I had nothing to say anymore. I couldn't think or write. I no longer wanted anything from life.

For Catherine, things were different. She went to classes, but constantly contradicted the professors. She became a troublemaker. The one who always had something to say, a remark, a comeback, a wisecrack. She was a pain in the neck. And yet that wasn't her. She had become that way after telling me about the "incident." Once that secret was out, a strange rage took hold of her. A rage that manifested itself in negativity. No to the professors, no to the administration, no to the system, no to herself.

One day when she came to visit me, I looked through the peephole before opening the door and had a fit of the giggles. I couldn't believe it was her. And yet it was. Her brown eyes, her glasses, her little nose, her wide mouth. Her face, fragile yet hard. Except that she'd shaven her head. She'd left nothing, not a single lock of hair. My friend was bald.

"What happened to your hair?" I asked, opening the door, a smile still on my lips.

"In the garbage."

I burst out laughing. I had an irresistible urge to touch her smooth skull.

"I can see you've shaven your head, but why?"

"Because I suddenly felt like it. Because I wanted to be in full possession of my body, and to feel that no one has the right to tell me what to do."

I didn't say anything. I didn't feel like laughing anymore. And she didn't either. I looked at her changed appearance without saying another word. I didn't know if I admired or pitied her. But I was shocked by her abrupt transformation.

We spent the whole evening talking about our relationship with our hair. I had never thought about it before. I thought of my hair as I did of my eyes or my mouth or my feet: what counted was the colour or the shape. Farida had always kept my hair short because I cried when she combed it in the morning before I went to school. Later, my mother wanted me to keep it a little longer, because "it's beautiful like mine," she would say with a touch of humour.

But Catherine saw things differently. "Without hair, I'm no longer prey, I'm neither male nor female. I'm just plain Catherine."

"But it's as if you're saying that you wanted to be a boy in order to have more power and to choose who you are."

She smiled. She wasn't convinced by my answer. "That's what everyone thinks, but no, I still consider myself a girl, only I no longer want to fit the norm. Who says women have to have long hair and men short hair? Huh, who says so?"

I didn't know what to answer.

"My new aesthetic is a way of rejecting imposed social norms. No to boys who want to attack me, no to society that dictates how I should behave, no to my parents' silence, no to my own silence!"

But it was short-lived, a kind of rite of passage. A few months later, Catherine let her hair grow back. It had been a phase she had to go through, a step she had to take from being immobilized by pain. The thought of Catherine's quest to find her way again was with me in my mourning. It helped me know myself better. Who was I? Jouda's daughter, Farida's, or both? And my father, who was he? Someone who was absent, or a social reject who was never able to find his place between Farida, who was too present, and Jouda, who chose to leave him? Loving them all without asking myself too many questions about what they had done to me was my daily challenge.

I survived the first semester without too much damage. Catherine almost got expelled, but Monsieur Lalonde, against all expectations, defended her. The person we secretly called a "know-it-all" went to battle with the administration for Catherine to stay in the program, and she stayed. I had gone to talk to him when things were at their worst for her, when her grades were dropping and she persisted in ridiculing the professors, including Lalonde. And he was the kindest and the most understanding of them. I didn't tell him everything, but I said that Catherine was not doing very well and that she was going through a difficult time. He didn't demand to know more. He didn't ask me questions. He just looked me in the eye and asked, "Why are you speaking on her behalf?"

I was paralyzed with fear. I expected him to tell me to mind my own business and leave his office.

"She's my friend, and I really care about her. I'll always stand by her."

He seemed surprised by my answer. He raised his eyebrow, glanced at his watch, and said, "I'll do my best. Friendship can't be bought, it's something to be defended."

And Catherine stayed in the program. I never told her what I'd done for her. But when she got the letter from the program director authorizing her to register for the second semester, she squeezed my hand so tight she almost broke my fingers.

Things went better in the second semester. Catherine gradually stopped her antics. She learned to deal with her pain. My own was beginning to subside as the weather got milder. It was as if with the passing of winter, I was able to lay my grief in a sunny corner of my heart. I visited it from time to time. Farida would remain there forever.

Regular phone calls from my mother also helped me get through the storm. They were sometimes short, sometimes long, but every Sunday at the same time, without fail, she called. The banalities we exchanged brought me closer to the shore from the place where Farida's death had dropped me. At first, there was anxiety in my mother's voice, anxiety about losing her daughter to demons or disease. But later the anxiety changed into concern, to finally reveal love. A mother's love seeking the daughter in me, the daughter she had once lost and then found, and a gnawing fear of losing her again. Her insistence, which in other times would have annoyed me and kept me at a distance, did me good. It allowed me to forget.

And then one day, I woke up. I once again felt like writing papers, polishing them down to the smallest detail, reading and rereading them to find a misplaced comma or a redundant word to delete. When Catherine left for Sudbury and I for Tunis, we were two girls changed by events and by life. Two girls still the weaker for our trials, but uplifted by our friendship.

I decided to go to the cemetery alone. My father, who had gotten much thinner and had a white beard, so that I almost didn't recognize him at the airport, explained to me at length how to get there. "You take the Jellaz gate, the one to the west, and walk straight ahead; when you come to where the path widens, turn left toward the cemetery fence. You'll see two cypress trees, one taller than the other, two metres from the fence. Your grandmother's grave is not far from there. First there's Uncle Habib's, then hers." He even made a little diagram. I took it without looking at it. He quickly added, "I can come with you, if you want."

"No," I answered almost brusquely. "I'll find the way, don't worry."

I didn't want to go there with anyone, especially not my father. I didn't want to cry in front of him, I didn't want him to hear me talking to Farida. I wanted to be alone, to talk privately with her.

I found her grave without getting lost. My father's directions and his little diagram were very useful after all. The stifling heat of the afternoon had dissipated, giving way to a gentle warmth that didn't bother me. My tears started to flow at the sight of the two cypress trees. Standing one beside the other. An incredible metaphor for those two lives, my grandmother's and her brother's. One who became a poet and literature teacher, and the other just a survivor. A woman without a profession who had left her mark. I was the living proof. I stayed at her graveside for a long time.

Chapter 19

Catherine

I returned to Sudbury reluctantly. The only person I wanted to see there was Guillaume. Not my parents, and not our house or our street. I didn't have a choice. I had to go back when classes ended in Ottawa. Leila left too. For Tunis. She was happy to leave, because she would see her grandmother again, or rather visit her grave. It was the missing part of her grieving process. My own was also late in coming. The confrontation with my parents was long overdue. I wanted only one thing: that they understand once and for all what I had gone through and what I had to overcome in recent months in order to survive. Silence was no longer an option.

Sharing my pain with Leila helped me. Now that she knew the whole story, I had nothing to hide from her. I didn't need to hide behind politics or the referendum to talk with her. I no longer had any need for pretexts or denial. I was facing up to my reality, including everything that was ugly and disgusting about it. Guillaume had promised to help me get an internship in the local member of Parliament's constituency office. He had told me they needed someone to organize the correspondence with voters. Political activity had made it possible for me to keep my head above water, but it did not completely save me from the danger of drowning. I came close to going under, and it was Farida's death coinciding with the referendum that allowed me to realize how fragile I was. Politics was just a mirage; I had to get past it.

There were no outpourings of joy when I went home to my parents. They were waiting for me, but I still dreaded seeing them. They were proud that I was going to university, but I had never forgiven them for their reaction to Paul's assault.

When I brought it up, my mother said I was complicating my life for nothing, that "these things happen," it wasn't the end of the world, and that, all in all, I had things pretty good.

I blew my top. "But at what cost? At the cost of hating my life and being haunted by that thing!"

"You refuse to put it behind you. You've always wanted to complicate things. Paul made a mistake. But he paid for it. He left his city and his family." My mother was talking as if Paul were the victim. She was all but begging him to come back to Sudbury.

My father, as usual, listened in silence to my conversation with my mother. He didn't feel it concerned him. For him, the matter had been over for years. He had done his part when he'd talked to Paul and Paul had denied everything. Paul's departure from the city was the end of it. When my father did decide to say something, it was a disaster. "Why are you still talking about it? Look around you. You went to university. You did a master's in literature. Soon, you'll have a well-paying job. What more do you want from life? Justice? There isn't any! You've come a long way, Catherine. Remember, I spent all those years working in the mine, ruining my lungs and my body for you, your brother, your mother, me, everyone . . . and you want to throw away what it took me years to build. Just like that, for a childish game."

A childish game. That was how my father summed up my years of suffering, with those words that sounded so innocent, so ordinary. My father had thought he could finally lance the boil, drain the pus, and restore health. While I, who went to school and will soon be earning my living in an office or a classroom, was still brooding about it and screaming for justice. I wanted to cut off the gangrened limb. I wasn't afraid of being an amputee. I refused to live with the rot of the past. My obsession with the past upset him.

"It was never a childish game, Papa. It wasn't mutual. It was an assault. An act of aggression, do you understand? A man who took advantage of our friendship, our being neighbours, our childhood spent together, to humiliate me, terrorize me, and silence me. I never played a game with Paul. And the education the two of you are so proud of. Do you know how much it's cost me and how much I'm still paying? Not in dollars, of course, but in dark thoughts, in suffering, in depression. If you think my life was so wonderful, you're sadly mistaken. I was at the edge of the abyss and I was almost expelled from my program. Did you know that? No, of course not! Of course not! Anyway, you don't didn't want to know. The only thing you're interested in is the fairy story of little Catherine, the daughter of poor people who became someone and who would be the pride of her parents in Sudbury. It's precisely that game I don't want to play anymore."

My mother broke down in tears. My father's face went pale. And I myself was surprised by what had come out of my mouth after so long. I hadn't thought myself capable of it. I already felt better. The silence had been burning me up inside. Breaking it had allowed me to rise from the ashes. I was finally freed from the wall that had surrounded me since the incident with Paul. The wall of fear and shame. My friendship with Leila had given me strength. I had broken down the wall, piece by piece, stone by stone.

Sudbury

Dear Leila,

Sudbury is its same old self. The nickel, the miners, and the mines. The people live from that crushing economy. My father did it for years, and so will my brother. I'm happy I won't be spending my life in the dark belly of the earth. The fact that I'm a girl saved me from that fate to take me toward another one just as dark. The fate of being an easy prey for some men. That was how Paul saw me. He tried to destroy me, as many other women have been destroyed before me. And he almost succeeded. My last years in secondary school were hell and my first months in university even worse. Politics with Guillaume offered me a lifeline, and for a few years, I believed I had survived the fear and humiliation. Guillaume helped me a lot. But the cleansing was only superficial; deep down, I still felt dirty and slimy. Unaware of the severity of the damage within me, I thought I had become "clean" through forgetting.

When I went to Ottawa to university, I tried to make a fresh start and forget the "incident." I was mistaken. The "incident" was still inside me, politics had only pushed it into a corner. It was lying in wait for me in order to devour me and finish me off. Then I met you. I finally found someone who was willing to listen to me. Guillaume did, but with you, it was different. You listened to me for what I was saying. I constantly pestered you with my stories about the political system, the referendum, Quebec and Canada. The anxiety and fear from what happened with Paul had become a morbid obsession. I thought I was surviving, but in reality, I was smothering one problem with another. Meeting you, Leila, brought me back to life. Real life instead of political games. Its joys, its fears, and its hopes. When I saw you weeping over the loss of your grandmother, Farida, I understood what it meant to lose someone very dear and I decided to be frank with you and tell you everything. Instead of hiding, I wanted to face the world. It's true that I flirted with revolt for a while. Shaved my head, talked back to the profs. I was groping in the dark to find my way. I had to go through that, it was part of my grieving process. Grieving the loss of my innocence and having to accept my parents' reaction.

Not anymore. Those months spent with you gave me the strength to look myself in the face and choose: to live or to die. I've never told you this, Leila, but it's thanks to you, to your friendship, that I was really able to choose. Yes, I decided that the time had come to talk to my parents. I decided that I would confront them and that I would no longer be ashamed of myself.

I did not clear up everything. My demons come back from time to time. But I face them, and above all, I know them, I can even name them. My parents are still shocked by my new frankness. They're at a loss. They're worried about me. Most of all, they're afraid I'll drop out of school. I'm still their only hope of escaping from the cycle of poverty. I used to resent them for only thinking of themselves. Today, in spite of everything, I accept that I'm their dream, and sometimes I'm even a little bit proud of that.

You know, Leila, it's sort of a crazy thought, but I'm grateful not only to you, I'm especially grateful to your grandmother, Farida. The next time you visit her, give her my best regards.

Catherine

Chapter 20

Leila

My stay in Tunis was coming to an end. Two months filled with emotions and thoughts. Two months during which I visited Farida's grave again and again. The first time, I didn't speak to her with words. I wept, and my heart did the rest. But the second visit was different. My father had ordered an inscription.

Farida Ben Mahmoud
(June 12, 1922 – October 30, 1995)
O serene soul!
Return to your Lord, well pleased, and pleasing in His sight!
Join My servant,
and enter My Paradise!

It was magical how a small marble plaque engraved with peaceful words could change an anonymous place to a grave with a name, a date of birth, a date of death, and verses from the Quran. The only thing lacking was Farida's face. The paths of death are narrow, but I had found a stone to use as a stool, and my time with Farida became longer. I would sit down on the stone, my face in my hands, and talk to her as if she were sitting opposite me on her bed with her legs crossed and the radio on the dresser.

Dear Farida,
You left without warning me, without a goodbye, with no way back. Last year at this time, you insisted that I leave the "hole" and I listened to you. I packed

my bags and left. You told me, Canada is better, you'll get a great degree and you'll find a husband. I still smile at your words. I don't have the degree yet, Insha'Allah next year. But about the husband, you were on the wrong track. Instead of a husband, I found a friend. I've told you a little about her. Do you remember, Catherine? But since you've been gone, we've become great friends. Your sudden passing caused me a great deal of pain, Farida. You were everything to me, mother, grandmother, friend, and suddenly I felt abandoned. Abandoned by the person who taught me everything, even how to read. I felt betrayed by your passing. Sometimes, I resented you for letting me leave for Canada and then abandoning me. Fortunately I wasn't alone. Catherine helped me survive. I didn't want to go to classes anymore. What did Victor Hugo matter without you? By the way, I discovered he had a mistress all those years while he was living with his wife and children. Did you know that, Farida? You admired him so much and wanted a man like him, are you sure you would have wanted to share a man with another woman?

But let me talk about my life. My life without you. Catherine became my friend, a friend who helped me find answers to many questions. For nine years, you were the only mother I had, and then my mother Jouda reappeared in my life. It's true I was happy to have a new mother who would sometimes come pick me up at school, who bought me nice things and cooked me my favourite dishes, but later, I became confused. Two mothers, one who gave birth to me and one who raised me. Which of the two to choose, which one was better? The real one or the replacement? I was caught up in a game I couldn't escape from. I blamed everyone. My mother, for abandoning me. My father, for not having done everything he could to keep her, and you, yes, you, Farida, for raising a man like my father. A man who lived in the past and didn't understand that his wife had needed more than to eat, sleep, and make babies. I put the blame on you, I believed you were responsible for all my ills. But, Farida, in that maze of complex emotions, I failed to look myself straight in the face and stop lamenting my fate. When Catherine told me how her neighbour had forced himself on her one night, and how she had survived in spite of it, I decided I, too, would survive. Survive my family's past and live with the present. Your death caused me too much pain, not only the pain of seeing you leave this world, but also the fear I had of living with only two parents, and not three, as I had until then. Without you, I didn't know how to behave with either my mother or my father. I had experienced those relationships through you. But gradually, I began to learn to live without you. My mother phoned me regularly. You liked letters. She preferred the phone, which

FARIDA 263

was quicker and more ephemeral. Before leaving, I resented her for remarrying and abandoning me again. I was very jealous, and I only understand it now. I've finally met her husband, Firas. Older than I thought, but not horrible, as I imagined. A normal guy. I sensed that my mother was happy with him, something I had always resented. I wanted her to be happy only with me. I was young and immature. Your passing made me understand that time is going by and I have to grow up. My father has changed a lot. The praying and the garden. He too has finally found his love. Not with women, but I would say in meditation. Perhaps that was his vocation in life, and it took him years to find it. So, I've understood that your passing was in a way necessary, that it freed us from the strained relationships among us all. I don't mean that your death was beneficial for us! What I wouldn't to do to see you again one last time! But I wanted to tell you that even your death, the worst thing that ever happened to me, gave a gift to each one of us. To my mother, to my father, to me, and, you know, even to my Canadian friend Catherine!

MONIA MAZIGH is the author of two memoirs, three novels, and a collection of short stories. She has written for *ONFr+*, *Radio-Canada*, the *Ottawa Citizen*, the *Globe and Mail*, and the *Toronto Star* and contributes regularly to *Islamic Horizons*. Her memoir, *Gendered Islamophobia: My Journey with a Scar(f)* was a finalist for the Governor General's Literary Award for Nonfiction in 2023. *Farida* won the Ottawa Book Award for French fiction. Monia Mazigh is an adjunct and research professor at the Department of English and Literature, Carleton University (Ottawa).